HONEYMOON
alone

HONEYMOON
alone

nicole macaulay

4B Pub

Providence

ISBN 978-1-7332769-1-7 (E-Book)
ISBN 978-1-7332769-0-0 (Paperback Edition)

Library of Congress Control Number: 2019910969

Artwork by Marilyn Sowinski
Author Photo by Moments by Mackenzie Photography
Book and Cover Design by Kerry Ellis

Printed and Bound in USA
First Printing December 2019

Published in the United States by 4B Pub
P. O. Box 6430
Providence, RI 02940

To John
For believing in me. Always.

"If adventures will not befall a young lady in her own village, she must seek them abroad."

– Jane Austen

chapter one

"The psychic is missing."

I don't have time for this. I so don't have time for this. I am supposed to be walking down the aisle in minutes. No, seconds! The music has started. The bridesmaids are going one at a time, all decked out in their purple polka-dotted dresses. But...the psychic is missing.

I gaze out at the congregation. All heads are turned in our direction. There are still a few bridesmaids standing before me, waiting for their turn.

"Walk slowly, girls," I say. I turn to Wendi and take a deep breath. "Is this something you can handle? I mean, you are the wedding planner."

"Well, that's just it!" she says, her brown eyes wide and panicked. "I have to oversee the wedding. Then I have to attend the photo shoot and ensure everything goes according to plan, that we get every single picture on our shot list. Then I have to –"

I touch her arm gently. "I'll take care of it."

She breathes a huge sigh of relief and rolls her eyes, smiling. "Thank you, Lucy! Marian was right – you are so reliable. I can see why she named you the maid of honor."

That's me! Reliable Lucy. It was actually the description of me in my high school yearbook: Most Reliable.

"Okay." I fix Wendi with my firmest gaze because she seems to be falling apart. Is this her first wedding? "Just write down the psychic's number. I will handle it."

"Thank you!"

"Lucy! What on *earth* are you doing chatting up my wedding planner when you should be walking down the aisle?"

Marian peeks her head in from just outside the cathedral doors, where she's waiting with my father for her big moment, and looks at me a little murderously.

I peer down the aisle. My sister Julie is nearly at the front and I was supposed to be right behind her. In a hurry, I walk down the aisle, my face bright red, wondering for the thousandth time where Marian found this wedding planner.

"You looked great in there," Ian, my date, says, as we step outside the cathedral into the cool, crisp December air. The bells on the steeple clang in celebration as snow begins to gently fall. Everything is beautiful. Magical. But I'm freezing. And now that the ceremony is over, I'm back on duty. A MOH's job is never done.

"Thank you," I say, scrolling through my phone furiously, barely looking up at him. Wendi texted me the number of the psychic but the woman really is MIA. She's not answering my texts and ignored my call the two times I tried her.

Google: Psychics Haley, MA

Instantly, results fill my phone screen.

Mall psychics, tarot card readers, online psychics, Magic 8 Ball interpreters…

"Earth to Lucy."

I finally look up at Ian. "Sorry," I say. "We lost our psychic."

Ian looks properly confused. I mean, weddings don't usually have psychics. But Marian's bizarre 80s themed wedding does. And she's been more excited about this psychic the past few weeks than making her wedding vows.

"Well, I'd fill in, but I'm already sort of playing a role today."

I flush, remembering how I cornered Ian in the teacher's lounge two weeks ago and basically begged him to come to the wedding as my boyfriend.

"You see, I have a large family and lately, like, everyone is married! Or having babies. I spend most of my time at weddings and christenings. And all anyone ever asks me is if I have a boyfriend. Plus, my sister is kind of a bridezilla, and it's been stressful. No, that's being kind. It's been hell. The woman booked two wedding venues because she's indecisive. And two churches. And two honeymoons. And she put me in charge of everything. She has a wedding planner, but somehow I ended up doing seating charts, creating programs, making cassette tape mixes of all 80s music for wedding favors, and buying neon scrunchies and banana clips for every brides-maid to put our hair up in when we dance the night away!"

"I'll go."

"You…You'll come as my date? You don't think I'm crazy?"

"Crazy, no. Stressed, very. I'm not doing anything that night. And…I love a good party."

So here he is. Ian. He cleans up very well, and it really was very sweet of him to come today. I'm an 80s themed mess. My hair is crimped. *Crimped.* I look like a bottle of grape soda in my purple, polka-dotted dress complete with shoulder pads. And having him here has been working just the way I'd hoped! People for once are not asking me about my love life (or lack thereof). They're asking me about my date! And that's what I need because I've been so frazzled by this whole wedding experience, I worried if one person lamented in front of me that I'm still single, I'd go all *Carrie* on the whole party. That's a little bit of almost-80s madness that no one wants to see.

I smile at Ian. "It's an easy role. Just fawn over me, pretend I'm the most fascinating woman you've ever met and obviously the most beautiful as well."

"Done," he says. "I've always loved a girl wearing purple and polka dots."

"Don't forget the shoulder pads."

"They're burned in my brain. No, really," he adds when I laugh.

"Lucy, you ready?" my brother Jake asks me, leaning out of the trolley.

I take a deep breath and smile at Ian. "I have to go take photos now. And find a psychic." The knot that has been tightening in my stomach for weeks now gets a little tighter. "I'll see you at the reception."

"I'll be saying wonderful things about you to anyone that I meet while I wait," he says with an easy smile, sticking his hands in his pockets.

I smile appreciatively and turn, joining my family in the trolley.

Entering the reception hall an hour later, I immediately pan the room for Madame M. I called three potential psychics before resorting to calling Madame M from the Haley County Mall. She seemed strangely excited to offer her services and said she would meet me here. Of course with two hundred guests milling about and no idea what she looks like, the task is a fairly complicated one. I don't see her. I do, however, spot my Aunt Velma scurrying up to me almost urgently.

"Lucy!" Aunt Velma says as she approaches, completely winded from her one-hundred foot speed walk. "I saw the boy you were at the church with. Very handsome, like John Stamos," she says in a conspiratorial kind of way. "Is he your boyfriend? I didn't think you had a boyfriend. At least, no one told me you did. But your mother never tells me anything. I mean, back when she was popping out the five of you, I had to be very aware of her weight gain to even know she was having more children. Can't she pick up a phone? And when Marian got engaged to this Tom fellow – do you think I got a call?"

She waits for a moment, looking at me impatiently. "Do you?"

"I don't think you did," I say, as if I sympathize with her. But if she ever logged on to the family blog, she wouldn't need to wait for her phone to ring with family newscasts. But I can't say that to Aunt Velma, of course, as she'll only launch into her rant about how communication is a dying art since That Devil, the Internet, took over.

"I didn't," she concedes. "So?"

I blink at her for a few moments. "So…"

"Is he your boyfriend?" she asks, like I'm the village idiot.

"Yes," Uncle Walter says, sauntering up to us and smack into the middle of the conversation he's been eavesdropping on the whole time. "I was wondering that too. Is he your boyfriend, Lucy?"

"Oh. Ian?" I ask innocently. "He's my...it's kind of like...you know...he tells me that I'm his...we're just... dating." That's *so* not how that went in my mirror at home. I've never been a very good liar.

"You really should hold onto him, Lucy," Aunt Velma says, tilting her head and furrowing her eyebrows. She touches my arm sympathetically for emphasis. "You're, what, 35 now—"

"26," I say brightly, hoping the fire alarm in the building will go off at any moment, giving me a legitimate excuse to turn and run away from this conversation which is exactly what I'd love to do right now.

"—and child bearing years don't last forever," Uncle Walter chimes in.

"As usual, you two make great points," I say, preparing to close this conversation up – because childbearing is usually where I draw the line. "In fact, I should go find him and then grab on like you said. And hold on tight!"

"Before you find him, Lucy, you really should find a mirror. Your hair is a mess!" Aunt Velma says, shaking her head sadly as if my hair is the reason I am unmarried.

I reach up and touch my hair and groan. It does feel all out of place now. After all our time this morning on hair and makeup, it seems to have all come undone during the photo shoot. An outside photo shoot (80s photo booth themed, of course!) on a frosty December afternoon may not have been Marian's most inspired idea. But she always dreamed of having her photos at Boston Public Garden.

The moment I turn to walk away, I see a glass of bubbly champagne dangling in front of me from the outstretched hand of my best friend, Mary.

"Every family has one," Mary says as I grab the glass and begin drinking its contents. Quickly. "Or two," she adds, nodding towards Aunt Velma and Uncle Walter.

"You're a lifesaver." I smile and relax a bit.

"I still don't get your family. It's like they're passengers on Noah's Ark, everyone's pairing up, and they're throwing life vests at you."

"They never watched Mary Tyler Moore totally make it on her own." I take a couple of pieces of shrimp cocktail from a passing tray. My phone vibrates and I look down to see a text message from my sister, Julie:

Almost speech time. Where r u? BTW, liking the new guy. He told auntie Doris that it's very serious...and of course she's been telling EVERYONE.

Oh God. I hope he's not overdoing it. Where *is* Ian?

"I have to say, I really like the '80s theme!" Mary says. "I've never been to a psychic at a wedding before."

"Oh good! She's here."

"Why wouldn't she be here? The invitation very clearly said there would be a psychic."

"And what did she tell you?"

Mary shrugs and smiles like a giddy teenager. "Madame M told me that I already met the man of my dreams."

"You've already met him? Then why aren't you guys together?"

"I have no idea," she says, shaking her head. "But later, when I go home, I may have to make a list of all the men that I know."

"Seems like the only logical thing to do," I joke. But she nods and I know for a fact that she will absolutely make that list later. It's one of the reasons we get along so well, actually. She has the same irrepressibly romantic spirit that I do. I kind of hope she finds someone on that list who can become her dream man. I've never known any couples who met because of psychic guidance.

"Speaking of dream men, where's Ian?" I scan the crowd again.

"I have no idea," Mary says. "I've been keeping an eye out for him the past half hour, but last I saw he was chatting up everyone he saw about how great you are. I think he used the words 'the most fascinating woman I've ever met, seen, or heard of.'"

Okay, maybe I should have told Ian to tone it down a bit. I don't want people to think—

"Lucy, speech time." Jake comes up to us and lightly grabs my arm to begin pulling me away. "Hi, Mary."

But Mary is too busy looking through her phone – obviously looking for any men that she knows already who could be her dream man to add to her list.

"Do you believe in fate?"

After the question is out of my mouth, I peer nervously over the piece of paper clutched in my hand and into the many faces of the crowd. I attempt to make the impassioned expression that I practiced in my mirror at home – the one that dipped this question in romance and intrigue. Faces both familiar and unfamiliar stare at me, seemingly unsure if my question was rhetorical. Some people shake their heads while others nod. Some people shrug. Some people just continue the conversation they were having before my speech started.

"Well," I say coyly. "I do." I turn and look at Marian and Tom. "Tom was supposed to go to Atlanta for work," I say. I push a strand of crimped hair off my forehead, tucking it behind my ear. Despite my best efforts in the ladies' room, my hair is still looking a bit unkempt. "But he got the flu."

"Because I babysat a certain little sick nephew the week before," Tom chimes in, eyeing his brother's five-year-old son playfully.

"He didn't end up going to Atlanta. He stayed home, got sicker and sicker and eventually went to the hospital to make sure it was indeed the flu." I gaze at my sister and smile. She looks so excited hearing her own story relayed to this room full of their friends and family.

"At the hospital, he met a young, enthusiastic, and beautiful nurse. She took great care of him. Possibly, once seeing he didn't have a ring on his finger, she spent some extra time taking care of him," I say and a small giggle spreads across the room. "Tom told me recently that he fell for her on the spot. He'd been feverish when he met her, but he assures me that his light-headedness had nothing to do with the flu. She obviously felt the same way in return." I shrug and smile. I do love their story. "And, well...they've been taking amazing care of each other since that day."

The room bursts out in applause as Tom and Marian share a short, sweet kiss.

"I've never met two people more perfectly suited to each other. Anyone who knows Marian knows that she has a *few* obsessive compulsive tendencies," I say, which earns me a laugh with most of the crowd and a cautionary look from Marian herself. "I mean, for this wedding, she booked two churches, two reception halls and even planned two honeymoons! She needed her options for all things wedding-related." I shrug and laugh and wave my hand like we're all great friends – the room and I. "She's a perfectionist."

Marian smiles and narrows her eyes at me, clearly wanting to get back to the lovey-dovey tone from the beginning of my speech.

"Tom is one of the most laid-back people I've ever met. He didn't care if they got married on the back of a pick-up truck. Anyone who knows Tom knows that he might've done just that and happily so, if it had been up to him." The room laughs again and I gaze at Tom and Marian. "But he went along each step of the way with Marian's plans. Together they picked *one* church, *one* reception hall – this beautiful place," I add, gazing around thoughtfully. "And *one* honeymoon. To the relief of everyone, especially Tom." More laughter erupts – and this time Marian joins in. "These two people are so unique and different and they balance each other perfectly."

Tom smiles and pulls Marian close.

"I love this," I say quietly, almost conspiratorially, nodding toward the newlyweds. "Boy meets girl. A little love at first sight. Because she's a perfectionist, today is *perfect*. Because he's so laid-back and gentle, today is very simple. Tom was meant to meet Marian. Fate intervened that day and made him cross her path. And that path led us all to this room to celebrate the best day in their lives."

Out of the corner of my eye, I see my mother wipe a tear and squeeze Julie's hand, smiling adoringly at Tom and Marian.

I look at Tom and Marian and hold up my glass. "I wish you both *all* the happiness –"

"OH MY GOD!"

I stop, my champagne in midair, to look at what the big ruckus is all about. Every head turns towards my aunt Velma in the back of the dining area. It seems she just pulled the curtain on the 80s photo booth and...and I don't know! What on earth would warrant an 'oh my God' in the middle of the Maid of Honor speech?

Then I see it.

Ian and Courtney. Courtney, my drop dead gorgeous 23-year-old cousin. She's getting up from sitting on his lap. And there's hot pink lipstick all over his face.

My arm goes all tingly with nerves and I drop it to my side, spilling champagne all over the floor.

"Isn't that Lucy's fiancée?" I hear someone yell out.

"He was supposed to pop the question later on tonight," I hear someone at a table right next to me say loudly to my great-aunt with a hearing aid.

Then I notice something that kind of hurts. My sister. She looks so disappointed. She told me months ago at her bachelorette party how fun it was that I'd be giving a speech about her. She's been a Maid of Honor quite a few times herself and was so excited that it was finally her turn to just sit and listen. This clearly was not how she expected it to go.

"Um. To recap," I say loudly into the microphone, gaining all of the attention once more. "Today we celebrate Tom and Marian." I smile at her with hope, but I think my smile is actually shaking. "Fate brought you together and it brings us here." I wink at Marian and she smiles appreciatively at me. "Just ask the psychic."

A nervous laughter creates a small din throughout the room as a waiter rushes over to refill my champagne glass.

⌒

People spend months and months planning for the perfect day – and in the end, it feels about as long as an episode of *Sex and the City* – and is filled with as many cosmos, too.

After a blur of dancing to Culture Club, the Eurythmics, Genesis, Debbie Gibson, and even the New Kids on the Block (I may have stressed about it, but I made a pretty good playlist in the end!), I sit at my table with Mary and look for Ian once again. I finally spot him slow dancing with Courtney to the Bangles' "Eternal Flame" – one of my favorite ballads of all time. The cat's basically out of the bag. Everyone knows he's not really a boyfriend of any kind. To me, anyway.

"How hard is it to obey one rule?" Mary asks incredulously, gaping at them on the dance floor.

"It seemed like a good idea in theory," I say, finally looking away from the couple. "I just forgot to factor in every girl not dressed like Barney."

"You're too good for him. Obviously."

Mary says this every time it doesn't work out with someone. If I'm still single when I'm sixty, I'll have to explain to anyone who asks that I was simply too good for *everyone*.

Ugh. I just should have come alone. So what if I had to bear people asking about my love life at a particularly stressful wedding? It's a hell of a lot better than saying I have a love life and then letting it explode in front of them so they can look at me like I'm the latest Lifetime Original Movie. I keep getting looks from family members – so many of them – filled with pity. Shock. Outrage. And in a few cases, a look that seems to imply, "I knew they weren't a real item."

I leave the table – and the line of vision to the dance floor and all these family members – and head to the front entrance area. There's not much going on here. Just the '80s photo booth and the psychic station. I am definitely not visiting the infamous photo booth, so I slip through the curtain and into the dark tent where Madame M sits, eyes closed, with her hands on a crystal ball.

On the phone, her deep voice made me think of a tall woman with black hair, penciled-in eyebrows and turquoise eyes. But before me sits a short, round woman, wearing what looks like pajamas, her hair tied up in a messy bun.

Was she in bed when I called her?

"You're Lucy Gray," she says and then she opens her eyes.

"That's right." I catch her eyes with mine for a split second and feel kind of strange. Her expression is nearly hypnotic. I'm not sure about her credentials, but she definitely possesses the ability to make people feel strange. That's a plus, anyway. "We spoke on the phone. Thanks for coming with such short notice."

She smiles. She reaches over the crystal ball and touches my hands. Hers feel like cold marble and send a shiver through me.

"You are waiting for your life to begin," she says slowly.

"Oh." I look at her as she closes her eyes and squeezes my hands tighter.

"It's going to happen. Soon. But Lucy, it can only happen if you stop ignoring them," she says, her voice dropping to an intense, low whisper.

"Ignoring…"

"The signs." She opens her dark, intense eyes and fixes me with a penetrating stare. Her eyes are so dark they seem black. "You talked of fate back there. You talked about fate to all of those people but you don't understand it at all! You don't listen. You need to listen. The signs are *always* there. Lucy –"

"Listen to fate," I say, furrowing my brows in confusion. I wish she'd just tell me something direct like I have already met the man of my dreams, so I could simply go home and make a list like Mary will undoubtedly do tonight. What does she mean, listen to fate?

When I blink again, that intense look in her eyes is gone. Vanished. Like it was never there to begin with. She says nothing more and so I thank her, leaving her tent and reentering the bright reception hall. The brightness momentarily shocks my irises and I squint, feeling very strange.

"How about a dance?" my father asks me. I'm not sure if he was waiting for me or just happened to be there, but knowing my dad, he probably guessed I was hiding out and wanted to be sure when I resurfaced that he was the one waiting for me.

I smile and take his hand and we walk back into the reception hall, straight to the dance floor. My dad says nothing about Ian, and I appreciate it. He simply holds me close and tells me my speech was nice.

The best thing about coming home on a winter's night is climbing into bed when every bone in your body feels frozen. I finally peel the purple, polka dotted dress off my body and pull on my steel gray fleece pajamas. Eventually my body begins to feel less like ice.

Ricky (Ricardo), my adorable tuxedo cat, is happy I am finally home. He jumps onto the bed and curls up next to me, while the black and white glow of TV Land lights my room dimly, buzzing quietly. I rub my feet together, and eventually feel my insides thawing.

Ricky purrs loudly. He loves the *Dick Van Dyke Show*. I try to focus on the show but my mind is still buzzing. I think about Ian. He actually left with Courtney. He didn't say goodbye – mostly because every time I spotted him I made sure to move far enough away that he couldn't spot me. But it's not Ian I really can't shake from my mind. I barely like the guy. Romantically, anyway. Honestly, he's a little too vain. I catch him checking out his reflection in clean windows all the time at work.

No, it's the psychic. The *mall psychic*. Hired like twenty minutes before the reception! Her words are echoing in my mind. I mean, why did she think my life hadn't begun? I have a great life. A fulfilling life! A good job. Friends. Family.

I close my eyes.

I'll just ignore her strange insinuations and drift off to dreamland! Perfect plan.

But the thing is, she said it was going to happen – "it" being my life starting. She said it would happen "soon."

Why am I still thinking about it? She was clearly just trying to play a part.

I close my eyes and try to go to sleep.

But...here's the thing: her "soon" kind of made me feel like I had as a kid when I thought I could hear the ocean inside of a seashell – like anything in the world was possible. And when I think about it now, I get this feeling...

Like something is about to begin.

the wedding of the century
Posted by: @Delores at 4:24 PM on december 18 on TheGrayBlog

Well thank God it's over. Tom & Marian get to relax poolside whilst I - who gave Marian life and also planned her wedding (except for the decision to have a DJ not a band - that was all Tom) - am a post-wedding bundle of nerves. The bride & groom get a honeymoon. The mother should get a spa weekend! Is there a registry for that?

Everything went off without a hitch. Well - aside from the fact that two people *got* hitched. L.O.L. Is that how you say it? I'm laughing out loud

Highlights of the day: My dear husband refrained from doing the chicken dance during the Macarena. And Marian and Tom looked insatiably happy.

Lowlights of the day: That awful boy who ditched Lucy! And for her own cousin. Everyone noticed. Lucy, if you're reading this: HE'S NOT WORTH IT. DON'T CRY. STOP EATING ICE CREAM.

All in all another MAGNIFIQUE Gray family event!

-Mom

chapter two

This December Monday brings me back to reality. Romantic scenes set inside cathedrals and insanely unromantic scenes set inside photo booths – that's all past. That was this weekend. *This*...is Monday. I look both ways and dash across the street, clutching my hot pink *I Love Lucy* umbrella tightly (It's not meant to be self-indulgent; it's just a tribute to the greatest TV show *ever*), and step right into a puddle on my way into Dunkin' Donuts.

I immediately look around in all directions frantically. What if the puddle is a sign? I look for a handsome man...or a lottery ticket. Anything in and around the vicinity of this elusive puddle. There's nothing out of the ordinary here. Except my soaking foot.

Well, that is probably not how Fate's signs work anyway. If I stepped in a puddle and fell right into the arms of my very own perfect match, Fate would lose its reputation.

All thoughts of psychics and signs really fly out the window as I walk up the cobblestone walkway and through the oak-wood doors of the Bradley Fitzhugh-Simms Elementary School. I finish my coffee a few minutes before my third graders begin to walk in and take their seats.

"Miss Gray, how was your party?" Cady asks sweetly.

Cady is an adorable little girl who wants to be a teacher *just like me*. So she copies everything I do and asks lots of questions about my life. It's very sweet, actually.

"It was a wedding," I say. "And it was very nice."

"Did you wear that dress that made you look like a purple monster?" Liam asks. He's Macaulay Culkin in *The Good Son*. Cute face. A little bit evil.

"Yes, I did," I say, smiling, reminding myself for the thousandth time since the beginning of the year to better control what I tell the children.

"It's my turn to share today," Cady says.

I pull my lesson planner out of my tote-bag and begin scanning my class list. "So it is!" I say excitedly. Because of the wedding, I never got around to finishing up today's lesson plan. A student geography presentation is the perfect way to start the day.

"Why do we have to do these presentations about places all over the world?" Liam asks.

"Because someday you might have to go to these places on important business trips or because you're heading to a destination wedding – or you'll be on a reality TV show like *The Amazing Race* and you'll need to know how to get around so you can win the big treasure. What you learn here might come in handy."

"You don't win treasure on *The Amazing Race*," Joey

informs me. "You get actual money." Three years ago, her great grandmother was on a dating reality show about finding love in your seventies, so Joey's always ripe with facts about all things Reality TV-based.

"Miss Gray, where have *you* been?" Liam asks. He looks pointedly at me and crosses his arms.

"Never mind." I look down at my daily syllabus. "Okay, Cady. You're on."

I sit in my chair and watch as Cady bounds up to the front of the class clad in a white button down blouse with a gray sweater and a long black skirt – an outfit I often wear to class. I smile inwardly. Her desire to be a teacher is one of the many reasons I love my job. And breaking through to kids like Liam who are a bit rough around the edges makes it pretty pleasing too. I notice that Cady has papers in her hands. Lots of papers, actually. I begin to wonder if she remembered that this was only supposed to be a very short presentation. But as I open my mouth to say something, she clears her throat authoritatively and slams the papers down on the podium.

"London, England: A Brief Overview, by Cady Mc-Ginnis," she begins dramatically. "The legend goes like this! In 60 AD, London was burnt to the ground by the forces of Queen Boudicca of the Iceni tribe. This was a tribe from modern Norfolk. Queen Boudicca was leading a major revolt against the Roman rule. So they say."

Oh dear lord. We're starting with London burnt to the ground? In 60 AD? I keep opening my mouth to cut in and remind her that she only has to tell us a little bit about her chosen destination and give a few facts about it within three to five minutes. But every time I do, she looks at me with the biggest smile on her face as if to say "this is surely A+ work, right, Miss Gray?" that I lean back and just let her go – reciting what she undoubtedly lifted from Wikipedia.

"The financial and economic equivalent of the governor was the pro...pro...cure...rator. *Procurator*. There is evidence that the offices of this official lay somewhere within the city of Roman London..."

❧

"Oh God, there he is," I whisper to Mary, quickly slinking behind the column that divides our teacher's lounge from the coffee station – on the coffee side, of course. I grab a banana from the bar a foot away and then resume my James Bond-esque hiding position behind the column.

Mary peeks around and fixes me with a disapproving look. She teaches kindergarten. Her kids are the most adorable little angels, not a Liam among them. Already, she's probably had a wonderful, cute-filled day. She probably didn't have to listen to a twenty-minute presentation about ancient London and the forces of Queen Boudicca. Her foot's probably not damp from stepping in a non-fateful puddle near Dunkin' Donuts. And she probably didn't just spot the date that ditched her at her own sister's wedding sitting on the couch in the teacher's lounge a mere couple of feet away, looking perfect. She should give me a disapproving look?

"Lucy, you can't avoid him forever," she says. "He works across the hall from you and we all share a lounge."

"Yet another reason it's not a good idea to go on a date with someone you work with. It might go badly and then you're stuck sharing a lounge forever."

"I believe that was one of the arguments I made when you told me you were going to ask him out," she says, crossing her arms.

"You're going to give me an I Told You So right now? Really?"

"Well...I did."

"Lucy," Ian says, peeking around the column, hands in his pockets and an uneasy smile on his face. I jump when I see him, and try to look like I was just leaning back, eating a banana, listening to Mary like she's the most fascinating person in the world.

"Ian, hey," I say casually. "How are you?"

"I want to apologize about the other night."

Mary walks away quickly, and I look back at Ian. "The other night...the other night...*oh* you mean the wedding?"

"Yes," he says – and he actually has the decency to look sheepish about the whole thing.

"It's fine," I say. "Really."

"I just met Courtney and...I guess, well...you see, she's completely my type and it all happened so fast and unexpectedly. When I met her, something went off inside me."

I'll bet it did. I nod understandingly all the same, wondering for the thousandth time in my life: what's so great about types? People act like we're all born with a predetermined prototype for our eventual match.

Ian Walker is predestined to end up with Type 242: leggy, dark-haired, turquoise-eyed damsel-in-distress who'd run over any one of her friends to get a guy to notice her.

I've never been a fan of the whole 'type' argument. It takes all the unpredictability out of the chase. Where's the fun in that?

"I think I really fell for her," Ian is saying. "If, you know, something like that can happen that quickly, which I believe it can. The only thing is," he continues, "and I hate to ask you this, Lucy, what with the way our date turned out – "

The way our date turned out? You mean when almost everyone I know saw my would-be boyfriend making out with my cousin at my sister's wedding?

"But do you have her number? I never ended up getting it and—"

Irritation courses through me and I feel my face flush completely. "Sure," I say. "Let me get my phone."

"Lucy, you really are the best," he says.

I walk back to my purse and grab my phone. Mary narrows her eyes at me. "You're not giving him her number."

"Why not?" I ask. "Who am I to stand in the way of...whatever that was."

Mary rolls her eyes. "You're too soft."

I sigh, texting the number to Ian, knowing she's right.

Instead of sitting next to Mary on the sofa in the lounge, I walk over to the globe in the corner. I place my forefinger on the map and look at all the colors and places, oceans and countries, islands and nations facing me and in one quick motion I spin it. As it turns, I hear Liam's question from earlier reverberate in my mind – *where have you been?*

The world spins before me – and all around me – and I'm here. Always right here. Standing still.

ॐ

It's a relief to walk out of the school with just four more

days to holiday break. The crisp air, the dirty snow, the empty parking lot behind the building. It's all very quiet and nice until my cell rings.

"Lucy, we're on our way to the airport. I need you to do me a favor! Quiet Tom, I can't hear Lucy! Lucy? I need a favor!"

"Wasn't my stellar performance as maid of honor enough?" I ask Marian, who apparently needs a favor.

"You need to go to our house. I think I left the door unlocked and the stove on," she says.

"You did not leave anything on, babe. We didn't even cook today. And I locked the door myself!" Tom says in the background. I know only too well that his assertions will do nothing to calm her paranoia. After the whole booking two reception halls, churches and honeymoons fiasco, he totally knew he was marrying a woman with obsessive compulsive behavior. I don't know why he's acting like this is at all shocking.

"I don't think either of us locked the door, honey," Marian says. "I just have this feeling that the door's unlocked and someone's going to break in and take something like our beautiful new china."

"Personally, I think they'd gun for your sixty inch TV," I add, getting into my car.

"Very helpful, Lucy," Tom says.

"Either way, you should go and check things out," Marian says. "And water my magnolias! I forgot to water them today. Could you do that every three days until we're back?"

Twenty minutes later, I unlock (read: it was locked) Tom and Marian's door and walk in, shaking my head. I check the stove. It's off, of course.

I walk into the living room and see plants and flowers

by the big window. She was pretty specific about watering just the magnolias. But are they the white ones, the green ones, the yellow ones, or the pink ones? I guess I'll just water every flower. Flowers love water, right?

I find her watering pot, fill it, and then proceed to unload its contents over the plants.

My cell phone rings a moment later. It's Wendi, the wedding planner. She called me practically daily in the month leading up the nuptials. What could she possibly want now?

A minute later, I play her voicemail, and feel that familiar knot of responsibility begin to coil itself all up in my stomach again. This knot was supposed to be all untangled after their knot was tied!

Lucy. It's me, hon. Wendi. Well, the wedding is done and Marian's off on her cruise through the Greek isles! Don't we all wish we could cruise off after everything we did for the big day? So now it's time for Thank You notes! To help our bride along, I am going to forward you the list of those who attended so you can fill out the envelopes with all of their addresses. And begin to detail for Marian who gave her what. The gifts are in Marian's foyer. So, you'll just have to rummage through them to get started. It should take a few hours max and our Marian will be so appreciative. She shouldn't have to worry about ANYTHING. After all, she is the bride. I know it's a bummer to do this over Christmas, but it would be best if she came back from her honeymoon without a worry in the world. I promised her this would get done. Thanks, hon. You're the best!

Okay, what exactly do wedding planners do? Is their number one responsibility to drive the Maid of Honor nuts?

I jump when Marian's house phone rings, and begin

to refill the water pot. They have a lot of plants. Tom and Marian's answering machine picks up. "Hi! If you call before December seventeenth, you've reached Tom Bolton and Marian Gray. If you're calling *after*, you're calling Tom *and* Marian Bolton! Leave a message!" Marian's voice squeaks excitedly, followed by a long beep.

I roll my eyes and smile, unloading the last of the water onto the white and pink plants.

"Hello, this message is for Marian Gray. Well, Bolton actually, it would seem. This is The Chaizer London calling to confirm your reservation for tomorrow night. We eagerly await your arrival and hope The Chaizer is to your liking for this special occasion!" a cheerful man says, sounding just like Michael Caine in *Miss Congeniality*.

I walk to the kitchen, putting the watering pot in their sink, humming to myself, wishing I had an exotic accent of some kind. It would be so cool to have a British accent. Or an Irish or Australian accent! There's just absolutely nothing great about American accents. You don't hear about Europeans wishing they could talk like an American....

My thoughts trail off, realization dawning. I slowly turn until I'm looking at the answering machine inside which that gorgeous accent just disappeared. I can't have heard him right.

"London?" I say aloud to no one.

Tom and Marian are going on a cruise through the Greek islands. As soon as the question forms, however, I remember. London was Honeymoon Option #2 for the OCD bride that is my sister.

Marian called me feeling like she forgot something and assumed it was turning her stove off or leaving her door unlocked when in actuality she forgot to cancel her honeymoon? For someone with obsessive compulsive behavior, that's a pretty laughable oversight.

I pick up the phone to call Tom and Marian. They probably haven't taken off yet. As I begin dialing Marian's cell phone number, I stop. They're taking off for their honeymoon. Marian is clearly already getting nervous about forgetting things back home. I would just be adding fuel to that fire. And they really should kick off their honeymoon stress-free.

Okay, new plan. I look at the caller ID, and dial the number in London. I will fix my sister's gaffe myself. I really am the best Maid of Honor because my job goes above and beyond just the wedding day. I'm more like a Maid of Honor for life.

"The Chaizer," Michael Caine says on the other end. Two words out of his mouth and I can just sense years of private school and a love of high tea.

"Hi!" I say cheerily. "I'm calling about a reservation that was made and...for Marian and Tom Bolton...um... the reservation...it was made...I'm calling...um..."

I've turned into a bumbling idiot. But I can't help it! As I get to the part where I cancel the reservation, I find myself thinking about her. The psychic from the wedding, I mean. I think about what she said about signs and how I'm supposed to give fate a hand so my life will begin and all that other mumbo jumbo.

I think about how Cady gave this entire, albeit painful, presentation about London only a few hours ago and about how my sister asked me to go to water her plants and check on her place because she's totally paranoid... and about how while doing that I just *happened* to hear a message from someone in London because Marian *happened* to forget to cancel her reservation – something she'd never do in a million years. If this isn't some kind of sign, then –

"Hello?" the man says, sounding a bit impatient now.

"I...I..."

I'm stammering, making no sense, and my thoughts are completely jumbled. If I could form a coherent sentence, I'm not sure if it would contain real words from the English language.

"Miss, are you alright?" the man asks.

My heart thumps rigorously inside my chest, feeling like it's in my throat, and I wonder if this man on the phone can hear it, it's so loud. "I am going to be there tomorrow night," I say finally. I swallow hard. "At your hotel, I mean."

"Okay, well, that's what we had called to confirm. That you'll be here."

"I will," I say quickly, my eyes darting back and forth around Marian's place. What am I doing?

"Yes. Well, we look forward to accommodating you for this special occasion," the man says.

When I hang up the phone and look around Marian's living room - at her flowers spilling over with too much water, her television and her striped navy blue and cream drapes that match her couch - my heart rate quickens and I smile.

"I'm going to London," I whisper to no one in particular. My stomach does flips deserving of an Olympic gold medal as a happiness laced with a little terror rushes through my body like a cold heat. I'm finally going somewhere.

chapter three

"*Y*ou're going to go on your sister's throwaway honeymoon?"

I swivel in my desk chair to face Mary. "Yes, and I just charged eight hundred and forty-two dollars on my credit card for a plane ticket so I'd love your unconditional support."

I click "Print" and my itinerary begins to become an actual, tangible thing one line at a time. I know that printing a document is not the same as flying away from home on an airplane, but at this moment, it kind of feels like it. This is the first step.

Mary tosses the *Entertainment Weekly* she was reading on the bed in my room and fixes me with her sternest look, which is pretty weak. I mean, she's the girl next door. Literally. She and I grew up right next door to one another and have been inseparable since we were in the third grade. "Generally when people go on honeymoons, they're married," she says. "Now, I myself am not married so I don't speak from experience, but I heard through the grapevine that they bring that special someone that they married with them."

"I won't actually be on Marian's honeymoon." I pull my itinerary from the printer tray, feeling like my head and body are suddenly disconnected. "I'm just going to the hotel with her reservation." Knowing Marian, she probably booked the most posh hotel in all of London.

"There are still a few days left of school."

"I already called for a substitute."

"What is your plan when you get there? Your name is not Marian Bolton. Or Marian Gray for that matter."

"I have her credit card from being a glorified errand girl for the past four months," I say brightly. "Not that I'd ever use it, but maybe if they need some kind of piece of plastic with her name on it −"

"It's not an ID."

"I'll explain. I'll…" I trail off. That won't work. Hotels require identification to check in. Nice ones anyway. I turn back to my computer and open Google.

London, England hostels.

Mary peeks over my shoulder. "Lucy, you're not going there and staying in a hostel."

I don't look back at her as I search through the list of hostels by price and amenities. "Why not?" I ask. "You stayed in like ten hostels when you backpacked through Europe after high school."

She laughs. "And I was eighteen years old. I didn't have any savings or know any better."

Now I look at her. "I want to go," I say desperately. "Even if I have to stay in some crappy, cheap place."

Mary places her hands on my shoulders and turns my chair around so that I'm facing her again.

"Why do you want to go right now? I mean...it's Christmas. And you love Christmas and all of your family's many, *many* traditions. Speaking of your family, they're definitely going to freak out if you take off without any notice to another country. Why not go this summer or something?"

I stand up and walk over to my sock drawer. I open it and scour through until I find it. My passport. I run my fingers absentmindedly over the golden emblem emblazoned on its cover and squeeze it in my hand. "Did you know that I got this when you went to Europe?"

Mary sits forward and looks at me.

"I wanted to go on that trip with you girls so badly. And...I didn't. I was nervous. The whole thing felt so spontaneous. So *not* me. So I didn't get my passport. That was my excuse. But when I got your first postcard, I went and got this right away."

I open the little book and see my own picture staring back at me. I look at the expiration date. "It's like I made a promise to myself that I never kept. This thing expires in two years and I haven't used it once! If I don't go now, will I just keep pushing this off? Because something will come up. It always does."

Mary nods, looks from the book to me, and finally, she smiles. "You should go, then."

I smile at Mary, relieved. If she's in my corner, then this must be a good idea.

My cell phone chirps. Charles, the oldest of us Gray siblings, is calling. "Shoot." I look at Mary, clutching the phone tightly in my hand. "Charles and Samantha were having a family dinner tonight to celebrate his big victory on the Mullins case."

I pull the cell to my ear. "Hey, Big Shot," I say. I've been calling him that ever since he passed the bar exam.

"Hi, Lucy," he says, sounding serious as always. "Are you coming tonight? Sam's about to serve dinner. And Cora would like to tell you all about her latest tween drama."

I can almost hear the eye roll on his end. Cora made me an aunt eleven years ago, and while I love my niece and nephew to death, she may be my favorite for that fact alone.

"I can't actually," I say quickly, looking for a little nerve. I'd never miss a dinner like this. Charles works hard and this was by far his biggest case. And my family is *that* family. If there's a reason to celebrate, we do. Most of the family manages to show up. And I always show up.

Silence.

"Are you sick?" he asks, sounding a little concerned.

"No. Not sick. Just not coming. I have a meeting."

Mary walks over to my desk and puts a mug of hot cocoa with marshmallows on it– our favorite winter habit.

"A night time meeting? You're a third grade teacher and it's days before holiday break. What kind of meeting do you have?"

I say nothing, wracking my brain for something that would make some sense. I can't say that I'm heading to London. Mary's right. My whole family will think something is really, really wrong. I've never left the country before. So it hardly seems likely that –

"I guess you heard, then," he says quietly.

"Heard?"

"That Courtney was coming tonight. And…"

Realization dawns. "And she's bringing Ian."

"Yes. But I'll tell her to stay home, Lucy. I'd rather have you here."

"I can't come either way," I say. "Like I said, I have a thing."

More silence. Despite the fact that I'm 26, live alone and take care of twenty-two third graders five days a week, Charles seems to still see me as the little kid he taught to ride a bike. He threatened my high school boyfriend's life (should he ever make me cry or lay a hand on me) – and I have to say, while he tries to act nonchalant about these things now, he's really not much better. I guess when you're the youngest girl of five and he's the oldest child – separated by ten years – this is the norm.

"I'm sorry to miss it," I say finally, before muttering a 'see you later' and tapping the phone off.

I dip a finger into my mug of hot cocoa, letting it barely touch the surface of the cocoa, the melted, gooey marshmallow sticking to the skin.

Mary takes a sip of her cocoa and sits beside me, grabbing my itinerary off the desk and scanning it. "You are planning to tell your family that you're leaving tomorrow, right?"

I look at her, my eyes wide. "I figured I'd call them from the plane and tell them then."

Mary laughs. "Why on earth would you do that?"

"Because when I was sixteen years old and wanted to go blonde – just to see if I'd actually have more fun – my mom and sisters held an actual intervention. 'But you have beautiful auburn hair,' they said! 'People would pay money to have your color!' 'We're all redheads. Why would you want to turn your back on your family?' 'It's a waste of money. The upkeep with roots is a real hassle. Dye it when you go gray.'

Mary nods like she's trying to follow.

"When I entertained the thought of taking off to Los Angeles to work in television, for weeks it was all I could do to avoid hearing, 'Everyone there is smoking the cocaine.' 'You have to sleep your way to the top.' 'What would you even do in television? All you do is watch TV Land. The shows you like were filmed in the '50s and '60s. You can't work for them! The actors are all dead!'"

I love my career. I love my loft right here in Haley, Massachusetts, where I grew up. I even love my hair color. I'm thankful to my family for always caring about what I do. They would do anything in the world for me. But to them, I am still a little girl in pigtails, my lip quivering as I get on the school bus on my first day of kindergarten.

I'm the reliable one. The constant. I shouldn't change my hair color. And I shouldn't jump on an airplane and take a spontaneous trip. When I wanted to take that backpacking trip through Europe with my friends, they said to wait, that one day I would go somewhere. On my honeymoon.

To them, "honeymoon" basically translated to "first vacation ever." My parents went to Hawaii. Charles and Samantha went to Costa Rica. Marian and Tom are going to the Mediterranean. I'm supposed to wait and go...well, somewhere. Someday.

Well, what if I never get married? I'll just never go anywhere? No. That is not good enough for me. I'm done standing on the sidelines. I'm done waiting for life. This time, I'm going after it.

I stand up resolutely and walk over to my window.
I see Mrs. Suzayaki sitting on her kitchenette stool by
her open window having a cigarette, looking at a trashy
magazine. She's my go-to for all the celebrity gossip
because she's pretty much a chain smoker with a lot of
subscriptions. I pull my window up, instantly chilled
by the winter air on my face.

"Hi, Lucy!" Mrs. Suzayaki says. "Weren't you going
to your family's for dinner tonight?"

"Not tonight." I smile, rubbing my hands up and
down my arms for warmth. "I'm actually wondering...
do you still make Fake IDs?"

⁓

Ricky is sitting inside my suitcase, attacking every article
of clothing I put in it, thrashing with his furry paws and
destroying any sense of order to my clothes—almost as
if he knows that they represent our impending separa-
tion. I pet him and look at *I Love Lucy* on my TV, and
the familiar sight of Lucy Ricardo calms me instantly.

"See that, buddy?" I say to Ricky, gesturing to the
TV. "The original Lucy and Ricky. Look at her, all wide-
eyed and mischievous, knee deep in shenanigans with
Ethel. In about ten minutes she'll definitely have some
'splainin' to do." I stop petting him and just stare at the
TV. "She'd totally do something like this."

Ricky stares at me.

I flip through the lonely pages of my passport. This
book is complete proof that the psychic was right about
one thing. I am waiting. I'm waiting to have a stamp.
I'm waiting to have a story.

I crawl into bed and gaze out the window at the

white lights adorning Mrs. Suzayaki's bushes. It's so peaceful out there. A night like tonight echoes for miles. It's crisp and still. And full of possibility.

∾

The next day, driving into Logan Airport, I feel a nervous thrill inside. As a plane overhead takes off for somewhere, I think of the psychic and clutch my passport in my hand. I look at Mary.

Thinking of the psychic reminds me of Mary's own run-in with the woman. "Any leads yet on your list of men you already know that may or may not be the love of your life?"

She rolls her eyes dramatically. "I scoured Facebook, Instagram, our high school year book and my phone for three hours the other night."

"And?"

She pauses. "Do you remember Evan Abbott?"

"Evan Abbott...your old guitar teacher?"

She nods. "He was a senior when I was a freshman and I had a huge crush on him. I never saw him after he left for college, but I found him on Instagram. He's single, handsome, and we used to make each other laugh a lot, which is why I never really learned much and can't play anything except 'Free Falling'. I sent him a direct message and we are actually getting together in two days for lunch."

I shake my head at her. She's such a romantic. I love it.

She pulls her car into an open spot by my boarding gate. "Okay, do you have your fake ID?"

I shake my head, grabbing the ID and Marian's credit card. I clutch them in my hand tightly. "I do."

I sigh. "And it seemed like a great idea last night, but I've slept on it and decided that I should just look into a hostel or find some kind of alternative—"

"You are not taking this trip and staying in a hostel. You deserve this. And anyway, I looked online last night. London at Christmas – all the hotels, even the crappy ones, cost an arm and a leg last minute. Marian booked this nearly a year ago. It probably costs as much as a hotel half as nice at this point. You've been saving for something like this for years."

"But—"

"Lucy, you need this. You basically handled every detail of Marian's wedding because her wedding planner was completely worthless. Your date made out with your cousin in front of the entire reception and now he's dating her." She folds my hands around the little pieces of plastic. "No one deserves this more than you."

"I'll figure it out," I say quietly, tucking the cards back into a pocket on the inner lining of my purse.

"Just remember, it won't matter on check-out day. They don't charge anything until check out unless you order room service or whatever. So don't do that, and just use your own card when you check out." She grabs my shoulders. "This will be fine."

Mary pushes the button to open her trunk and gets out of her car. I follow.

"Thank you for cat-sitting for me." I grab my bag from the trunk and look at her. "I owe you one."

"How about a few promises and we'll call it even?"

I narrow my eyes at her.

"Look up Cary Stewart when you're there. Maybe he can show you around so that you're not alone."

"Cary Stewart, the drama snob from high school? I

haven't seen him since graduation. Why would I look him up?"

"Because he is in London," Mary says excitedly. "When I was researching all of the men that I already know, I checked out his profile. He studies acting in London on and off all year and he's there again now."

"That's nice that you're Facebook friends with the guy," I say, beginning to step away from Mary. "But I'm not, so it would just be weird if I called on him to show me around." I smile at her. "I'll be okay."

"He's really nice," Mary continues, like she didn't hear me.

"He laughed at me when I auditioned for *Our Town* in ninth grade."

"He takes his craft really seriously. And I'm sure now that he's an adult, he doesn't laugh at people."

I grab Mary by the shoulders and look into her eyes. "I can't make any promises on that. What else have you got?"

"Promise me you'll be careful. Promise me you will call me when you get there and at least a few times after that."

"If you promise me that you'll play with Ricky every day and if he wants to sit on your lap, you won't do what you normally do." Which is throw him off.

"Fine. Deal."

"Deal," I say back.

"If he chooses to sit on my lap, I'll let him."

"And you'll cuddle him."

"Like he's a teddy bear."

"Okay, don't overdo it." I take my bag and look at Mary.

"Promise to relax a little. After everything lately, you deserve to take a deep breath and really relax."

"I relax."

"You're a planner. Read up a bit, jot down some ideas – but don't plan out every minute that you're there. Let things just happen for once."

I nod. "I can try."

"One more promise," she says. "When you check in using this ID to stay at the nice hotel – which you'd better do because I'm telling you, a park bench seems to be the only other affordable option – then when you're *in* that hotel, you're Marian. The minute you leave that place, you can be anyone you want to be. But when you're inside that place, just keep it simple and be Marian, okay?"

I look at her uncertainly.

She tilts her head, her face knowing and determined. "Promise."

"Fine," I say. "I promise."

Sitting at the gate, I mentally check and re-check my list to make sure I packed everything. I have coffee and magazines for the flight, and now the very last thing (the one thing I've been dreading) left to do is call my mom and tell her I'm, well, honeymooning solo.

She answers her phone with a loving, "What is it, Lucy?"

"Is that any way to greet your own flesh and blood?"

"Well, when it's 6:45 in the morning it is. Is everything okay? You don't usually call anyone in the morning until you've had at least two coffees."

"GATE B2 IS READY TO BOARD," the speaker directly above me blares.

"Where are you?" my mom asks.

I take a deep breath. Here goes nothing. "I'm just calling to say goodbye actually because my plane for London – you know, the one in England – is about to board, and please don't send me to the mental hospital when I get back. I'm honestly just trying to do what that old psychic lady at the wedding said and take my life into my own hands and make it happen. You know… seize the bull and all that. So, anyway, give everyone a hug and kiss for me and tell them I love them and Merry Christmas."

I don't do well under pressure. So what? There are lots of things I'm very good at. I put a hand against my free ear, to block out the noise of the airport, and pull the phone tighter against my other ear, straining to hear my mother.

"Lucy," my mother shrills, finally. "You are joking, right?"

"Actually, no. I'm really at Logan, about to take off. I'm going on a holiday for the holidays." I pause. "It's poetic, don't you think?"

"You're leaving your family for Christmas?" she asks.

"Yes," I say quietly. I mean, there's really no sugar coating that one fact.

Through ambient airport bustle, cellular air waves and motherly silence, I can hear, loud and clear, her total incredulity, practically feel her nerves shredding.

"NOW BOARDING GATE B2."

"Okay, Mom. I love you. I'll…call you when I get there!"

Once I get into my seat and get comfortable, I take out my iPod and switch on the playlist I made for Marian's wedding. Belinda Carlisle booms in my ears, "Heaven is a Place On Earth" becoming the anthem to the beginning of my adventure.

chapter four

I 'm tired, and it's late. I check my phone. 10:25 PM.
That's *London time*. I'm here. I'm in London! The
woman at Customs most likely thinks I am certifiably
insane, because as she stamps my passport, I gasp and
tears - actual tears - fill my eyes. I purse my lips tightly,
gripping the countertop, in a feeble attempt at trying to
keep my emotions in check. But she sees me. In all of
my blubbering idiocy. The goofy smile, the tear-filled
eyes...I look crazy.

"Welcome to the UK," she says, still eyeing me curiously.

I open my mouth to thank her, but – and I'm not
sure how it happens – what ends up coming out is,
"You have the best accent. And thank you so much for
the stamp. It's my first stamp."

I take the proffered passport back and put it in my
purse. "Thank you," I say casually, before clearing my
throat and looking around, trying to seem important

– cool – like I am here on business all the time. Like I didn't just make a complete idiot of myself two seconds ago. But when I walk away, I can't stop the smile from taking over my face. I'm in London.

The taxi line is long, but, tired as I am, I'm fine with it. For one thing – the taxi line is in London—and for another, there is a truly beautiful man standing not ten feet away from me, scanning the line, completely oblivious to the fact that I am staring at him. I imagine his gorgeous accent and glamorous British life. He's most likely looking for his fiancée, who's just arrived back from her business trip to Rome. Or Milan. She's probably a fashion designer. He looks like someone who'd be in love with someone who owns her own clothing line. He has black hair and tanned, golden skin. He's pretty tall – definitely a little over six feet. He seems to be in excellent shape. There's a familiarity about him, too. Like he's someone I've known my whole life.

Suddenly, the man looks my way and our eyes lock. In embarrassment, I close my gaping mouth and stare at a puddle on the ground with immense interest.

"Lucy?"

"I'm sorry. I really didn't mean to stare…" I trail off. "Do I know you?" I ask foolishly. I mean, obviously he knows me. He knows my name. The person behind me makes an awful noise to alert me, I guess, to take a few steps forward in line. The man walks over to me and stops, smiling.

"Well, we did go to high school together," he says easily and I suddenly realize that his inherent familiarity is because, well, I'm actually familiar with him.

"Cary?" I say, gazing up at him, my eyes wide—I'm incredulous. He was good looking in high school, but he wasn't exactly a Greek Adonis back then. He was just a cute theater snob who had the nerve to laugh at a little ninth grader during an audition preventing her from ever getting the courage up to try out for another production.

"It's nice to see you again," he says, chuckling at my bewildered face, obviously amused. "I thought it was you in that line." He clears his throat and gestures toward the Heathrow terminal behind us. "I'm just here coming back from a trip myself." He stares down at the ground for a moment before lifting his head to catch my eyes. "Can I offer you a ride?" he asks casually.

The pieces begin falling into place instantly, and my cheeks burn with humiliation. I note his distinct lack of suitcase, his very unruffled attire, and his shifty disposition. He may have studied acting for the past ten years, but he's not that good. "You just came back from a trip...or Mary called you and told you to make sure I didn't naively hitch a ride to my hotel with a murderer?"

He says nothing but smiles softly, his eyes glowing in acknowledgement.

"I'm going to kill her," I mutter. She told me to go have myself an adventure and then hired a babysitter? I look back up at him. "I'm really sorry she put you out...but you really don't need to give me a ride. I was just going to take a cab." My cheeks actually feel hot. It may be cold out, but I am sweating profusely. "Thank you, though, for agreeing to come," I add hastily. "I mean, you barely know me." I look up at him and smile, blushing. "It was really nice of you."

Cary shrugs and smiles. I do not remember his smile ever having an effect on me in high school, which could have been because of his bitter teasing. But here, in the cold London air, under the blinking lights of passing taxis, his smile sends warmth coursing through every part of my body. "I always thought Mary was the sweetest girl. I got her Facebook message and wrote back saying I'd give you a ride, welcome you to London."

"You probably don't even remember me." I peer up at him. Everyone knew Mary, who had actually been crowned Miss Congeniality. At our ten year reunion, I realized that while everyone remembered her, no one outside of our closest friends remembered me. I participated in everything, but...I guess I just blended in well.

He chuckles a little. "To be honest, you're right. But when I saw you, you looked familiar. I figured it must be you."

I really wish the ground would just open up and swallow me whole. "I'm really okay on my own," I say desperately. I cannot stand to extend this awkward interaction any longer than necessary.

"Miss?" the taxi attendant calls to me.

I look up. It's my turn. I take a step forward and move to grab my suitcase, but Cary beats me to it. He takes the suitcase and steps out of the line.

"It would be my honor to give you a ride," he says. "I don't often get to catch up with an old high school acquaintance on this side of the pond. This will be nice."

I glance at my suitcase – the little betrayer that it is, sitting there in his hands. I'm beaten. "Okay," I agree, and step out of the line.

"So is this your first time in London?" Cary asks as he merges his car onto the motorway.

"Actually, it's my first time anywhere." Seeing Cary may have jolted me from my adventure for a bit, but the shock is wearing off. I'm here in London now. And it is kind of nice to share that with someone.

He smiles and continues staring at the road. "Well, you picked a great place to start. This is my ninth time here."

"Wow," I say, and glance at him, looking for a sign that he's showing off or something. But as he smiles kindly at me before turning his gaze back to the road, I realize he's just making conversation.

"I'm an actor," he explains after a moment. "During the holidays, I head to London for a three-week workshop. Summers too, for these five-week workshops that I have been part of for a couple years now." He sighs wistfully. "There's an energy here. And a great history for the arts. Shakespeare, Tolkien, Laurence Olivier, Richard Burton, Charlie Chaplin, J.K. Rowling –"

"I know what you mean," I say honestly. "I was an English major in college and fell in love with so many British authors."

"What do you do now?"

"I teach. Third grade," I add. "We don't exactly read Shakespeare, but...I love the grade. I feel like it's a definite turning point in growing up. It's a pivotal year."

Cary lifts his eyebrows and smiles, shrugging. He peeks sideways at me. "What do you plan to do while you're here?"

I open my mouth to answer him but close it as realization dawns. I don't have a clue what I will do now that I'm actually here. I've just been so focused on getting here, I neglected to think of anything else. "I guess I will do all the touristy things."

"Buckingham Palace, Westminster Abbey...all that?"

"All that." My eyes are starting to get heavy and a

calm washes over me. The peaceful sound of the motor mixed with the quiet streets…I could take a nap right now.

"I'm a little envious of you, actually," Cary says, breaking through the quiet.

I look at him, confused.

"You're seeing this for the first time," he explains, looking wistfully out the window. He turns back to the road and squints. "I love coming back, but I know what to expect. Not much surprises me at this point. Not much fun in that."

I smile into the darkness, pleased and humbled. This man may have laughed at me in the ninth grade and made me cry. But he's turned out to be pretty nice.

We ride in a companionable silence for a few minutes more, while I look out the window, seeing the city lights of this foreign place stream by as we sail down the road on the left side. I wince as cars pass and assume we are going to die, because we're clearly on the wrong side of the road.

"Here we are," Cary says, as his GPS signals our arrival at The Chaizer. His cell phone rings as the car comes to a stop and I look happily at the sign for my hotel: *The Chaizer: Honeymoon Suites.*

Wait, honeymoon suites? As in all of the guests are honeymooners? Okay, I feel like I should have known that. "Oh God," I mutter.

I look at Cary nervously. Surely he'll think it's odd that I'm at a hotel for honeymooners. Fortunately, he's too busy staring at his phone to notice. When he puts the phone down, he leaps from the car and quickly pulls my suitcase from the trunk.

"If you need anything, I am staying at Kensington

Hostel," he says. He pulls out his wallet and retrieves a business card. "Here's my cell phone number as well. Call for anything. Tips on where to eat, what shows to see…" He catches my gaze and smiles. "Anything."

"Thank you so much," I say, smiling ear-to-ear. "For that and for the ride," I add. I look down at his card. Cary Stewart. Actor. I smile. "And the card."

"Any time," he says.

As Cary drives away, I look around and remember that I am standing outside of a honeymoon resort. What am I supposed to do now? It's one thing to check in as Marian to stay at a nice hotel. It's another thing to walk into a couples' resort completely alone.

A man dressed in a suit emblazoned with *Chaizer Honeymoon Suites* on its front pocket walks out through the hotel's revolving door and looks around the premises, regarding me curiously when his eyes land on me. And why not? I've just spent a couple of minutes staring absently at the hotel's sign. I roll my bag over to him.

"Hi," I say brightly, standing in front of the man now. "I'm a new guest– "

"I'm not a bellboy," he says, before walking back up the front steps and disappearing inside the hotel, leaving me standing there, gaping.

I glance around, flabbergasted, but there doesn't seem to be a bellboy in sight. I grab my bag and drag it up the twelve steps that lead to the lobby. The bag and I get a little stuck in the revolving door, but we eventually manage with a shove.

When I enter the lobby, I notice the man from outside, sitting at the concierge desk engrossed in a magazine sporting Victoria and David Beckham on its cover.

"I hope you get paid the big bucks for all the work

you do," I say. Exhaustion mixed with irritation definitely seem to lower my inhibitions.

He never glances up from his magazine. "Actually,
not nearly enough."

I roll my eyes and walk over to the reception desk.
I lean in to talk to the man behind the counter quietly,
my eyes darting back over to the hotel's sad excuse for
a concierge.

"He isn't very nice," I whisper. I look back at the receptionist. "And I don't mean for a concierge. For a person."

"Please just ignore him," the man says, and I realize
that it's Michael Caine! Not the actual actor, but the man
from the phone call yesterday. He looks more like Mr.
Bean than Michael Caine.

"He's only here temporarily. A concierge, uh, for the
moment." He glances over at the rude guy, looking like
he can't wait for that moment to be over. "Anyhow." He
looks back at me, his smile wavering but never leaving
his face. "How are you this evening?"

"Fine," I say, smiling again. I am not about to let one
bad-mannered person ruin my night. Not when the
rest of London seems so nice. I yawn – feeling nearly
bowled over with exhaustion. "Actually, very tired," I
correct myself. "I'd like to check in."

"Yes, of course. Name, please?"

"About that," I say. "I'm just curious about a few of
your policies here."

The receptionist arches an eyebrow and gives me
his full attention.

"Can a reservation be switched from one name to
another? And is this place really *just* for honeymooners?"

He looks a bit startled at my questions, but bends
down to grab something from below the desk. He hands

me two brochures. One seems to be a history of the place and the other a list of couples' activities.

"Due to our extremely lengthy waiting list, all reservations are non-transferable. And our mission since we were founded eighty-three years ago," he says, gesturing to The Chaizer history brochure, "is to provide accommodations for honeymoon couples only. When guests make their reservation, they check a box acknowledging this mission, with the understanding of our long waiting list. Surely, you saw that box?"

I scramble for what to say. He clearly thinks I am some kind of imposter. Which I am. But I am too exhausted to go anywhere else. Tonight, anyway. "Right," I say at least. "My husband checked that box. He, um...he made the reservation. I was just asking because I wasn't sure if I'd be able to check in without him, if it was just under *his* name."

He smiles. "It would be under both your names. What is your name?"

"Marian. Marian Gray."

I look in my purse and find the fake ID. I hand it over to him, my heart beginning to race.

"Oh, yes," the man says, his expression clearing in recognition. "I think I spoke with you on the phone yesterday."

Oh God...this guy must think, after that phone conversation and this interaction that I am completely off my rocker. "Probably," I say, blushing.

He taps a few buttons on the computer and then nods at the screen. Here we are. Marian Gray and Thomas Bolton."

"Yes," I say, in a mild panic. "That's us," I say, gesturing to the air behind me.

He looks at me, one eyebrow now raised. He thinks I am crazy. It looks like I have an imaginary husband. Which isn't entirely untrue.

Oh God. I *am* crazy.

"Um." I clear my throat and look at him. "What I mean is, Tom will be along later. His flight was delayed."

"You didn't fly together?" he asks. "For your honeymoon?"

"Oh...we never fly together," I sputter out as my eyes dart back and forth. "In case of a crash," I add. Brilliant.

"So one of you could die alone and the other one could be miserable over it?" he asks, his face twisting in confusion.

I glance quickly towards the concierge from earlier, who's now staring right at me, clearly eavesdropping. "You know, the hospitality here really leaves something to be desired."

The receptionist smiles reticently and looks back at his computer. "My apologies, ma'am. You will be staying in Flat 708."

"Flat?" I ask. I lean forward, over the counter. "I'll be staying in a flat? Like the one that Bridget Jones lives in?"

"I'm not sure if it's exactly like that, no. We have flats for our honeymooners, for a true London experience. They are very nice. I'm sure Bridget would approve."

"I'll be staying in a flat," I gush to myself. My excitement seeps into every word, even though I try – I do – to contain it.

He looks around, ignoring me.

"Well, the bloody bellboy has gone missing. I guess I could – "

"I'll show her to her room."

I look up and see the rude concierge from before standing beside me now.

"Alright, Oliver, if you want to show her to her room that would be fine." The receptionist sounds like he is losing his patience (although with whom, I am not sure). He shoots the concierge what I can only call a warning look.

The annoying concierge nods at him curtly and that is that. He grabs my bag without so much as a glance in my direction and stalks away.

In my haste to keep up with him – and my bag – I only get a brief look around at the lobby as we walk through. There's an old-fashioned bar in one corner and a fireplace in the other, with brown, cozy love seats and large, comfy-looking chairs around it. The rug has pink and red heart designs all over it. It's so lovey-dovey, I almost feel nauseous. Tom and Marian would have loved this. Too bad they're off in the Mediterranean on an actual honeymoon and not living it up in London, like me, on a fake one.

We step into the elevator and he pushes the button for the seventh floor.

"So," Oliver says after a few moments, "you and your husband flew here separately? That's kind of strange."

"And you eavesdrop. That's kind of rude," I reply. The elevator doors open and Oliver turns away from me, leading me down a long hallway. "And lots of couples fly separately," I add. "Kings and queens, for example."

"I see," he says, looking over his shoulder at me his eyes squinted slightly, his mouth forming more of a frown than it had before, if that is even possible. He stops at the door that reads 708 and glances down at my suitcase. "Marian Bolton, isn't that what Geoff said?" he asks.

"Yes," I answer, a slight quiver shaking my voice. Why is he asking so many questions?

He hands me my key after opening the door, and places the suitcase in the doorway.

"If you're Marian Bolton, how come your bag says Lucy Gray on it?"

Oh God. The jig is up.

"My maiden name is Gray," I say with sudden inspiration. "In fact, I plan on keeping the name. And all my friends call me Lucy," I add. Lying clearly doesn't come easy to me. The moment the words are out of my mouth, I realize that it would have been easier to say I borrowed the suitcase.

"Why do your friends call you Lucy? It doesn't sound a thing like Marian."

"Well...the man downstairs said your name is Oliver. What do people call you?"

"Oliver."

"Really?" I ask, trying to peek over his shoulder and into my flat.

"It's incomprehensible, I know. "

"No one calls you Ollie or anything?"

"No, thankfully."

"Well, Oliver, lots of people have nicknames. It just so happens that Lucy is mine."

"Okay, well, why?"

I am sure my face is completely red by now. "It's... my middle name. And I like it better than my first. And I love the show *I Love Lucy*."

His eyebrows shoot up. I am definitely crossing the line dividing sanity from insanity. You can guess which side I am on. It's not my fault. I didn't sleep a wink on the plane and clearly need to go to bed.

I try to save face. "Thanks for taking my bag, being you're not a bellboy and all."

He stares at me for a long moment, not saying anything. He looks like he is studying me. He knows I'm lying. He's going to get me kicked out. Tonight. Right now even. I'm never going to sleep again. I have been in the hotel for twenty minutes and already it all seems to be coming to an end. They say you're never prepared for the honeymoon to end, but this is ridiculous.

"Okay, Lucy," he says eventually, making a slight face when he says my name. "Goodnight."

I take a deep breath, relieved, and finally walk into the flat with my bag.

I close the door with my foot and swivel around to take it in.

There is a little basket on a corner counter to put my key in when I first walk in and then a short hallway. As I walk further, turning on a light, the rest of my flat reveals itself to me and my breath catches. I can't believe it. My flat is perfect. It's honestly perfect.

It's a true, bona fide London flat. Hardwood floors cover the place – dark, shiny pine wood, the color of mustard, that remind me of the floors in the studio where I took ballet classes as a girl.

To the right, there is a full kitchenette. A tiny, round table, only big enough for two, sits right outside the kitchenette, a gorgeous bright green vase filled with colorful flowers in its center.

Beyond the kitchen, there is a living area, complete with a cozy love seat the color of burnt umber. It looks so soft, I feel like if I sit down in it, I'll only be found once I've died because I'll never want to get up again. The love seat faces a fireplace. One of those that's remote controlled, perfect for people like me who couldn't start an actual fire without burning the building to the ground.

To the left of all this glory is a king-sized bed. Pink and red throw pillows are spread about the dark blue silky comforter. It looks so snug, backlit by the moonlight coming in from the large picture-window. It is dark outside, so I am not exactly sure what the room overlooks, but I can see lights outside. All the beautiful lights of the city.

To the other side is a bathroom. I stand in the doorway and smile. Black and white floor tile give it a retro vibe. Even the bathtub is old-fashioned looking. The knobs are labeled in French – *chaud* and *froid*. It's all so darling. I still can't believe that I am here, that this is mine for a little while.

Remembering my promise to Mary, I walk back into the bedroom, collapse into the love seat and pick up the phone, dialing the familiar number. She answers on the first ring.

"I've arrived," I say, when she answers.

"Oh good." I can hear the relief in her tone. "You're at the hotel?"

"Yes," I say, narrowing my eyes. "Cary drove me here."

"Cary Stewart? From high school?" she asks innocently.

"Drop the act. I know you got in touch with him."

She laughs and immediately begins apologizing. "I just wanted you to see a familiar face on arrival."

I remove my sneakers and put my feet on the coffee table, relaxing back into the cushions. "I wouldn't exactly call his face familiar after all these years," I say. "I completely ogled him as he was scanning the crowd."

"Isn't he so handsome?" she gushes. "He was sort of cute in high school, but he's completely gorgeous now. I've cyber-stalked his profile page a time or two."

"Well, I hate you," I say, closing my eyes happily. It's so good to hear Mary's familiar voice, which sounds tinny and far away but it's soothing all the same. "I had him painted in my memory as a jerk and now I have to reset it all."

"What do you mean?"

"He was very nice," I confess. "And handsome. I'll agree with you there. He was really sweet. I couldn't hate him now if I tried."

She laughs at that. "I am glad it worked out. And that you're there," she adds.

"How's Ricky?" I ask.

"Well, he's biting me. I keep trying to pet him like you said I should, but he keeps biting me. Not hard, but – "

"He's hungry! He's biting you to let you know that he'd like to bite food. Didn't you give him any dinner?"

"Of course I did." She pauses and I can almost hear her shuffling around my loft. "Where do you keep his food, again?"

"Cabinet by the fridge," I say, sighing.

"Okay. And Lucy, you really should call your mom. She's a bit...nervous," she starts. "About you taking off like you did."

Oh boy. After I hang up with Mary, I dial another familiar number. Jake answers, much to my relief. I'm not ready for my mom just yet. "Ciao from London." I say, hoping Jake will adopt my infectious enthusiasm over this whole thing.

"Hey, Luce. Mom's having a minor fit," Jake says.

I ask why he's over at my parents' house on a Tuesday

night, and he informs me that all my siblings are there – minus Marian, of course. Apparently, they're trying to calm my poor mother down and find a solution for what I've done. I cannot believe they've called a cross-continental intervention because I took a vacation.

"We are all kind of confused over here. You're gone?" he asks quietly.

"I'm in London on vacation," I clarify, exasperation leaking into every word. "And I'll be back on January third."

"But, it's Christmas. You went by yourself to London?"

"I'm twenty-six. I didn't run away from home. I just had to – "

"Lucy. Where are you?"

I've switched on to Charles apparently. I gather he grabbed the phone from Jake. And he sounds totally panicked.

"Charles, relax. I'm just in London."

How did I think for a second that they'd all just laugh and think it was amusing and wonderful for me and just continue about their lives?

"Give me your reservation number, and we'll get you a flight right back. What airline did you take for this fool's mission?"

Fool's mission? "Charles, I'm not coming back until January third," I say calmly and patiently. "Why do I feel like I'm having the same conversation with everyone? Maybe you can just spread the word and spare me saying it all again."

"You worry too much, Charles!" I hear my dad say, his jovial tone bringing a smile to my face. "You do you, Lucy!"

"And you don't seem worried at all that your young-est daughter just left the country very suddenly without telling anyone, Dad." He takes a deep breath, and I can hear movement on his end. He's probably walking away from my dad. "Lucy, we'll pay the fee. Don't worry," he says, using his removed, all-business voice on me. That's never a good sign. I shudder to think what he'll be like when his actual kids grow up.

"I'm not worried," I assure him. "I'm just not coming back until January third."

"Lucy – "

"Charles, please, tell everyone to stop worrying. They'll listen to you. Tell them all to go home. You, go home. Prepare for court tomorrow. Enjoy your family. And leave me alone." The words are harsh but my tone is soft. He is my big brother. "Please."

He is silent for a second. "Is something going on? Are you okay? It's not exactly normal behavior to hightail it out of town to another country at a time of year that usually brings families together. Were you upset about – "

"This is just something I wanted to do."

He sighs loudly and says nothing. He is probably fuming. Lawyers – and big brothers – hate it when things don't go their way. "Julie wants to talk to you."

"Hey," Julie says, and I can just tell she's on the verge of laughter. "I won't keep you. I know you got enough of an earful from Charles. I explained that you need your sister at a time like this."

"A time like what, exactly?"

"You know, I'm not sure what to call this."

"I can't understand why everyone is so unnerved."

"It's just unlike you," Julie explains simply, almost

defensively. The family's not crazy, her words convey. I'm just that predictable, that...comfortable.

I glance around my loft and take it all in.

"That's why it felt so good," I tell Julie. "Can you understand that?"

"I think I can."

When I hang up the phone, I look around the flat. It feels quiet here right now. Not a peaceful quiet, either. It's the kind of silence that can make your ears ring. My cheeks and neck are burning. I should not have to defend myself to anyone about taking my life into my own hands and doing something different. This is my life, after all.

I crack open the hotel window and lean forward, letting the crisp air cool me off a little.

My phone begins buzzing and beeping like crazy and I look down to see a flood of text messages coming in.

Charles: Call me back. Your phone is going right to voice-mail.

Mary: How'd it go...

Mom: Lucy! You called home and didn't talk to ME...

Julie: omg Lucy! I can't believe you left...

3 New Messages from Charles Gray

12 Text Messages [swipe to read]

"Stop!" I yell, squeezing my phone tightly. Before I can stop myself, I hurl the phone as hard as I can out the open window and into the night. My mouth falls open and I take a deep, steadying breath.

Everything is quiet and cold. I look out my window at the lights of the city and smile. I don't think I've ever felt so free in my life.

my children hate me

Posted by: @Delores at 7:04 AM on December 20 on TheGrayBlog

I cannot believe that Lucy has left me for Christmas. And to go to London! Aunt Velma sent me an article just last month about how the London Bridge was built on the remains of human children! CHILDREN. And that a crazy couple called the vacationers, or the honeymooners, or something like that was in London very recently murdering people in their hotel rooms! Not to mention they drive on the other side of the road there. Lucy, you can barely stay in your lane in America. Do NOT rent a car over there. Of course, if you take public transportation, watch for pick-pockets. They're everywhere in Europe and Great Britain. Everywhere! And I think London may have been the place where the subway cars just fell off the tracks one day a few years ago.

Everyone is telling me to relax. I have a daughter who's missing. You tell me to relax!

And Marian has still not thanked me for planning her entire wedding. And Charles and Samantha are going to her family's again for the 25th.

I gave them life. They give me heartburn.

No presents this year, children. No presents.

-Mom

Go, Go, Go, LUCY!

Posted by: @Dad at II:OI AM on December 20 on TheGrayBlog

Ah, to be young again. Go, live it up, my girl. When you want something, you have to go for it. Like Tom Brady. You don't win six Super Bowl championship games by sitting on the sidelines.

Love, Dad

Lucy

Posted by: @Charles at 12:12 PM on December 20 on TheGrayBlog

If she calls anyone, forward her to me.

-Charles

the mediterranean rocks

Posted by: @Marian at 12:24 PM on December 20 on TheGrayBlog

Hey everyone.

It costs a fortune to go on the internet, so I'll keep this quick. I could only barely skim through all the latest blog posts. Santorini is absolutely stunning. A sun-drenched island paradise. I am completely sunburned. I hope our future offspring can tan like Tom. No - that was not a hint at things to come in nine months. I am actually drinking a martini right now.

Mom - I thanked you about a thousand times for my wedding. Didn't I? Just in case, THANK YOU. It was the wedding of all weddings. So be kind and give Christmas to us all. Haha-

Okay, back to cruising, tanning and EATING. No more dieting to fit into a size 6 Vera gown. I can eat what I want.

Love and hugs,
Marian

PS: Did Lucy go somewhere?

---

chapter five

I don't notice immediately what's happened. I open my eyes, and the sun's glare nearly blinds me. I stand up and stretch in front of the picture window. When I turn to look at the bedside clock, I nearly fall over when I see that it reads 12:58.

I slept in. Scratch that. I think I actually fell into a mild coma. It's one in the afternoon. How could I not set an alarm? My first full day in London is now completely wasted.

Well...it's only eight in the morning in Massachusetts. I had a *very* exhausting day yesterday. And I barely slept a wink the night before, thinking about the trip.

I close the door to my flat twenty minutes later, showered and ready for the day, and jump when I spot a couple across the hall making out against their door.

"Dan. Dan, stop," the woman says between giggles. She sees me out of the corner of her eye. "Someone's watching." Her husband doesn't seem to care, but she pushes him off of her and straightens her hair.

"So what?" her husband mutters, frustrated. "She's on her honeymoon, too," he says, casting a quick, very conspiratorial glance my way. "She gets it." He goes in once more for the kill, but his wife swats his face away playfully.

"Dan."

He pulls away reluctantly and looks at me as she walks toward me before I can sneak away from the awkward situation.

"Sorry," she says, rolling her eyes. She holds her hand out to me and I take it a little cautiously. "I'm Kiki," the woman says.

"Lucy." I shake her hand and look past her to her husband who is now leaning on their door. "And I take it you're Dan."

He smiles at me, giving me a quick nod, before turning his attention back to his new bride, seeming to want everyone in the world to disappear so he can continue showing his new wife just how much he loves her.

I take the hint and zip up my coat. "Nice to meet you both," I say, before turning on my heel and heading towards the elevator to officially begin my day.

"Hi," I say, walking up to the reception desk once I'm downstairs until I'm standing in front of the man who checked me in last night.

"Hello, Mrs. Bolton," he says, and I come up short for a moment. That's right. That's me. Mrs. Bolton. "You can call me Miss Gray, actually. I'm not planning to change my name just yet."

"Miss Gray," he says, tapping some keys on the

keyboard. "I'll just make a note of that for the staff." He smiles at me when he's done typing his note. "We like to keep things as friendly and personal as possible here. Which is why I do want to apologize about last night." At my confused look, he adds, "The concierge."

"I appreciate that." I smile, though my mind trails back to the strange interaction. "He asks a lot of questions."

"It's just...well, his, um, his father owns this place, and he can pretty much do whatever he wants while he's here." A nonchalant shrug implies that this is just how it is. He returns his attention to the computer screen and begins typing urgently. Apparently the case is closed for further discussion.

I sigh and put my hair behind my ear. I grab a couple of brochures for what look like city sightseeing opportunities. I was going to make a list on the plane of all the places I want to see, but I kept hearing Mary in my ear, urging me to relax for once, to not plan – to let things happen. I look at the brochures and London travel guides and walk away from the reception desk. It's time to see which options will get me to the most places.

❧

Kensington High Street is so very British, lined with boutiques, cafes, cell phone stores, music shops, and designer clothing stores. It's at the same time ultra-modern sophistication and old world charm.

I'm donning my bright turquoise parka over a heavy ivory sweater. The sun is beaming right now but the chill is biting. I check in my purse for my folded yellow umbrella. Practically every guide said to always prepare for rain in London. And honestly, even if I get completely drenched, I cannot wait to experience a London rain myself.

I pop into an Internet café and get into the long line for coffee. I glance down at the brochures I grabbed from the lobby. Tomorrow I will be a good traveler and see all that London has to offer. I spot a theater brochure in the pile. I browse the list of shows and circle *Mamma Mia*. There is always time for more Abba in my life. To think, I will actually get to see a show in London's famous West End.

"Two large iced coffees, please," I say to the barista.

"Sure thing," the girl says. I am obsessed with the accents of these Londoners!

"Two?"

I turn to see Oliver standing there, disheveled, and a little out of breath.

"We meet again," I say, flashing my sweetest smile at Oliver in hopes that he'll leave me alone and haunt another hotel guest. "Hello, Oliver."

"Why two? Is your husband around?" he asks, looking around the coffee shop suspiciously.

"Just out of curiosity, do you always ask so many questions to the people that visit your dad's hotel?"

His smile disappears in a nanosecond. "My...what?"

"Geoff, that guy at reception, told me."

"Did he?" he asks, distractedly. He looks pretty upset. I pay the cashier and take my two iced coffees.

I sit down, and begin downing my first iced coffee, hoping to get out of this cafe before Oliver finishes paying for his own coffee and comes over to play a new round of twenty questions with me. When my first coffee is gone, I begin putting my coat on quickly.

My plan: grab the second coffee and book it. It's a good plan. And I almost make it, too.

"You do know it's not going to rain today," Oliver says, walking over to where I'm seated, eyeing my umbrella, which is peeking out of my purse.

"I'm tempting fate."

"Your husband still not here yet?" he asks, sipping his coffee, not taking his eyes off of me. He doesn't seem to get the whole socializing thing. He's not very good at it. And, quite frankly, he makes me a little uncomfortable.

"Not yet. His flight was – "

" – delayed. I remember. I'd like to meet him. When is he due in?"

"Later today," I say impatiently. I grab my stuff and stand up. "Well, Oliver, I'd love to stay and chat, but I'm missing all that London out there."

"You don't seem too concerned. You slept half the day away," he says.

"Well, that wasn't…" I trail off, something occurring to me. Is he spying on me?

He smiles. "I worked the morning shift. It's not that big of a hotel," he explains.

I regard him skeptically. "Okay. See you later," I say, and walk quickly out the door.

I instantly wrap my arms around myself as the chill outside makes me shiver. I look over my shoulder, just to be sure Oliver is not following me. He is going to blow my cover. I just know it. His dad owns The Chaizer. From the moment he met me, he knew I was lying. Finding out someone was lying about who they were was probably the most exciting thing going on in his life! He is probably a spoiled, rich brat, just bored enough to want to make someone else's life miserable. Oh, he will definitely find me out. And then it will be revealed that I am not my sister and I'll probably be thrown in jail for identity fraud! Oh God...orange really is not my best color. Black and white stripes I can do, though. I wonder if I'll have a choice.

I sigh, seeing my breath in the chilly air. My cheeks and nose begin to turn numb as my eyes water. Maybe iced coffee wasn't my most inspired idea. I take one more sip as the effects of the caffeine and cold have definitely given me the jolt I needed – and throw the cup in the trash bin on the street. I continue my walk down Kensington High's cobblestone streets, enjoying the scene of tourists and locals alike doing their holiday shopping and walking around with their families. A guitarist sits on the front steps of a brownstone, snug in about four different scarves, and an old, weathered brown coat, playing Christmas music.

"Silver Bells" fades into the distance as children laugh and people pass (meeting smile after smile), and I finally arrive at *Kensington Hostel* where Cary is staying. I hold the card that Cary gave me in my hand and debate calling him. Well – without a phone, I guess I'd have to have reception call him. Except I don't think hostels have a reception area. Do they?

I really should just explore this city on my own. Buying Cary a thank-you coffee is silly. He basically did Mary a favor and I should—

"Lucy?"

I look up and see Cary standing before me, exiting the hostel, looking even more handsome in the daylight than he had last night.

"Hi!" I say, smiling widely. I'm forced to admit that

Mary was right. I mean, knowing someone in town really isn't a bad thing.

"How was your first day in London?" he asks, walking up to me.

"I slept in and wasted it mostly, but have promised myself to start fresh tomorrow." I hold up the brochures. "I will see it all."

He smiles at that.

"How are you?" I ask.

"Okay. They ruined my reservation," he says, nodding towards his hostel, "and I'm being forced to share my room with these three other guys. I have to take my bag with me wherever I go." He rolls his eyes, his annoyance clear. "Normally, I stay in a loft with two of my friends who live here, but they have family in town for the holidays and, well, this is all that's really available at a normal price at this time of year."

I look down and there it is. A bulky black suitcase sits beside him on the sidewalk. "That must be annoying," I say, lamely.

"Just beyond annoying, actually," he says. "You know, I realized something last night after I left you." He tilts his head and narrows his eyes kind of playfully. "Isn't The Chaizer some kind of deluxe honeymoon spa or something?"

I feel my face instantly flush. "How did you know?"

"It's world-famous," he says, laughing. "I knew it sounded familiar but I'll admit I was a bit distracted last night so I didn't realize it until I was brushing my teeth before bed."

Cary was thinking about me as he brushed his teeth? Something stirs in my stomach and I groan. I did not come to London to fall for an old acquaintance, so any feelings of hope or pure admiration for his handsomeness must die. They must die now. I'm here for me. And that's it!

I shrug, realizing he's waiting for some kind of an explanation. "I came here kind of spontaneously," I explain. "My sister and her new husband were going to come here for their honeymoon but decided not to. When I realized what happened, I called the hotel to cancel the reservation, but – "

" – you decided to come in their place instead."

I shake my head, embarrassed, half expecting him to call this a fool's mission like Charles did. "I'm a honeymoon thief."

His grin changes at that, and he looks like he's fighting the urge to burst out laughing.

"I just wanted a vacation, honestly. I only realized The Chaizer is exclusively for honeymooners when I got there last night. I actually tried to find a new hotel too, but you're right. Prices are a bit astronomical. Plus I completely fell in love with my flat, so I'm stuck pretending to be my sister because there is no way I can stay anywhere else now."

He takes his hands out of his pockets and crosses his arms, looking amused. He gestures for me to continue. "Did you explain all of this to the hotel staff?"

"I started to, but they have this policy about honeymooners and non-transferable reservations, so here I am." I smile and shrug casually.

"They didn't question your lack of husband?"

"They did. So, I am going to lay low, be virtually unnoticed."

He laughs. "That's probably a good idea."

"Anyway, I wanted to see if I could buy you a cup of coffee as a thank you for driving me last night."

He checks his watch. "I actually have to run to class right now. Could we do a raincheck for tomorrow? Same time, same place?"

I smile at him. "I'd like that."

⌒⊙

The thing they should tell you about psychics is that once you read the signs they warn you about, and make irrational decisions because of them, you are pretty much on your own. There are no psychics in your honeymoon suite to tell you what to do or where to go next. It's all up to you.

An actually adventurous person would have no problem making what could otherwise be a boring night in a foreign city into a memorable occasion. Me?

I went to a bookstore, picked up a book entitled *The Cat Who Went to Paris*, and took it to a pub. A cold beer, fish and chips, and a relaxing dinner by book in an English pub - it's a pretty okay way to spend a first night in a new city, especially if you're still completely exhausted.

Reading seems the perfect way to while away the remainder of what I've dubbed my "settling in" day. I keep smudging the same pages with my greasy fish fingers, unable to fully concentrate on the lighthearted story when so much is going on in the local pub.

A young couple in the corner seems oblivious to the fact that anyone else is in the pub. The bartender looks like she's about sixteen – though I'm sure she's older – and she jumps every time the bell rings over the door, like she's waiting for something. Or someone. A young man is asserting that Tony Blair was the greatest Prime Minister ever. His two friends completely disagree (it was John Major). And a woman with silvery blonde hair wears a Christmas sweater and sits in a corner, watching every scene unfold unashamedly, like she does this every day.

I return to the hotel at ten. I see that my lovely neighbors, Dan and Kiki, are making out by the fireplace in the lobby. It is kind of sweet, actually, that they can't keep their hands off each other. I've never really witnessed newlyweds like this, who seem physically unable to stop making out. They must have had a very quick courtship.

I make it successfully to my room when I realize I forgot my key inside. I walk back down to the lobby, making a beeline for the front desk.

"I locked myself out of my room," I say to the teen-aged girl behind the desk. This is clearly her after-school job. Her feet are propped up on the counter as she reads *Jane Eyre* though she seems to be keeping one eye on the reality dating show on the television in the lobby.

"It wasn't the smartest thing to do," she says, without looking at me. It is so unfair that the British can say anything they want and it all sounds like Shakespeare.

"So," I say after a long moment, looking at the book cover staring me in the face. "Should I wait for the house to burn down?"

She looks up at me, finally. "What?"

"I locked myself out of my room," I repeat. "I was wondering if you might have another key for me."

She sighs loudly, drops her feet from the desk and looks up at me. "There will be a fine next time."

"Won't be a next time," I assure her, hoping to convey

friendliness since she's looking at me like she wants to hit me with *Jane Eyre*. The hard cover version. They must have not gone over the hotel's mission to be friendly and personable with her during her training. "Promise."

"And I will need to see identification."

I smile and open my purse, grabbing the appropriate ID and handing it over to her.

She types something on the computer. "It says here to call you Miss Gray because you are not planning to take your husband's name and not to mention that to him if he ever shows up in case it's a sour point."

I laugh. "The note really says all that?"

"It does." She reminds me of Liam but ten years older and a girl. She has an almost sweet looking face but a prickly personality to go with it.

"Prepared for an indoor shower, Miss Gray?"

I roll my eyes, recognizing the voice. Stupid slow receptionist. Stupid Charlotte Brontë.

"Oliver. Hi," I say, turning.

He smiles. He actually has a nice smile. It's slightly crooked and kind of boyish. He should spend more time smiling, instead of being so absolutely annoying.

"Hi, Oliver," the girl behind the counter says, a big smile on her face, clearly pushing away thoughts of *Jane Eyre*, reality shows and misplaced flat keys.

"That's flat 708," I say to her. She just stares at Oliver, perfecting her Shyest Girl in All of London act.

"Hi, Polly," Oliver says, looking past me.

She types quickly onto the keyboard for a moment and grabs a new key out of a drawer and hands it to me.

"Great. Thanks." I walk away, optimistic that Oliver will strike up a conversation with Polly and leave me alone.

"Is your husband still delayed?" he asks, falling into step beside me, his inherently polite British accent covering up what I can only assume is a very snarky tone.

"You will be the first to know when he arrives," I say, picking up my pace a little.

"You know, I am starting to think that – "

"Lucy!"

I stop and turn to the foyer where Cary, in a sleek leather jacket and wind-ruffled hair framing his face, smiles at me, dragging his suitcase with him.

What on earth is he doing here?

"I'm sorry it's taken me so long to get here. I hope you weren't too bored," he says.

"I..." I don't know what to say. I am so confused. Were he and I supposed to meet up tonight?

Before anything coherent can even begin to form, he grabs me and pulls me into a passionate kiss. Okay, Cary has obviously gone *mad*. But my God, what a kisser. It can't hurt to just go along with it. I throw my arms around his neck as he wraps his arms around my waist.

I'm so going on vacation more often.

When he finally comes up for air, he turns and holds his hand out to Oliver.

"Pleased to meet you. I'm Lucy's husband," he explains.

Yes. He's my...

Wait, *what?*

Oh. Dear. Lord. I'm not sure who looks more surprised, Oliver or me. Or Polly, for that matter, who's looking from Cary to me repeatedly, clearly thinking, "*He* married *her?*"

And really, who can blame her? Cary looks like James Bond. He's the kind of guy that my mother used to warn me and my sisters about. He's the definition of tall, dark, and handsome.

But I am not exactly one of Bond's famous girls, at least not today. Ever since I arrived in London, my curls have been out of control. My untrimmed copper-colored ringlets are all over the place. After trips up and down the stairs (thanks to the forgotten room key), I'm not-so-gently perspiring under the several layers I'd put on this morning to combat the wet cold of London. I'm just praying that it all comes across as a rosy-hued glow instead of a sloppy mess.

In my experience, guys like Cary never look twice at me. But if he wants to kiss me like that again, I could go along with it.

"What do you think you're doing?" I ask him, the moment the door to my flat is closed. Or is it *our* flat? Oh God.

"It came to me all at once. Why didn't we think of this when we were chatting earlier? Okay." He sits down on the love seat and turns on the fireplace, making himself at home. He looks at me. "I'm stuck in my hostel with three guys. One pees in his suitcase. One is an aspiring opera singer who likes to practice. A lot. And the other guy's name is Gorilla. *Gorilla*. I have to take my suitcase with me everywhere lest my clothing be pee-washed. I mean everywhere, too - the bathroom, restaurants, coffee shops, acting class, phone booths. It's absolutely insane."

"That is kind of insane," I murmur, my mind a blur of rom-com fantasies and mind-blowing kisses, the kind that can stop time.

"And *you*," he continues. "You're pretending to be a

honeymooner at the most famous London honeymooning spot and you have no groom. You said there was someone who was onto you. I am guessing it was that guy downstairs who asked me all those questions?"

"Oliver, yes. By the way, smart move storming in here like that, not knowing *anything* about the guy you decided to pretend to be. I almost died on the spot when Oliver asked you what your name was and you answered, 'Right now just call me Tired because I have the worst jet lag.' Real smooth."

"It's called improv. We're spending this whole week in class on it." He aims one of his most disarming smiles my way and I feel short of breath. "So you, my dear, are in luck."

"Yay," I say, feigning enthusiasm. I sit down in a dramatic huff. Crossing my arms, I look up at him.

"Hey," he says. "If it makes you uncomfortable, it's off. I just thought it was a decent solution for both of us. And I'll obviously pay you. I can give you what I would have otherwise spent on my hostel and work toward adding a bit more to that. Because this," he says, looking around at everything – the kitchen, the fireplace, the king-sized bed and love seat, "is obviously a bit more expensive than that."

I'm quiet for a moment, taking it all in. I came here to vacate my comfort zone. But this – sharing a flat with someone I barely know – is really, *really* far outside of my comfort zone.

"And I'll sleep on the couch here, obviously," Cary adds, as if reading my train of thought. "But again... if you're uncomfortable, just say the word and I'll go."

I watch the fire crackle and roll the whole situation over in my head. It *does* makes sense. It's an easy solution for me, that's for sure. Finally, Oliver will have to leave me alone. That is a good thing, anyway. Plus, I'll get to stay in a honeymoon flat with a guy that looks like *007* himself. I may even get to see him shirtless.

"Alright," I say, like it was a hard decision for me to come to.

"You sure?"

I look at him and picture him shirtless. Oh, I'm sure.

"No funny business," I joke.

He chuckles and I feel just a little offended. "I'll try my best."

Has anyone heard from Lucy...

Posted by @Charles at 9:53 AM on December 22 on TheGrayBlog

...since the night she called? If you hear from her, tell her to call me RIGHT AWAY. And Courtney, I am not sure you're reading this but I have a feeling that Lucy's asinine decision to run off to London like she's Bridget Fucking Jones stems from you having walked off with her date to Marian's wedding. I was annoyed then, but now I'm pissed. You are her cousin and he was not some guy....he was her date. So, I better hear that it was love at first sight and the two of you are marrying. Because if this was just for a meaningless roll in the... you know what? I'm going to stop there.

Remember, whoever hears from Lucy first - one message. Call me.

Charles, the role of Officer Ass has already been filled.

Posted by @JakeG at 11:04 AM on december 22 on TheGrayBlog

Courtney just called me wondering if she should change her locks or just move altogether. Leave her alone. I'm sure she's only partially responsible for Lucy leaving.

Lucy, if you're reading this, you should come home. Charles has gone to the bad place. Remember when he made your seventh grade boyfriend cry and then that kid told all the boys in your class not to go anywhere near you because your big brother was 'postal'? Yeah

- that place. Anyway, I'm heading to your apartment in a little while to fix your sink - in case it was feelings of family neglect that made you leave.

---

chapter six

*O*kay, when London calls, it beckons. Cary – my old classmate, new roommate or new husband, depending on who you ask – gave me two great pieces of advice last night before drifting happily into dreamland, far away from roommates named Gorilla or aspiring opera singers.

"Number One: a trip to London is worth nothing without a trip to Abbey Road and a picture taken on the zebra crossing to document it."

Cary is a big Beatles fan. I'm not sure if it was when he asked me to pass the salt and Sgt. Pepper to him this morning or when he offered me a Penny Lane for my thoughts that tipped me off.

I stored that advice away for another day. Walking across a landmark in musical history is not number one on my London to-do list. Cool as it would be. Now his other piece of advice –

"Number Two," he said, as he placed his pillow down on

the love seat, preparing to go to sleep, "if you want to get all of the major sightseeing done in one fell swoop, sit on the top deck of a red two-decker bus and buy the hop on/hop off pass. You'll see everything."

– is why I am freezing my butt off. I am sitting on top of this stop sign red tourist bus and it's only thirty-two degrees outside. No one else is up here. At the last stop, a woman who couldn't get a seat downstairs came up here, sat down, and before the bus could even start moving, she hopped right off to wait for another one. I stopped feeling my nose about an hour ago. My eyes are so watery, I feel like I'm watching *Titanic*. I'm so cold, I feel like I'm *on* the Titanic. I feel like the wind is seeping right through my skin like osmosis practically refrigerating – no freezing – my bones, muscles, ligaments and basic internal makeup.

I'm wearing my favorite red hat that my grandmother knitted for me twelve years ago. Donning two scarves (one red, one green) on over two sweaters – I embody Christmas spirit in my efforts to keep warm. My granite-colored trench coat is buttoned up to my neck. With all these layers, I am still completely frozen to the spot.

I think my brain is frozen too. I cannot for the life of me focus on what the guide is saying. I know some cute market is to my left and some political building or old palace (or both) is to my right. I know it's all important but I can't focus on anything other than the wonderful feeling that accompanies the knowledge that I am on a red, open bus in London – the same kind I have seen in movies and on television. White Christmas lights twinkle from stands in the local markets and I spot a few carolers making rounds throughout the city.

Somehow, right now, the scenery seems less important than the scene.

I get off the bus at Buckingham Palace – also known as Her Majesty the Queen Elizabeth the Second's house. As I approach the main gates, I feel my blood thawing a little. I spot the famed guards standing outside in their high bearskin hats and long red coats, keeping watch over the Queen. I wonder if they're as cold as I am. Suddenly, music starts to play and I realize I'm about to witness the Changing of the Guards. They are playing "Yellow Submarine." Cary would love this. I'm sure he has done this before, though. For the first time since arriving, I really wish I had my phone back. Not to call home and tell everyone I've ever met about everything I'm seeing. But for the camera app! My life is completely undocumented without my phone and now I have no idea how to capture any of the great moments I'm about to encounter. I know I'll never forget this moment, but without a video camera, I can never relive it over and over again to remind myself that I was here and witnessed a piece of history.

I walk for a couple of blocks and enter a quaint coffee shop, determined to defrost. This place – Hugging Mugs – is most definitely not part of any chain. It's so tiny and homey, definitely a mom and pop shop. Each brown and lavender chair is shaped like a large round coffee mug. Locals seem to be right in the middle of business – stopping at this neighborhood hangout to refuel.

Today, I am in no mood for two iced coffees sans sugar. I order a caramel mocha latte with a dash of cinnamon. I want something steaming and sweet. I sit down in a dark brown mug, relishing in the warmth of the drink and the indoors as jazz music buzzes softly in the background. My ears ache with relief at being away from the bitter cold.

I glance down at my map. Where to next? More of Cary's winning advice streams into my mind.

"Ride the tube. It'll make you feel like a local. Oh, and visit Hyde Park. That's where the Beatles shot their photography for the album Beatles for Sale. It was the autumn of '64..."

You'd think he'd been at the photo shoot with them. Or alive at the time.

I look at my map of the London Underground. It sounds so much cooler than The T in Boston. I've never been very good at reading maps. Another drawback to not having my phone is that I have to actually read a map. I turn it sideways, pull it closer to my face, then further away again, like I'm doing a *Magic Eye* exercise. How do I get over to Hyde Park?

I walk to the nearest tube station and decide to kill two birds with one stone. I will ride the tube to Hyde Park.

It's a good plan, but unfortunately my inability to read a map properly and the fact that I am in a foreign country add up to me jumping on the wrong tube line heading in the wrong direction. At least that is what the old woman next to me is telling me.

"You clearly needed to go the other way." she says, pointing emphatically at my map.

"I was intimidated," I explain. "I was being yelled at about this gap, and it kind of scared me so I just hopped on – "

"Americans can never handle the overhead announcing 'mind the gap.' It's that announcement that prevents you all from dying," she says, waving a finger in my face. She eventually begins talking about her granddaughter who apparently looks about my age.

" – But she's very good with maps. And married. Are you married? You look single."

I look single? Fantastic.

"I'm actually on my honeymoon," I say. Part of me wants to put her in her place for assuming I'm single on sight – and for making singlehood sound like a disease. The other part of me wants to get used to saying it, so the next time I see Oliver and he asks me a bazillion questions, I won't stammer and turn completely red again.

"Oh. Where is the lucky young man?" the woman asks.

"Oh...he's...working," I say lamely.

"On your honeymoon?" she asks, one eyebrow raised suspiciously. She's certainly not impressed by me.

I sigh. It seems everyone in London has a real opinion about my fake marriage. We sit in awkward silence until I get off the tube. After I get on the wrong line one more time, I realize it's easier from my new destination to just walk to the park.

After getting lost on foot, I eventually spot another red open bus and jump on, making the most of my all-day hop on/hop off pass. The bus driver seems completely astounded that I got that lost trying to get to Hyde Park from Buckingham Palace. Apparently I could have walked there in about twenty minutes.

An hour and ten minutes and three pounds after I first set off to find the park, I walk in through the Grand Entrance. It definitely lives up to its name. Three massive archways are separated by gorgeous columns, looking like something you might find in Ancient Greece. Trees line the outskirts of this vast and massive stretch of park. Children are running around, their parents yelling for them not to run too far. In the freezing cold, couples, friends, families and those going solo like me are here, enjoying the open arms of the park. It's hard to believe it's right in the middle of such a busy city.

I sit down against a tree and look around. I spot a couple that looks like actual newlyweds, or at the very least, a couple in love. The man dips his head to plant a tender kiss on the woman's lips and then they smile and he takes her hand. I think back to the kiss I shared with Cary last night. He's every bit as good a kisser as he appears to be. You don't often get the opportunity to know something like that for sure. I haven't really allowed myself to think too much about the new situation I'm in now.

I'm "married" to Cary, someone I knew in another world, another time and place. Back then, he didn't know I was alive and I thought he was a complete jerk.

But now my mind is running away from me and I can't help but think about it for a second, in the words of Mary at my future hypothetical wedding:

It was so sweet. They pretended to be newlyweds. They pretended to be in love. And then...they realized they were not pretending anymore, that somewhere along the lines, they really did fall in love.

I sigh, smiling to myself. I did not come to London to fall in love. I came here to try something new. I came here for me.

Besides, Cary is pretending to be my husband for one reason and one reason only.

He doesn't want some weirdo to pee in his suitcase.

Back on Kensington High Street, I pop into a little camera shop. A woman with yellow and pink hair and a black leather coat walks up to me and smiles.

"Are you looking for something in particular?"

"Something cheap," I say. "I just need something that takes pictures."

"Lucy, this is Anne Benedict," Cary says, when I meet him outside of the school building his class is in. "My teacher." He recommended after my tour de Beatles that we meet up and hang out a little. He didn't really mention meeting up with his classmates though…

"I think it is just wonderful what you and Cary are doing," she says, before I can even shake her hand. She's beaming at me, her long, golden-blonde hair in a messy braid.

"I told her about me being your husband," he explains, raising his eyebrows with a look of intrigue.

"Just fantastic," she says, shaking her head in seeming awe.

"Lying?" I ask. I just want to clarify so she realizes what it is she is so happy about.

"Oh, it's not lying, dear. This is pure acting at its best. Improvisation. Living the scene."

"She says this is the perfect exercise for me," Cary says, smiling. "I've recently struggled a bit really getting into my characters."

Great. My ultimate fantasy is the perfect classroom activity for him. I am trying to get a lifetime of love out of this whole thing and he is trying to get a little gold star next to his name on the bulletin board.

"I've made a list of things for him to try to do for the remainder of your time here."

When Cary and I arrive at Emerson's, a quaint little restaurant near The Chaizer, I browse the list. Hand-holding, PDA, date nights...okay, it's a little weird, but it'll be nice to have company for some of my trip. Then I notice another list item. "We have to stage a public falling out?"

"Yes, but look at the next item."

"Stage a public make-up." *That*, I can deal with.

"I want you to come with me tomorrow," he says. "To my class. Everyone wants to meet you."

"They do?" I ask.

"Of course. You're my wife."

I take a swig of my beer. This is all getting very strange, very fast. Normally right now I'd be Christmas shopping with one of my brothers or sisters or Mary. I'd be decorating the loft. I'd be pretend-boxing with Ricky and yelling at him for trying to bite the tiny lights around my window. And then he'd hide under the tree, looking cute. But I am in London sitting with my fake husband on my fake honeymoon and I'm his Show And Tell project.

"Okay, fine. I'll stop by your class," I say, popping a French fry into my mouth. "After my sightseeing."

"I wouldn't stand in the way of you and London."

"You couldn't. We're in love."

He laughs and takes a sip of his beer, the same dark local brew I'm drinking. It has a kick and just a hint of the winter season in its flavor. "So, what will our public falling out be over?"

"Oh," he says, his eyes lighting up. "I was thinking that it would be about how I cheated on you the day before our wedding."

"Then I guess I'm acting too, because the real me would never stay with you if that was the story."

It has to be said that no one else in history has ever had a honeymoon quite like this.

chapter seven

*D*ecember twenty-third is generally a very busy day, but when you are in the center of one of the most famous cities in the whole world, it's downright ridiculous. Everyone's running around (and sometimes literally into each other) frantically doing their last minute shopping. I can barely bend my arms without my elbows hitting someone.

It probably doesn't help that I'm standing in the entranceway to Harrods attempting to take a selfie with my new camera. This thing is amazing! It's a pale pink digital mini camera – a Christmas splurge gift to myself. I scan through some of the images of my day – the tube, the London skyline, the London Eye – amazed at the beauty in the shots. I admit I feel a little lost without my phone –literally (I never realized how much I relied on my many map apps) and figuratively (I keep reaching for it to text Mary, Jake, Charles, my mom or to take pictures with it). But it's kind of nice seeing photos that are incredible on their own, without an Instagram filter applied. I'll get used to being disconnected. I hope.

After being bumped into by two bustling shoppers, I realize that taking a selfie without a smart phone is simply not working in the Harrods doorway, so I finally walk in to the massive store. Ever since I was twelve, my mother has dreamed of owning something from Harrods. Anything. She hasn't outright admitted to this fact, though. But I know it. That was the year my Aunt Velma returned from a trip to London and showed off her Harrods *everything*: designer jeans, earrings, a rose-gold key ring, platinum teapot with Harrods engraved in its top, and Harrods tea to serve with it. You name it, she bought it.

My mom would say things like "that's nice...if you like that sort of thing," and casually shrug, brushing off Aunt Velma's showy behavior. But I saw the way she looked at the pieces. She ran her fingers over the details of the teapot and stared at the key ring like it was a piece of buried treasure in the palm of her hand. She and my dad plan to explore Great Britain and Europe when he retires, but we all kind of secretly think he will work forever. He loves his job too much to stop.

I now hold a bona fide Harrods souvenir wrapped safely in tissue paper: a tiny wooden Christmas ornament of Harrods' famous storefront, the year emblazoned in brilliant gold. I know it's not a glamorous platinum teapot or a finely engraved watch – but it made me think of my mother. I love decorating the tree with her every year, while Bing Crosby or Andy Williams provide our Ye Olde Christmas soundtrack. The first of December is one of my favorite days of the year for that reason. Ever since I can remember.

Clutching my souvenir, I walk into a nearby Starbucks for a hot caramel macchiato. It's official. Boston Lucy is on vacation and London Lucy takes her java hot.

"Miss Gray."

I jump at the sound of my name and turn to see Oliver stride up and get into line behind me. Where did he come from? "What a surprise," he says casually, sticking his hands into his pockets and just staring down at me with that annoyingly penetrating glare.

"Hi, Oliver." I smile and look up at him. "I won't lie. I'm not that surprised."

He smiles, unraveling his black knit scarf. His brown eyes are bright from the cold. With a little five o'clock shadow, and his dark wavy hair windswept, he kind of looks like he just rolled out of bed. And...he actually looks kind of handsome. "You know, you're in England, not America," he points out.

"And here I thought everyone had forgotten the basic rules of traffic, all at once," I joke, wondering where he's going with this train of thought. "Hot caramel macchiato," I say to the barista.

"What I mean is why not go to a local coffee house instead of an American chain?"

"This was closer."

Once I pay and get my drink, I head to my table and sit down, pulling out my camera and snapping a picture of my drink next.

"So, where's your husband?" he asks, sitting down at the table after buying his own drink. Walking away without a word was meant to discourage him. Maybe I'm being too subtle.

"Please leave me alone, Oliver," I say, turning the dial on the top of the camera to Portrait.

"What's that?"

I groan. "Honestly, there's *got* to be something else you could do with your day."

He looks at me expectantly.

"It's my camera," I say, exasperated. "Haven't you seen a camera before?"

"Yes. It's just most people take pictures on their cell phones these days."

"I'm not most people."

He laughs quickly. "I'll agree with you there."

I put my camera away and look at him. "I hope you've come here to tell me that you took the next week off for the holidays and this is 'goodbye.'"

"You don't enjoy these talks?"

I smile and just shake my head as I stand up and fix my scarf. Without a backward glance, I'm off.

❧

TO: Gray, Lucy
FROM: Gray, Julie
RECEIVED: Friday, December 23
SUBJECT: Your trip

Hey Lucy. I just wanted to say that I think it's great what you're doing. I thought about it. I mean, you are seeking inner harmony and you are out looking for yourself. It's inspiring. We'll miss you on Christmas. But I get this. I get what you're doing. Okay, I'm going home to do some more prenatal yoga with mom. It's really fun actually.

xoxoxoxox
-Jules

I smile at Julie's email, suddenly feeling fantastic about being away from home, on my adventure of self-discovery. I am looking for inner harmony out here in London. I am an independent woman and many people will look at my journey the way Julie does...in awe. Though I'm sure some might look at it the way my mom does...with concern for my sanity.

Tingling all over with feelings of total independence, I click open an email from Charles. I don't have much time left on my internet pass, and I can't afford to buy another today. I sincerely hope Charles isn't writing to impart his overprotective 'wisdom' upon me. Again. I see immediately that it's not from Charles at all, though.

TO: Gray, Lucy
FROM: Gray, Charles and Samantha
RECEIVED: December 23
SUBJECT: Come home.

Auntie Lucy. Its Cora and Tristan. Y did you go 2 London? Dad can't stop talking about it. He wants 2 come out there 2 get you. Was this because I said u couldn't ice skate? Because u were fine. For a beginner. You can come home if thats all it was. WE LOVE YOU. Oh Tristan wants me 2 tell you he made a clay thing for you at school for Xmas and will give it 2 u when u get back. It looks really weird, but he can't read so he doesn't know what I just wrote lol.

LOVE,
CORA & TRISTAN

I shoot the kids a quick email back to let them know that I did not hop on a plane and skip countries because my eleven-year-old niece suggested I'm not the best ice-skater. With my remaining two minutes, I open an email from Mary. Hopefully she sent a picture of Ricky.

TO: Gray, Lucy
FROM: Trino, Mary
RECEIVED: December 23
SUBJECT: Your brother...

...Jake came by. He's trying to fix your sink, but he ended up making it worse. He's about as handy as your dad. So anyway, he'll have it fixed he said by the time you get back. You know, he's really very nice. Is it me, or has he kept that part of himself hidden since we were kids??

-Mary

PS: Pooper scoopering is like sifting through the city dump. Just FYI.

PPS: Are you having fun?

PPPS: I'm heading out to have lunch with Evan soon – wish me luck!

I send along some good luck for her lunch date with Evan and assure Mary that I am definitely having some fun and ask her to send me a photo of Ricky in her next email.

As I arrive at Westminster Abbey, the next place on my day's agenda, I gape at its pure magnitude. The gothic church stretches skyward, towering over me, almost like it's greeting me on arrival. I step inside, immediately hearing the heel of my brown suede boots echo softly on the hard wood floors inside. It's not exactly warm in here, but it's not the outdoors either. Sitting in a pew, I take off my gloves and look around at everything. The stained glass windows, the religious statues, the gorgeous architecture. This place is amazing. It's somehow more than I expected even after seeing it in movies and reading about it in books. Red candles run along the wall on the side, ready for Christmas Eve mass tomorrow.

Before she died, Grandma Lucille always came to midnight mass with me. My family used to come, too, but when Cora was born, they all wanted to go to a mass she could go to as well. Grandma Lucille knew how much I loved the magic of midnight mass, so we went together, just us. Last Christmas was the first time I went to the early service with the rest of my family. It was nice, but some of the magic was definitely missing. I miss her a lot. And I know she'd be cheering me on right now.

After checking out the grave of the "Unknown Soldier" by one of the doors, wondering at the mystery of this man, I eventually put my gloves back on and head outside to make my way to the Tower of London aboard another red bus.

There's no line at the Tower. I enter directly behind an American tourist group. I nonchalantly hang back a couple of feet from the guide, hoping to hear some of the history she is sharing with her group.

What I do hear is kind of shocking. There were all these deaths that took place here. A bunch of people were just beheaded right here, in the exact spot I am standing now, looking around innocently, not a guillotine in sight. They did not cut you slack if you were a woman *or* a queen. In the sixteenth century, Queen Anne Boleyn (one of Henry VIII's six wives) was beheaded for treason.

"That's not the worst part," the tour guide continues. I nearly balk out loud at that, but suppress the sound. I am still trying to pretend that I am not tour crashing, so I gaze at something away from where the group is looking, while my mind wonders what on earth could be worse than being married to a king who allowed your head to literally get cut off.

"They say that she haunts this place still, carrying her head under her arm."

Okay, that's just creepy.

One of The Tower's many towers is actually called The Bloody Tower because of the insane amount of murdering that went on here. Apparently, there's also this guy who Shakespeare once said drowned in wine here. *Wine*. They should call this place the Tower of Horribly Unfortunate Deaths.

I trail the group to an area where there used to be a moat and learn that when they drained it in the nineteenth century, human bones were found at the bottom. So basically, people were losing their heads, drowning in wine and moats, and there was a Bloody Tower so as to not forget all of this was going on. The Tower of London is a disturbing place...though unbelievably fascinating.

Staring at the empty moat area, I imagine all of the

unlucky people who thought they were going on a fun and harmless boat ride but were actually getting a boat ride to their deaths. The group begins to walk into another part of the fortress. As I move to follow, I catch a disapproving look from a middle-aged man in the group. He totally knows I'm listening to his guide for free. The group moves away and I smile at him, embarrassed. I stop in my tracks. I get it. He paid for the tour. I didn't. When the group is long gone, I grab my camera and immediately begin documenting the former moat.

"Lucy?"

I jump at the sound of my name. I've been alone for most of the day, so it just sounds strange, penetrating my quiet bubble like that. I see a familiar looking woman heading towards me.

"It *is* Lucy, right?"

"Yes," I say, trying to place her.

"Kiki." She points to herself as she stops in front of me. "From The Chaizer."

Ah, one of the impatient newlyweds from across the hall. I didn't recognize her all decked in her winter gear and without the husband ravaging her. "Sure," I say, "Kiki, nice to see you again." I put my camera back in its case.

"This has to be your first time in London," she says. Her cheeks look red. So do her dark eyes and her nose in fact. Long dark brown waves spill from her cream-colored knit cap that matches her totally cute cream and black checkered coat. She looks like she's about twenty-one years old. In the hotel with her husband, she somehow seemed older. More mature. Now that I see her clearly, she reminds me of a young Mary Tyler Moore. Graceful, classic, and naïve.

I smile. "Is it that obvious?"

"You just have this look on your face, like—"

"—a kid at Disney?" I offer. She nods, rolling her eyes at the cliché. "I can't help it," I say, wrapping my arms around myself, as the wind picks up slightly, chilling me. "You're right. It's my first time here. And I can just imagine what my face looks like. Have you heard the history of this place? It's like a bad episode of *Days of Our Lives*. But in a good way, because it actually happened."

Kiki grabs a tissue from her pocket to wipe her nose. "I know. Everyone killed everyone. And they married, like, a thousand people before they died," she says in agreement. "I love the architecture here. Dan and I, we've been all around Europe the past couple months, but I like everything here the most. I mean, that fortress was built so long ago. Like, before machines."

I look out at the fortress she's gazing so adoringly at. "It is pretty amazing," I concede.

She shrugs and turns to face me. "I majored in architecture." She continues looking toward the fortress, though her eyes now seem about a million miles away.

I look around. "Is your husband here, too?"

She nods with a smile. "He was, but he went back to rest. He had a headache. He always gets them when he travels." She turns to me and forces a smile. "Looks like us little wives are on our own today."

Did she seriously just say *us little wives*? I...I can't even formulate a response to that.

"Have you seen the Crown Jewels yet?" she asks, clearly not noticing my perplexed expression.

"I haven't."

"Maybe we could check them out together."

Her eyes are so wide and eager, and she seems kind of lonely. I decide to take her up on her offer. Besides I need something to do for the next hour before I head to Cary's class. And I can't leave the Tower of London without seeing the Crown Jewels. I think a first-time tourist could get beheaded for that.

❧

An hour later, a taxi takes me about six miles from the Tower of London to Anne Benedict's studio. Six miles is apparently the distance it takes to go from skyscrapers and walk ups to avenues of cottages and farmhouses. I pull up to an old, converted farmhouse. It looks like something out of a Jane Austen novel. As I make my way inside, I realize why Cary comes here year after year.

The white ceramic tiles lining the walls look like they were painted on by my third grade class yet that's the charm of it – like a silent homage to the most simple joys of art. It invites you right in. The hardwood floor gives way to a shag area rug that looks like it, too, was decorated by my class. Artificial lighting is hardly needed as schoolroom-styled windows open outward, casting sunlight into the bright space.

The most noticeable feature of the room is the furniture. Or rather, the lack of it. Without a couch or seat – or desk – in sight, everyone sits cross-legged or lies on their stomachs. This room seems like the most peaceful place in the world.

"You made it," Cary says, jogging over to me.

As he approaches me, I notice that he's sweaty. Like, really sweaty. "Do I want to know what you were doing before I arrived?" I ask.

"Pilates, to loosen us up for class," he says. He puts a hand on my shoulder and turns to look at his classmates. His eyes land on his teacher, and he stops scanning the room.

She catches his eye and smiles in acknowledgment before noticing me and waving. Inside her studio, Anne looks almost radiant. When I met her outside, she seemed almost elfish – tiny, pale, long hair in braids. In here, she looks more relaxed and natural. Her complexion is healthy and glowing, her hair tied in a messy bun that actually looks incredibly stylish. She's at least ten years older than Cary. And among all of her students in here, she seems worldly. Almost regal.

"What's her deal?" I whisper, leaning into Cary.

He follows my gaze. "Anne?" He looks down at me, surprised at the question. "She's great. She used to rule the London theatre circuit. Years ago." He shrugs and looks at Anne again. She's chatting with a student. "She never liked the limelight, though. I'd give anything to have even a glimmer of the success she's had. Or just to know what she knows, to exude that confidence."

He takes my jacket off my shoulders and leads me into the studio, and we take a seat on the floor. Class begins with "simple meditations," as Anne explains. It *is* actually relaxing. I breathe deeply. In and out. In and out. I've been so worked up for the past couple of days, living a lie and missing my family and all, it feels nice to just close my eyes and listen to my own deep breaths. As Anne announces the topic of the day, however – my marriage to Cary Stewart – I feel myself tense, the meditative state I was in leaving my body almost instantly.

In the end, Cary did all of the talking with Anne cutting in periodically to tell me not to look so surprised every time Cary revealed a new piece of our history. But...it was all so horribly unromantic.

"We met in the frozen food section of the grocery store?" I ask Cary, as we walk out of the studio. I really couldn't hide my mortification upon learning the "truth" of our grand first meeting.

"I should've thought of something more original," he says, placing an arm around me as we head outside. He hails a cab and directs it back to the Kensington High district. "It's improv, though," he explains, once we are seated and off. "Whatever comes to you is what you go with. Whatever drove you to say it had some other motivation driving it. When I looked at you, I thought, 'grocery store, aisle six, frozen dinners.'"

Well, that's just great. Why can't a guy look at me and think something exciting, like that I'm in the witness protection program or something?

"So what do I do?" I ask finally. "Am I a mime or something?"

"A mime?"

"I pretty much said nothing throughout the entire class, so they probably think I'm of the silent variety. There are so few professions for silent people."

He laughs. "I'm sorry if I talked too much. It's just...I'm the actor. You were sort of like a prop."

"A prop," I say, narrowing my eyes at him. I turn in my seat to fully face him. "This is getting more romantic by the moment."

"I'm the one who needs practice with improv and acting, because I'm hoping to make a career out of it. You aren't."

"Fair enough." I slouch in my seat and look at the scenery whisking by us just outside, a gnawing feeling in my stomach.

"What's wrong?"

I look at him. "Oliver."

"Who?"

"Concierge. Annoying. Nosy. Ring a bell?"

"Ah, that guy," he says quietly. He looks at me, waiting for me to continue.

"He asks so many questions just like your class. He was onto me before you came, and even now that you're here, he's still so pesky every time he sees me. He's obviously got issues with his dad and is just trying to impress him by catching *me* in a lie. It'd no doubt be the biggest drama The Chaizer has ever seen, and he'd be the star."

"Well, now you sound a little paranoid," Cary says, smirking and doubtful.

"I'm serious, Cary. He obviously thinks that I'm a honeymoon crasher, which I totally am, but that is beside the point."

"What is the point?"

"I've checked online. There's nowhere else to stay because it's Christmas, without coughing up a fortune. I need him to back off. I just wish I were a little better at that whole improv thing."

"I didn't think about it, but I guess you need to be," he says, tapping his knee with the fingers of one hand, while the other coils around me. I know he's just trying to get comfortable with me, get into the role. But I like to pretend, anyway, that it's more than that – that he's just...into me. He leans forward toward the driver. "Actually, can you take us to Oxford Street?"

When the taxi stops, he pays the driver and offers me a hand, helping me out. "Let's figure this out." He looks around at the many shops and boutiques lining the street.

"Figure what out?"

He ignores me, still scanning the street. "Here we go." He grabs my hand and leads me across the street to a small shop on the corner. The mannequins in the front window stare back at me with their haute couture gaze.

"Cary—"

"We are going to reinvent Lucy Gray."

<hr />

"So, who are you?" he asks me, as we browse the racks at Blue Montgomery, UK, the clothing boutique. The clothes inside are even cuter than the ones being modeled in the store front.

"Lucy Gray. Your make-believe wife." I look at a price-tag hanging off a tee-shirt at the entrance. Seventy pounds. "Why exactly do I need a new outfit? My clothes are fine."

"You need to get into character," Cary says firmly, noticing my apprehension. He leads me further into the store. "For starters, forget make believe. If you don't believe it, Oliver won't either."

I think about that as I grab a very pretty pale gray dress off of a rack and hold it against me in the mirror.

Cary grabs it out of my hands. "How about something with a little color?"

"My hair is all the color I need in my life," I say. I've always been self-conscious about how red my hair is. "Earth tones are sort of my thing," I explain to Cary. "They tame the whole picture – in a good way."

"Well, brighten the picture up a bit. Step outside your comfort zone. I mean – isn't that what you've been doing since you arrived in London?"

I stop and look at him, the dull gray dress clutched in his hands. "Since right before I left actually. Deciding to come here on my own was so far outside of my comfort zone that I'm still expecting to wake up in Haley at any second."

"You were trying something new," he says. "That's something most people are too scared to do. Ever. Because it's not *easy*."

I nod slowly, my mind working fast. "Fine. No gray." I turn to start scouring the racks again and sigh. "I guess I should look for polka dots and purple."

Cary's smile lights up his gorgeous blue eyes. "That's pretty random."

"Well my sister, Marian – "

" – Now she's the one who really got married?" he asks, following closely behind me as I move to a new rack.

" – yes."

"Okay. Stop there. Marian is on her honeymoon right now, right?"

"She's on a Mediterranean cruise as we speak with Tom."

"So you're not actually on *her* honeymoon?"

"Of course not," I say, like he's the village idiot. "But Oliver thinks – "

"Forget Oliver. Forget Marian. Do you like polka dots?"

"God, no. After Marian's wedding, I'll never like them again," I say.

"This is why you can't get into it. This is why you can't get through those talks with Oliver."

"Because of the polka dots?" I ask doubtfully.

He puts the gray dress away on a nearby rack. "Because you're trying to be some kind of hybrid of yourself and your sister. Just focus on yourself. See, Boston Lucy wears gray colorless numbers. She's single. London Lucy is married to me and she has a colorful history that *you* need to figure out. Base it on what inside of you drove you to take this trip, to try something so adventurous, in the first place."

"London Lucy, huh?" I think about that as he waits patiently for me to continue. "She is a bit of an adventurer I guess. I mean, she'd fly to another country at Christmastime just to get a stamp in her passport." I grab a wool sweater with red and pink stripes. It's very colorful and Cary seems to approve. "Just to have a story to tell someday to her grandchildren or her cat."

"What about us?" he asks, putting his hands in his pockets and looking at me like he's incredibly interested in anything I might say on this matter.

Knitted brows, crossed arms, and tilted head, I'm completely ready to come up with something elegant – something borne out of my girlhood romantic fantasies, but Cary stops me. "The *first* thing that comes to your mind. Now."

"I, uh...I first realized that I loved you when you sat by my side for days on end after I had knee surgery. And...you had to cancel loads of important appointments to be able to be with me."

"That's kind of sweet. Did you really have knee surgery?" he ventures.

"Yes, when I was sixteen. Nothing glamorous," I add at his interested look. "Let's just say that my family takes sledding very seriously."

Cary laughs, wincing a little.

"I was out of commission for a few weeks, and while my mom took excellent care of me, I did sort of fantasize about a handsome love interest dropping everything to take care of me himself," I admit sheepishly. I feel like my face has turned the color of the red and pink sweater I am clutching.

Cary grins and rests back on his heels, bobbing his head once at my silly confession. "Very sweet," he eventually says. "Staying on track, what was our first kiss like?"

"That's a big one," I say, looking imploringly up at him. "As a girl, it's my *right* to come up with something amazing – since I get to invent this bit of our romantic history myself. You already took all the magic out of our first meeting."

"What did you have in mind?"

"We were...under the stars...and music was playing," I start.

He shakes his head. "Remember. This is real life."

"*This* is real life?"

He smiles. "You know what I mean. I'm looking for something a little more..."

"...grocery store, aisle six, frozen food?" I offer.

"A little more typical, yeah." He hands me a dark emerald-colored dress that is casual yet surprisingly flirty. "Here. Try this on."

I walk into the dressing room and undress quickly, putting the dress on. It's tighter than the clothes I normally wear. And much more vibrant. Immediately I'm self-conscious about how it looks, since I can't see it. There are no mirrors in the dressing room – just outside where Cary is waiting.

I step into the waiting area and Cary turns. He takes a step back to really appreciate the outfit as I take a couple steps to the wall where three mirrors stand, bridal-shop style.

Immediately, I like the dress. It's different. Pretty. And I feel sexy wearing it. "We had just gone to a movie," I say, looking at Cary now through the reflection. "It was our first date and the conversation had been a bit awkward. I honestly thought that it was all over, that we had nothing in common. But when we stepped outside, you saw that I was cold and you gave me your jacket." Cary nods, something in his eyes lighting, excited. I know the look. It's how I feel when one of my students finally understands something they were struggling with. "You let your hands linger on my arms just a moment too long, and right when I thought you were about to let go and turn away, you bent down and...and kissed me instead. Right outside of the Cineplex."

I turn away from the mirrors to really look at him.

"Very nice," he says, looking mesmerized. He looks at me again, his expression clearing. He eyes the dress up and down. "Very nice," he repeats. Only this time I know he's not remarking on my story.

"I think I'll take it." I look at myself in the mirror once more and smile. "It's really London Lucy, don't you think?"

෴

Three stores and two and a half hours later, Cary and I walk through the doors of The Chaizer. My credit card company is going to suspect theft for sure. The fraud department is probably calling my cell at this very moment. I just bought two new sweaters, a new skirt, and that dress. Cary is holding two boxes filled with Christmas decorations. We decided that since we are going to be together on Christmas, we should go all out. We might be in a flat that isn't ours for the holidays, we might be lying about everything under the sun, and we might be far away from home...but that doesn't mean we shouldn't fill the place up with holiday spirit anyway.

"Hi," Polly says, when she notices us. She closes *Jane Eyre* immediately and stares wide-eyed at Cary. "I didn't catch your name the other day. It got sort of crazy once you started sucking face with your wife here."

"Tom," Cary says smoothly. He holds his hand out. "Tom Bolton." I'm pleased he remembers his name this time around. She takes his hand. Honestly, she's acting like she's just met Justin Timberlake.

While she pumps him for pretty much every detail about his life, I walk away from the counter and place my bags down, looking at some of the lovebirds in the lobby right now. Kiki and Dan are nowhere to be seen.

"*No.*"

I jump at the sound of Oliver's voice, feeling something in my stomach clench. I turn to see that the door is open a crack to the back office, behind the reception desk. It sounds like Oliver is talking to someone on the phone.

"Would you let me alone? I know all of this. I just have to catch them." Catch who? "Oh, sod off," he says, sounding really angry at whoever he is talking to. A loud clang implies he ended that phone call pretty abruptly.

I walk quickly back toward Cary, who is telling Polly about what it's like to be an investment banker.

After a moment, Oliver walks out of a back room

looking very upset. I can see his jaw clenching and he runs a hand through his hair, trying to regain his composure. When he notices me, he stops in his tracks, his mouth falling open slightly. We just look at each other – in his eyes, I see it. Clear as day. He's onto me. And he's not stupid. He'll catch me in my lie. It's just a matter of time. And who knows what kind of trouble I'll get in? I mean, is what I'm doing considered identity theft? I'm not sure.

I wonder how well London Lucy can handle jail.

chapter eight

The flat is all dressed for the holidays. Cary and I made sure to cover all the essentials: a colorful wreath hangs on the door, white twinkling lights trace the perimeter of the room, and a small, sorry-looking build-a-tree stands pathetically by the window. Plus, of course, mistletoe! After all, we are supposed to be honeymooners. Looking at this veritable winter wonderland, I almost forget that I'm a thousand miles from home this Christmas. Almost.

"I'm going to see Anne for a bit," Cary says, stepping out of the bathroom, clean-shaven and freshly showered. "To give her her Christmas gift. I forgot to give it to her earlier."

"Okay," I say.

He bends down, kisses my cheek and smiles. "Bye, darling."

I roll my eyes. "So long, sweetheart," I reply, before closing the door.

I turn, facing the empty room and think about what I can do to kill time. If I were at home, I would still be sleeping, Ricky snuggled up against me. And then I'd wake up and head over to the house I grew up in. Slowly the house would fill to the brim while Burl Ives and Brenda Lee crooned Christmas favorites in the background. It's the same every year.

Except this year.

Okay, festively decorated or not, I can't be here right now. I need a distraction. I grab my coat and leave the room quickly.

Stepping into the lobby, I spot Oliver, doing what he does best. Sitting at a desk, pretending to read a magazine but totally people watching in that Barnaby Jones way of his.

I take a deep breath for confidence and head his way purposefully. He's as good a distraction as any. Feeling annoyed is better than feeling sad, any day.

Oliver looks perfectly shocked as I approach him. And why not? Normally I speed walk past his desk, a hand cupping the side of my face.

"Miss Gray," he says, collecting himself and pushing his chair back.

"Merry Christmas Eve, Oliver," I say. "So, you seem to like coffee." I admit it sounds random. He has every right to blink at me several times, confused about where I could be going with such a statement.

"Sure." He sits forward, crossing his arms, looking interested in the very least.

"So how about it? You. Me. Coffee. At a London coffee house, since it was brought to my attention that we are in England, not America. You know what? We can go to your favorite coffee house."

"And here I thought you hated me, that spending time in my company would be physically painful," he says, even as he stands and grabs his coat.

"Well, it's that charitable time of year."

"I see." I follow him toward the door, and glance over to the reception area where Geoff is eyeing us suspiciously.

"Don't you have to tell anyone that you're going?" I ask.

In lieu of an answer, he opens the door, gesturing politely for me to go before him.

"Oh, that's right. Your dad owns this love nest," I say before walking out.

He smiles reticently at that, but bites his tongue.

As we head down Kensington High, I feel more confident with Oliver already. Apparently my reinvention with Cary worked like a charm. Maybe it's the new London Lucy wear. I'm keeping warm with my new deep green wool sweater, with a sailor collar and festive threads of silver strewn into the fabric. The silence isn't uncomfortable, which surprises me. Oliver is walking, hands in pocket, a thoughtful look on his face.

Why isn't he with his family today?

After a couple of blocks, he indicates that we are at the coffee shop. I immediately realize that it's Hugging Mugs, the place I'd discovered the other day.

"I love this place," I say, happily walking in.

"You know it?"

"I'm full of surprises, aren't I?"

He shakes his head, looking a bit taken aback, but smiling. He still says nothing. I stop to look closely at him. His usual arrogant face now appears sullen and pained, like he has the weight of the world on his shoulders.

We order our drinks and he pays, which I wasn't expecting. I thank him for the surprisingly kind gesture. After we take a seat he looks out the window. He scans the street, almost like he's looking for someone.

"You are a complete mystery to me," I say finally.

He shoots me the half-smile I am growing accustomed to. "Nonsense." He sips his latte and shrugs at me casually. "I'm an open book," he says.

"I don't even know your last name."

He shrugs. "Maybe I haven't got one. Like Madonna and Cher."

"Ciccone and LaPierre."

He looks at me blankly.

"Madonna Ciccone and Cher LaPierre." I think for a moment and add, "Actually, Cherilyn Sarkisian LaPierre Bono Allman." He stares at me, wide-eyed.

"I'm a big fan. I've been to all her farewell concerts."

He laughs at that. "I can see why she opted for just Cher."

"Everyone has a last name," I press.

He looks down. I can see a muscle in his jaw clenching, like he's trying to maintain control of himself – or the conversation. "Burke," he finally utters. He looks back at me. "Satisfied?"

"Oliver Burke."

"Do you approve?"

"It's a nice name." I lean forward and drop my voice to a conspiratorial whisper. "I think it should be used for good, not evil."

He seems amused, but still, as usual, says nothing. The man really keeps a tight lid on his thoughts.

Maybe he just needs prodding. "So, do you like working at your dad's hotel?"

His smile fades so fast, I almost wonder if it was there to begin with.

"You're like a broken record, you know that? Why do you always ask about that?"

"About what?"

"My dad." I feel a little bad. His carefree attitude from just moments ago has fallen away completely, instantly. He's all tense again. I make my point anyway. "It annoys you when I ask the same question, over and over, even though it's clear you don't like it?"

He laughs bitterly. "All right, point taken."

I smile and look around at the bustle inside Hugging Mugs. Everyone is ushering inside for reprieve from holiday madness and bitter chill.

"Finish your latte, and let's get out of here."

I frown, something sinking within me. He obviously didn't like that I asked him about his dad again. And I'm sure he has better things to do today anyway than enjoy a long coffee break with a near stranger. "If you have to get back to work – "

"Actually, I want to show you something," he says, his voice light, almost like he's attempting to sound friendly. "I think you'll find it worth your while. So hurry up."

"I can take it to go," I say, putting my coat back on. "I'm not burning my insides downing this, thank-you-very-much."

I follow him again through the cold streets of London. He knows his way around here. I'm happy to follow someone around instead of attempting to decipher maps.

Since I keep tripping on the cobblestone streets, I look down as we make our way to – wherever. When we finally stop, I look up and see a very tall Christmas tree standing tall in an open, busy plaza.

"What is this?"

"Christmas in Trafalgar Square," he says. After a thoughtful moment, he looks down at me. "They put this tree up every year and tourists come from everywhere to see it. Kind of like your Rockefeller. It's a gift from our friends in Norway."

I look back at the tree, which stands proud and tall, a deep green, cloaked in tiny, twinkling white lights. I take a long sip of my latte.

"It's amazing." I smile at Oliver – really smile at him. He stares at me for a moment, but then quickly gazes at the ground, closing his eyes for a moment, like he's counting.

We walk around Trafalgar Square for awhile, listening to the carolers singing by the tree in the freezing cold. I make my way into almost every tourist trap store for souvenirs for my family.

"Mind the Gap pens, magnets, T-shirts," Oliver reels off, looking at my latest purchases. "Why do Americans love that so bloody much?"

"We just do." I look proudly at my new purchases – souvenirs for my students and family.

"Well, thanks for clearing that mystery up for me."

We walk to a bench and I take a seat, grabbing my receipt from one of the shopping bags. "You know, everything's pretty reasonably priced here," I say, glancing at the receipt. I look up at him. "I got this great dress yesterday for about eighty dollars."

"Pounds."

"Hm?" I say, distracted, still scanning the receipt.

"Here in London, we use what we like to call pounds."

"I know. That's what I meant."

"You are familiar with the exchange rate, then," he says very seriously, though something very playful lights his eyes. He takes a seat beside me.

"Of course." I think back to the London travel guide I read on the plane. I believe the exchange rate was currently at $1.30 to the UK Pound. "Though I admit I did forget to consider that when shopping." I look at my purchases – and price tags – with a little bit of alarm.

Oliver looks away for a moment, and when he looks back, a wide grin has spread across his face. Here's the thing. Oliver actually has a nice smile. He smiles like he knows a secret or a joke that I'm not privy to. This smile makes its way all the way up to his mysterious dark eyes. From being outside all day, those eyes are brighter than usual, and his cheeks are rosy. His tousled brown hair falls messily over his forehead. I want to reach up and smooth it out, but I stop myself. That would be highly inappropriate, under the circumstances.

"So eighty pounds is over one hundred dollars," I say, thinking about the cost of that emerald green dress. Before I can stop it, my mouth falls open. I am going to kill Cary. He knows that this is my first time here. He might've double checked that I was thinking about the exchange rate during our little London Lucy makeover spree.

"And your Mind the Gap purchases," Oliver says, grabbing the receipt from me and studying it. "About seventy *dollars*." Is he enjoying this? I grab the receipt from him and stare at it. Factoring in the plane tickets, the flat at the Chaizer, all the fish and chips and caramel macchiatos that London Lucy so loves, and my two-day shopping spree, I am pretty sure I'm going flat-out broke.

"Still love that Mind the Gap overhead?"

I narrow my eyes at him. "Yes, I do," I say stubbornly. At least I'm thinking about the exchange rate now. I'll definitely be more careful with my shopping. For the entire rest of my trip.

"Let me ask you something," Oliver says, looking at my raincoat with a confused expression on his face. "Do you always wear a raincoat when it's not actually raining?"

"London is known for its rain."

"I'm sure you've noticed we're having a bit of a dry spell."

"I'm nothing if not optimistic," I say, airily.

He regards me strangely. "You actually want it to rain? Most people are hoping it won't."

I shrug. "I'm not most people."

He nods and smiles in that secretive way of his again. Almost as if realizing that he is letting his guard down, relaxing – *talking* – he stands up quickly and checks his watch. "We should probably head back."

I feel a small twinge of regret that our time together is ending but think of Cary. Maybe he's back at The Chaizer so we can enjoy Christmas Eve together.

❦

For awhile, I'm happily curled up on the couch in the lobby, reading *The Cat Who Went To Paris* as the crackling fire warms me. Oliver disappeared almost the moment we returned. He probably was meeting up with his family after all.

"Hey," a familiar, deep voice says and I look up, seeing Cary approach, looking as if he's on the edge of a major life decision. He sits beside me on the couch, heavily, unwrapping his scarf and unbuttoning his jacket. "Sorry that took so long. I hope you found something to do."

"I did," I say happily, closing the book, my finger holding my place. "I did a little souvenir shopping with Oliver."

His eyebrows shoot sky high. "Crossing into enemy territory?" he jokes.

"I figured if I made him like me, he'd get off my case." While that was not entirely the motive, perhaps it would be a fringe benefit of my outing with Oliver today.

Cary shifts on the couch and faces me, eyeing me uncertainly.

"What?" I ask impatiently when he says nothing. "Are you going out again?" I know I came to London at Christmas on my own and I can very well handle spending the holidays just like that. But now that Cary and I made our plans, the thought saddens me though I try not to show it.

"No," he assures me quickly. "In fact, I was thinking of abandoning our original plans and doing something spontaneous, something you'll always remember for the rest of your life."

"What's that?" I ask, bracing myself. The last time Cary had an inspired idea, we wound up married.

"Let's take the Chunnel to Paris."

"Paris?" I ask before his words even fully process. My mind buzzes with thoughts, implications, concerns...

"Paris." He grabs my hands and squeezes them reassuringly. "Tonight."

chapter nine

Apparently, it's that easy. You step on a train in London and three hours later, you get off in Paris. The one in France. So I'm doing it. Well, we're doing it. As Cary and I travel beneath the English Channel, anticipation races through my veins. I was excited to get *one* stamp in my passport, hoping it alone would symbolize millions of stories for the rest of my life. I never fathomed a second one.

"Thanks for my stamp," I say, possibly too excitedly, to the woman at the customs station. "My first one was from England," I explain since she's regarding me like I've just disembarked from a spaceship. "See, I only thought I'd see England on this trip and now I'm seeing France, too." She just continues staring at me as I wait for some kind of reaction from her. *"That's a completely different country."*

"Come along, honey," Cary says, laughing as he pulls on my arm to lead me away from the woman. I don't miss the wink he offers to her, though. "It's her first time traveling," he offers quietly.

"Hey," I say, swatting him playfully. Truthfully, nothing can temper my excitement. I'm walking through a train station in France. I'm going to see the Eiffel Tower. The Seine. The Arc de Triomphe. I'll eat a croissant in its own native country. Back in London, paying for my Chunnel ticket did give me a moment of pause until I remembered the reason I came on this vacation to begin with.

"So now what?" I ask Cary as we exit the train station. "Are we jumping in a taxi? Taking a bus? Where to, *le capitaine*?"

"Um…"

He crinkles his brow and stuffs his hands in his pockets, shrugging. He smiles reticently at me. That smile could win him the title on America's Next Top Model, but I won't be distracted. He said he had a plan. I'm beginning to think he doesn't. "Cary, where are we staying? You said you had a plan."

"I do. I have a general idea." He looks at his phone kind of nervously and smiles at me after a long moment. "We'll figure it out," he says smoothly.

Oh my God. We're homeless! I clutch my duffel bag close to my chest and look around anxiously. This was a bad idea—I just ran with Cary's impulsive whim to visit Paris for a couple days, not questioning anything back in London. Where we had a hotel. And a plan.

"This is all part of the adventure," Cary says, although he seems a bit distracted. He looks like he's looking for someone. He should be looking for a brochure desk filled with cheap hotel options.

"I'm all for adventure," I say as a sudden gust of

wind blows my hair forward, whipping Cary in the face, which succeeds in returning his attention to me at least. It's freezing out. "However, when evening rolls around," I continue, more loudly, "I'd really like to have a place to stay."

"Hey, isn't that the concierge from The Chaizer?"

I swivel around on my heel and look casually in the direction Cary is pointing. And there he is – Oliver Burke, talking with four people, gesturing to a piece of paper.

"You have got to be kidding me," I mutter, thrusting my duffel bag into Cary's chest. I march straight over to Oliver. When I'm standing right in front of him, he looks up from the paper. Unreadable as ever, I can't tell if he's surprised or unsurprised to see me standing there before him. In Paris.

"What are you doing here?" I demand when he says nothing. I hope I look as outraged as I feel.

"Excuse me," Oliver says to the people he's talking to and suddenly I notice that two of the people are Kiki and Dan. They're poring over a map, looking around. What on earth –

"Miss Gray," he says quietly in acknowledgment. He clears his throat and nods his head quickly toward Cary before turning his attention back to me.

"What are you doing here?" I ask.

Before he can say anything, Kiki looks at me and smiles. "Lucy! You came for the Paris getaway, too?" Her husband wraps his arms around her from behind and rests his chin on her shoulder, looking as in love as ever.

Oliver pulls a piece of paper out of his back pocket and hands it to me. It's a notice from the Chaizer, like the ones all around the front desk promoting couples yoga and sightseeing tours of London.

CHAIZER COUPLES: ENJOY A PARIS CHRISTMAS GETAWAY AT A DISCOUNT

"I assumed you were also here for this," Oliver says at my quizzical expression.

Cary clicks his tongue as he reads the fine print. "We could have gotten a discount on the train," he says. I read as well, still suspicious. I mean...I leave the country and the guy that's been there every time I turn around is suddenly here too?

"It doesn't say that this is hosted by The Chaizer. Just that the hotel offers the couples discounts on their train tickets."

"My sister lives here, if you must know." He shrugs. "I offered to escort these two couples and give them tips about what to do when they got here."

"We're going to a can-can show and then dinner at the Eiffel Tower," Kiki says, excitedly. Dan laughs at her excitement and gives her a quick kiss on the cheek, squeezing her to him.

"We should actually jet, Babe," Dan says. He looks at his phone quickly. "We need a little time to get ready."

"If I don't see you beforehand, I'll see you back in London," Kiki says to me. The two of them rush off and I look at Cary, wondering what we will be doing with our time here.

"Oliver!" A young woman, who looks to be in her mid-twenties, bounds energetically towards Oliver. Her long brown hair falls in two perfect braids that trail halfway down her back. She's striking, but in a very natural way. Her freckled face seems completely bare of makeup. "You came," she says, approaching Oliver. "I really didn't think you'd make it."

Oliver stares down at her, his frown deepening. How

can someone look so upset on Christmas Eve? "I told you I would come to your apartment later. I didn't want you to come here," he says quietly.

"When I got your text, I said to myself, 'if my big brother figured a way to be here with me on Christmas, I will greet him myself.'"

Oliver closes his eyes and shakes his head. Her arrival obviously was not part of his plan and seems to have completely unnerved him. If I liked him even a little, I honestly think I'd get him a spa day for Christmas. The man needs to relax.

The young woman spots Cary and me standing a couple feet away, totally eavesdropping. "I'm sorry, I'm being rude," she says. "Are you two friends of Oliver's?" she asks, walking toward us with an outstretched hand. "I'm Jessie, little sister extraordinaire."

I laugh, taking her hand. "Lucy," I say. I can't hide my look of shock that Oliver wasn't lying. He really is visiting his sister for Christmas.

"Tom," Cary says confidently. "We're acquaintances of your brother's," he explains to her earlier question. "From the hotel."

"Jessie, come on. Let's go," Oliver orders, walking toward his sister, clearly trying to put an end to our bare introductions.

"Is this your first time in Paris?" she asks Cary and me, waving off Oliver.

"Yes," we answer simultaneously.

"Where are you staying? What are you planning to do? Christmas in Paris, what a fun time." Jessie's dark eyes match her brother's – except the way his are darkened by a sort of mysteriousness, hers are lit with a free-spiritedness.

She's so friendly. I look at Oliver in shock. "Were you two raised by the same parents? She's actually civilized to people she's just met."

"Civilized?" he scoffs, looking at his sister in a disapproving way that reminds me of how my brothers sometimes look at me. "Chatting away with complete strangers is civilized?"

"On Christmas Eve, it is," Jessie explains. "So spare me the lecture, Oliver, please."

"To answer your question," Cary interjects politely, "we don't really have a plan. Do you know of a decent, cheap place we could stay, since you live here?"

Jessie eyes Cary and me wondrously before slapping Cary's arm playfully. "Duh, just stay with me. I have another guest bedroom that never gets used."

There is no way I am spending Christmas with Oliver Burke. One look at him tells me that he absolutely refuses to entertain that thought, too.

"I don't think that's a good idea," I say. "But thank you for—"

"Nonsense. The rates will be murder on today of all days."

Cary laughs. "You wouldn't mind housing two complete strangers at your house?"

"Of course she would," Oliver says, grabbing his sister's hand. "Jessie—"

"Please," Jessie says to us. "Last year we hosted a homeless family from a local shelter for Christmas. Was quite nice, actually."

How are these two people brother and sister?

"I need to have a word with you privately," Oliver says in a low voice to her.

"All right, I get it. Details in a moment. But, Oliver,

if these are acquaintances of yours, I'm sure you don't want to see them with nowhere to go tonight. You don't mind, do you?"

Oliver puts a hand agitatedly through his hair, his mind clearly racing. "I guess not," he finally says.

"It's settled then," she says. "Shall we?"

❧

Oliver is quiet for the entire walk to his sister's place. Well, mostly quiet. He continuously tries to call someone on his cell phone and then mutters under his breath when he gets no answer.

"You're sure this is okay?" I ask him. "Because we can find other arrangements."

"It's fine," he says, looking like it's anything but fine.

When we arrive at a charming chalky-gray stone one-story duplex, with colorful flowers in a basket on the front window that overlooks the sidewalk we stand on, Jessie bounds up the front steps. Before she can finish unlocking it, the front door bursts open and a stocky, friendly-looking man wearing an apron looks on at Cary, me and Oliver happily, not even a little fazed or curious about who we are. "Merry Christmas," he says in a thick accent that I think might be Italian.

"That answers my question," Oliver says quietly to his sister, "about whether or not you're still with him."

She rests a hand on Oliver's forearm and squeezes lightly – a warning gesture I recognize well having brothers of my own and all. "Honey, my brother and his friends came for Christmas." she says to the man in the doorway.

"Ah, magnifico," he says, looking at Oliver closely.

I can see he's looking for Big Brother Approval. Well, good luck, buddy. My big brothers are pretty overprotective. I imagine Oliver is about ten times worse given his general personality.

"Everyone this is Giancarlo. Gian, this is Lucy and Tom. And you know Oliver."

Giancarlo smiles at us all. He's shorter than both Oliver and Cary and adorably boyish looking. "Come out of the cold," he says ushering us inside.

"Bathroom's round the corner and straight ahead," Jessie says, once we're inside. "Make yourself at home. Ma maison est sa maison."

When we get to the guest room, Cary starts rummaging through the phone book, a determined look on his face.

"I hope you're looking for another place for us to stay," I say, sitting beside him on the bed.

"Is there a problem?" he asks, not looking up from the phone book.

"Only Oliver," I say, looking at him closely. "You know, the guy who asks a lot of questions and sulks when I'm around." I sigh loudly, dramatically. "I don't really think staying in the same place as him is a great idea."

"Don't worry about Oliver." He meets my anxious gaze. "Just think, the money we don't waste on a hotel here, we can use for more souvenirs."

I shake my head, not liking this one bit. "I hope you have lots of plans for us to do here. I really don't want to get in the way. His sister is being so nice. I don't want to put her out at all."

"I have plans for us," he starts. Immediately I know there's a catch. He has that tone.

"But first," he says quickly. "I need to run out for a

little bit. Just to say hi to a...to a friend." He rips a page out of the phone book. I hate when people do that, especially when it's not their property.

"You can't leave me alone here, Cary," I say. "This whole Paris idea was yours. I am here because of you—"

"I won't be long." He runs a hand through his hair and checks his phone, his brow creasing. He looks back up at me apologetically, and I feel for him.

"Where am I supposed to say you went?"

He smiles that million-dollar grin of his. "It's a great chance to work on your improv," he suggests.

I groan. Does he think improv is the answer to everything?

Maybe if the world could just improvise, act like they're not hungry, world hunger would just go away!

Cary notices my look and makes a remorseful, albeit impatient, face. And then, he's gone.

⌒

Since wallowing isn't exactly in the essence of Christmas spirit, I'm just going to get ready for my night. I plug in my hair straightener and summon some excitement for my unique holiday this year. Christmas Eve and Christmas in Paris. This is once in a lifetime. Maybe when Cary gets back we can go to a fancy restaurant and really celebrate.

The thought puts a total spring in my step as I jump in the shower. The hot water tingles my skin as I mentally rummage through my duffel bag figuring out what to wear later. There's the emerald dress that I purchased with Cary. I also brought a burgundy turtle-neck sweater. It's warm and Christmasy...and much more me. I could wear that with dark jeans—

A loud bang from inside the bathroom makes me jump and shriek. What the hell was that? I grab the shower curtain and wrap it around my body as I peer out. Oliver is standing there screaming...well *something*.

"I'm showering. Oliver—"

"There's a fire in the bathroom. What did you plug in?"

"My hair iron," I say, defensively. "It fit in the plug..."

"How did you not smell this burning?" he yells as he moves quickly to yank the plug out of the socket. "Or hear the fire alarm in the hallway?" he adds when he's done.

"Well, the shampoo was still in my hair...all I could smell were citrus fruits and all I could hear was the sound of water."

I stare startled at the mess that used to be my hair iron. Something that looks like black tar is pouring from it now. Oliver grabs a towel and begins pounding on the small flames. "I can't believe you used an American hair iron."

"I had the converter," I explain. "It's right there. In the rubble."

It's then that I notice that Oliver is not wearing a shirt. Just a pair of sweats. It's definitely not the time to notice that under all that annoyingness, the man hides a pretty nice picture. But before I can stop the thought from forming, it's there.

"This isn't the only thing you needed." His voice cuts into my thoughts with razor sharp precision. "This makes it so your plug will *fit*, but it doesn't change the voltage."

I look at the mess in shock, beginning to feel the tips of my ears burn in humiliation. "Why would they make it so the plug fits, but the voltage doesn't change?"

He looks at me and seems to notice my makeshift towel for the moment. I look down at the shower curtain, realizing the plastic is nearly see-through.

"Oh!" I yelp, bending forward so my body is further away from the material. "Seriously, Oliver, don't you know how to knock or just wait until someone is done showering before barging in?"

"I'm sorry, should I have just let you burn?" he says. He turns away slowly, exhaling deeply. His cheeks seem a little flushed.

"You could have banged on the door and told me to put it out," I argue, trying to focus on my anger rather than his sculpted back. "Instead of barging in here like a big gorilla."

"For all I knew, it was you that was burning in here," he says, staring at the wall. "And anyway, *you* probably would have tried to put it out with that plastic shower curtain and burned the whole place down." He lifts his hand, squeezing the bridge of his nose. "You know, Miss Gray, I come in here to help you, you've ruined my sister's countertop, and you have the gall to yell at *me*."

"Can you please get out?" I say, my voice quivering. My body is starting to shake from the cold.

He looks down at the mess on the counter one last time. Deciding that the bathroom can survive the remainder of my shower without his help, he walks out without a word or glance, thankfully, in my direction, closing the door behind him.

My knuckles are white from clutching the curtain in a death grip. I let it go, rearrange it and step back under the hot water, feeling cold water from my hair trickle down my back. I stand still for a long while, letting my body warm up. Tears cloud my vision as my nose turns numb and I begin to tremble.

How could I have done that? Jessie has been so nice to me. She opened her house to me and I've honestly *ruined* her bathroom counter. That was not quite how I imagined thanking her for her hospitality.

I shudder a sigh as tears threaten to fall and I wonder for a moment what Christmas would have been like if I had just stayed home.

⌓

Okay, so my plan to look like an elegant Parisian with sleek hair has completely backfired. I'm sitting on the bed in the guest bedroom and my hair's curlier than ever, almost as if to spite me. After that awful shower, I was in no mood to throw on the emerald dress, which is why I've donned my warm burgundy sweater and dark jeans for my Christmas Eve night on the town. Except Cary's still prancing through Paris without me. Outside the room, I hear the distant rattling of dishes and chatter. The Burke clan is getting ready to sit down for dinner.

Oh, where is Cary? He was only supposed to step out for a little while and it's already been two hours.

There's a soft knock at the door. It's about time. I swing the door open expectantly, ready to grab Cary by the collar and turn him around so we can slip right by Oliver and right out of this house. Only it's not Cary on the other side of the door. It's Jessie. She smiles and looks past me.

"Still no sign of your petit lapin d'amour?"

I can only assume she means Cary. "He should be

back any second," I say. I sigh and meet her gaze with my own. "I'm so sorry, Jessie, about the bathroom." Hot embarrassment weaves itself into tight little knots in my stomach. "I feel like one of my students right now, hiding from the teacher," I explain as my cheeks warm instantly. "I'm totally hiding in here," I admit sheepishly.

"You really don't need to hide from me. Oliver's the scary one of us," she quips, laughing lightly.

I walk over to the nightstand and snatch up my purse, opening it. "Don't worry," I press. "I have my checkbook. Just let me know how much you think it'll be."

"Well, that depends," she says very seriously. "Are we taking into account exchange rates?" She waits and stares at me expectantly, before bursting out laughing.

"Oliver mentioned that, did he?" I say, relaxing a little. She really doesn't seem too bothered by my accident earlier.

"He did," she says, squinting at me, like she's considering me. "He mentioned quite a few things, actually. Right up until the bathroom caught fire." She laughs again and I drop my purse by my side, clutching it tightly. I really don't know what to do here. I need to repay her for what I did. Surely, she must want some compensation for the mess in the bathroom.

"Jessie—"

"Look, it's Christmas Eve. Forget all about earlier. Join us to eat." I open my mouth to explain that Cary will be back any moment but she holds up a hand. "At least join us until your husband returns."

❧

An hour later, I sit back in my chair and stifle the urge to unfasten the top button of my jeans. That Giancarlo can *cook*. I am completely stuffed. Jessie is one lucky girl because she's found herself a man who apparently will gladly spend hours in the kitchen, simmering a dish to utter mouthwatering perfection.

"The trick is the red wine," he explains. Because I can't stop complimenting his spaghetti sauce. Sheer self-restraint is the only reason I am not drinking it. "Plus, you must simmer the sauce all day, and cook the sausage and meatballs in it to add flavor."

Normally I'd be eating ham. At my mom's house, I mean. Christmas Eve dinner every year is the same. Ham with an orange glaze, turkey, cranberry sauce, mashed potatoes and veggie casseroles. This year, it's an Italian feast in Paris and my mouth has gone to heaven.

"You'll have to give me the recipe," I say to him.

Jessie laughs. "If Gian weren't here, we'd be eating cinnamon oatmeal."

Oliver smiles and looks at his sister curiously. "Didn't we do that one year?" he asks her.

She nods, but her smile falters a little bit. "It was the Christmas after we lost Dad."

"Ah," he says simply, his own smile dissipating as he stares at an invisible spot between himself and his younger sister.

"It wasn't all bad," Jessie says lightly. "We added tiny marshmallows to the oatmeal."

Something in my stomach tightens. I've mentioned Oliver's dad to him a bunch of times. And every time it's seemed to bother him. I just assumed his dad was busy running the hotel, letting Oliver annoy guests and do as he pleased. No wonder he was always so guarded when I mentioned his dad.

"I'm sorry," I stammer, looking just at Oliver, hoping he understands. "I didn't know."

He waves his hand dismissively, offering me a small, appreciative smile.

"Lucy, where are you staying in London?" Jessie asks, lifting the heavy mood that's threatened to settle over the table.

"The Chaizer."

At the mention of their dad's hotel, Jessie looks confused, which just confuses me. "You know, where your brother works…"

She looks quickly at Oliver and then back at me. "Right, right. The famous Chaizer." She chuckles at Oliver. "God, that must be a nightmare for you."

I look at him, utterly lost, not missing the look of exasperation he gives his sister.

A half hour later, I sit curled up by Jessie's quaint, adorable fireplace reading my book, an afghan keeping me warm. Jessie and Giancarlo are cleaning in the kitchen still.

"*The Cat Who Went To Paris*?" Oliver asks, peeking at the cover of my book.

"Yes."

He has that look on his face, like he wants to laugh but thinks better of it.

"What?"

"Nothing. Just…who would bring their cat to Paris?"

I close the book, my finger holding its place. "Ricky would love Paris," I say.

"Who?"

"My cat. Ricky. He'd love it here. Though he wouldn't enjoy being quarantined."

"I see," Oliver says. He rewards me with one of his rare grins.

I return the smile and put the book down. "I don't think I thanked you for putting the fire out in the bathroom earlier."

"You yelled at me," he says lightly, a teasing glint in his eyes.

"Well, you walked in on me in the shower," I reason.

He looks at me for a long moment. "Well, you're welcome," he finally says.

"I'm going to pay Jessie for the damage."

"I know my sister, and I really don't think she'll let you—"

Before Oliver can finish his sentence, the front door bursts open and Cary shuffles in looking disheveled and utterly upset.

"Hi," I say, getting to my feet. I clamp my book shut and hold it to my chest, looking worriedly at him.

Cary looks at Oliver and me, and then at the floor. He walks down past the living room and begins heading toward our room.

"Are you okay?" I ask, walking behind him. "Where were you?"

"Don't start with me," he says. "Please." Reaching our room, he opens the door. I place my hand on his shoulder, stopping him in his tracks. He turns to look at me and what I see behind his eyes gives me chills. He looks so unlike himself. So dark. So...unhappy.

"Start with you?" Oliver asks and I notice then that he's also decided to follow Cary down the hall to do what he does best: make everyone else's business his own. "She asked if you were all right, man. You've been gone half the day, it's Christmas, *and* you're on your honeymoon. Or so you say," he adds, looking quickly and pointedly at me.

"I *am* sorry," Cary says to me. "Let's talk in here."

The moment the door is closed, I turn to Cary and attempt to lighten the mood. "Was this our big public falling out?"

He smiles sadly and shakes his head. But still, he says nothing.

"If it was, I'm going to tell Anne to give you a big, gold star for your performance. You did really well."

"Please don't...don't mention Anne," he begs, sighing. He sits slowly on the edge of the bed and leans forward, resting his head in his hands. He finally looks at me again. "I'm sorry I was rude, especially in front of him. I should have known better. I should have done better."

I kneel beside him on the bed and put a hand on his shoulder. "Are you kidding? Walking in, getting mad at me for no apparent reason...we've never looked more married."

He laughs and puts an arm around me, searching my eyes. "You are forever the optimist." He kisses my forehead and rubs my arm, seeming to relax a little.

"We're friends, Cary," I say when our eyes meet. "So dish."

He drops his arm, and takes a deep breath, groaning on the exhale. "I hate him," he finally says, so quietly it's barely audible.

"Oliver?" I ask, looking at the door. "I'm thinking that a lot of people feel that way."

"Not Oliver."

"Who?"

"Jacques Marchand," he says in a way that suggests that Jacques Marchand is a hoity-toity French jerk.

"I already hate him too," I say in what I hope is an encouraging way.

Cary smiles, but looks kind of far away. "Well, Anne doesn't hate him," he says, shaking his head angrily. "You might even say she loves him."

"Anne...your teacher?"

"She's not just my teacher, Lucy," he finally says, squeezing his eyes shut. He turns to me. "Do you honestly think I'd spend nine Christmases in a row away from my family if she was?"

"I thought you were a committed actor."

"I am," he says, growing frustrated.

I don't quite understand. "Are you two together?" I ask.

He shakes his head, looking the perfect picture of rejected. He's so gorgeous that rejection just looks wrong on him. "We're friends," he says, putting a hand through his hair. "Very close friends." He turns away from me again, looking at the door like it's Anne herself. "I've dated girls. Lots of girls. I'm pretty confident when it comes to that stuff. But with Anne, I've never felt so... paralyzed."

I nod, taking this in. "Does she return your feelings?"

"I thought so." He sighs "I've never been brave enough to ask her out. I just keep coming back to her stupid classes. I keep coming back, thinking this year will be the year that I do something already."

"You never said anything. I had no idea you had feelings for her."

He sighs. "That was on purpose. You see, I was actively trying to get over it, but she keeps—she just makes it so hard." He looks at me. "It's so easy to just talk about her the way that I want to view her. Teacher.

Inspiration. Friend. I never really let on that it's a lot more complicated than that. And that's on purpose."

I sigh. "She's in Paris?"

He nods. "She used to live here." He turns and stares at me. "She encouraged me to come here. She talked about the City of Lights like it was this place that, I don't know, gave someone who's scared shitless the strength to make a move already. I *assumed* she was talking about me. That's why I dragged us here."

"I actually don't see why you needed to have me here. You've spent most of the time running away from me."

He smiles. "I thought you might like seeing Paris at Christmas. I was coming and thought it might be good for you to come, too."

I smile appreciatively. Coming to Paris is the second most spontaneous thing I've ever done. I rub his back, realizing that somewhere in the middle of this mess we're both involved in, Cary's become a friend. I hate seeing him like this. I prefer the guy who smiles and jokes all the time.

"Jacques is her boyfriend," he finally spits out, the word 'boyfriend' seeming like acid on his tongue.

"Oh," I say stupidly.

He moves to the floor and lays his head back against the bed, eyes closed. "How idiotic am I?"

"She never mentioned Jacques before?" I ask, joining him on the floor.

"No." He looks at me again. "That's what is strange about the whole thing. I didn't know she had a boyfriend at all. We talk all the time. On the phone. In email. I've never heard of him."

"That doesn't make sense," I agree.

Neither of us says anything for awhile.

"What are you thinking?" he asks, after a long while.

"About something my grandma Lucy said to me when my college boyfriend broke up with me."

Cary looks down at me, stoic and interested.

"She said, 'your heart can break, but if it's still beating, you'll be okay after all.'"

He laughs, and pulls me closer to him. Relief courses through me. His smile says it all.

chapter ten

How exciting – Christmas day in Paris! A sparkling blanket of calm cloaks the city. It seems everyone is staying in today. And why not? It's a day for family and loved ones. Oliver, even, stayed back to enjoy the day with his sister. At least that is what I hope he's doing. I sort of left while he was in the shower, telling Jessie to wish him Merry Christmas for me.

I finish my hot latte and warm croissant from a tiny little Parisian café and make my way down the avenue that borders the River Seine. Little strings of colorful Christmas lights twinkle above, tracing the charming espresso shops that line the street. Intoxicating aromas of coffee and baked goods waft out into the street. Boutiques display the kind of clothes I've only ever seen in magazines while vendors sell paintings that bring the City of Love to life with colors I've only imagined in my most vivid dreams.

I take a deep breath. This is what I came here to do.

It's just me here in these quiet, nearly deserted streets. Everyone seems to be closing shop early for the holiday, ushering down the streets to family and traditions. This year, my traditions have gone out the window. This is my honeymoon. Alone. Well – technically Cary was supposed to be hanging out with me today, but he was such a downer on account of the whole Anne-having-a-hoity-toity-French-boy-toy thing that I sent him away to go find her and talk before she left for her own Christmas festivities. Because at the very least, they are friends. And I know feeling reassured of that fact will (hopefully) save his Christmas spirit a bit.

But he did leave me his phone, in case I get lost. And to "completely remove the temptation to text Anne or stare at it waiting for her to text him." They agreed on a place and a time to meet, and he decided to take a page from my book and disconnect while he made his way there, letting me know that I should call anyone at all since he did drag me into his personal love problems quite literally.

I'm on my way to The Eiffel Tower. I have one day here and I will see as many famous landmarks as I can. There it is now, in the distance. It's a long walk, but I can't think of a better way to warm up.

Continuing along the river, the tower is my own personal north star. Compared to the bustling streets of London in the pre-Christmas craze, these streets are quiet, but they still have people, sipping coffees or eating croissants, bundled warm, cozying up to one another. I watch the lovers, the artists, the families, the locals and the tourists. Some walk around me. Others sit on the wall along the river, lost on their own little adventures. I wonder what I look like to other people. I lift my chin and toss my hair. Maybe I look worldly and adventurous. As I stare at the people and the sights, I realize that it's far more likely that I look like the world's biggest tourist.

Finally, I'm there. At the Eiffel Tower. I can't breathe. I mean, I, Lucy Gray, am in *France*, standing before the Eiffel Tower, surrounded by many people who look like they've popped out of a storybook. This is definitely a moment to document.

I pull my camera out of my backpack and focus the architecture of the tower in the viewfinder. I begin snapping away. I walk a few steps forward and put my backpack on the ground by my feet. I lay down on my back, resting my head on the bag and look up. Some passersby regard me strangely, though most just walk around me as if someone sprawling out beneath the Eiffel Tower is totally normal.

As I gaze up, the tower disappears into a cloudless sky. Peering at the scene through the lens, sunlight renders the people around me mere silhouettes darting around before my eyes. I smile and take the picture of what I can only describe as the most perfect moment. Ever.

⁂

"What do you mean you saw the Eiffel Tower?" Mary asks me an hour later. "Aren't you in London?"

"Mary, pay attention." I clutch Cary's cell phone tightly to my ear and tear off a piece of a croissant I bought at the only café that I passed that was still open, and take a bite as I walk down a winding, charming avenue. "I'm in Paris now."

I purchased a calling card because while it was really sweet that Cary lent me his phone, and even sweeter that he keeps insisting that what's his is also mine, I simply cannot take advantage of his loyalty to his craft. He's a little too caught up in his role as husband.

"You're in *Paris*?" Mary shrieks. "I can't believe you."

"I can't believe me either," I say. "How's everyone?"

"They're good. Christmas Eve was interesting."

I stop in my tracks. "You saw my family for Christmas Eve?" I ask, looking around at the street names, not understanding any of them. I thought I was heading back to that street where the taxi driver dropped me off but nothing around me looks familiar. At all.

"Well, just for a few hours," Mary says quickly, "because Jake and I...we..."

"We?" I interrupt, biting my lip. "You and Jake are a 'we'?"

"Um..."

"Mary," I say, trying to sound calm. She doesn't say anything, which only proves one thing to me. "What's going on? Last time we talked, you were going out with Evan Abbott to see if he was the missing love of your life."

She sighs. "He wasn't. He came to our date with his guitar for 'old time's sake'. And he wouldn't stop playing 'Free Falling.' He kept saying it was our song. And even after the wait staff repeatedly asked him to stop, he said that he could not and would not. Lucy, I panicked and called Jake. Before my date, he was arriving at your place to fix your sink so, I don't know, I guess he was fresh on my mind or something."

"Uh huh," I say, struggling to keep up. I mean, Mary and Jake have known each other for two decades and barely talk to one another. And they're total opposites. She's a bookworm and he loves to go out to parties and bars. He loves dating. I can't even picture him settling down with anyone. Not yet, anyway.

"He told me that he'd come help me out of my date, but when he got here, he literally sat in another booth, ordered lunch and laughed quietly at me and Evan for like thirty minutes. Finally he came over and told me that my house was burning down and that I had to leave the restaurant immediately."

I smile at the idea of a man taking Mary out and playing the same song on his guitar for an hour straight. "That was nice of Jake to finally rescue you. How like him to make you suffer first. He'd do the same thing to me."

She's quiet for a moment. "It's weird. I don't think that we have ever hung out without you there. And he's not what I imagined *at all*. It's so easy to talk – we stayed up until three in the morning talking. And I always pictured him as this smooth operator. But he gets tongue-tied and he blushes. A lot. He's actually tripped at least twice. He spilled a drink on me." She takes a deep breath and I can sense her struggling emotionally. Despite being a romantic and so open to love, she doesn't fall easily, ever since her last boyfriend crushed her heart into about a million tiny pieces. "These *cannot* be his moves," she explains, a slight quiver in her voice. In a whisper, she adds pleadingly, "there's something here."

"You've known each other forever," I say quietly, a nervous laugh escaping before I can help it. I'm never nervous with Mary. I want to be supportive. I do. And honestly my brother would probably kill a guy who was bad to Mary. She's family. I clutch the phone tightly to my ear and look around at the unfamiliar surroundings, wondering if Jake actually could change. Fall in love. It would be fantastic if he finally settled down. And to fall in love and settle down with Mary? That would be a dream come true. She has the biggest heart of anyone I've ever met and she's beautiful – not that she gives herself any credit on either front.

"I'll just have to see this to believe it!"

Mary breathes a long sigh of relief and laughs. "In one week, you'll see it all. You know, I can hardly believe it myself."

"Now tell me why you said Christmas Eve was interesting and make it quick. This is very long distance because I am – "

" – in Paris, I know," she says, feigning annoyance. "Okay, well...are you sure you want to hear everything from me and not your family?"

"I'm dying over here, Mare."

"Charles and Samantha are expecting another baby."

Samantha's pregnant again? I can't believe it. I mean, two years ago when Tristan was born, they said they were done. They had two amazing, healthy kids. They always loved the idea of two children. And yet...Charles has been really stressed out lately now that I think about it. Not unhappy stressed either. Just overwhelmed and definitely overprotective, if his behavior regarding Ian and my vacation is any indication. Oh yeah. He's in daddy-mode, big time.

"Lucy?"

"That's so cool," I finally say, my heart pounding with excitement. They make the cutest children. Though I may be slightly biased. "Is there anything else?" I ask. Because I know there is. Mary could always give away too much by barely saying a word.

"Julie has decided to become a professional makeup artist."

"But she's a doctor." Is Mary messing with me?

"Your mom was not exactly thrilled."

"I can imagine," I laugh. "I think it'll be quite the pay cut. And Jules loves her vintage dresses and designer jeans."

"Your mom brought that up as well."

"What did Julie say? Did she give a reason for abandoning her life's work out of nowhere?"

"Well, she sort of implied that your little international jaunt motivated her to be more true to herself."

"You're kidding," I say, throwing my hand to my forehead. As if I hadn't given her enough ammunition lately, my mother is going to kill me. She takes unbelievable pride in telling anyone who will listen that her Julie is a 'real doctor'.

"She gave your mom a beautiful makeover before the night was over and I think that softened the blow a little," Mary says, stifling a laugh. She's always loved my family. As an only child, she sort of adopted us in grade school and fancied herself an honorary Gray ever since.

I hang up with Mary and stare at the phone for just a moment, taking in everything she told me. Just two weeks ago, everything was normal. Now, it's just all changed around back home. Is this what happens when you make spontaneous decisions and take a leap? Does life completely go haywire when you aren't looking? Does everything get turned upside down when you're out taking pictures of the Eiffel Tower?

Major things are happening with the people I love the most at home. And here I am in Paris....

I look around.

Here I am in Paris *completely* lost. At some point during my conversation with Mary, I wandered without paying any attention. I can't even spot the Tower in the distance anymore to get my bearings.

And – everything is closed. Most people are gone now except for a few, and there don't seem to be any taxis around anymore. Plus, it's getting colder by the minute. I jab at the map app over and over, but the wheel just turns, searching for a WiFi signal.

From the pocket of my faded blue jeans, I extricate the business card Jessie handed me as I headed out the door this morning – 'in case of an emergency!' I dial the number she gave me and am happy to hear a distant ringing on the other end.

"Hello?" answers a male voice that I'm coming to know only too well.

"Hey, Oliver," I say, trying to sound cheerful, like he is just the person I am calling to talk to.

"Ah, Miss Gray," he says, and while he tries to sound bored, I can detect a note of interest in his tone. "Merry Christmas."

"Merry Christmas. Um...is your sister there?"

"She's not."

I sigh. He's purposefully being difficult. I can hear it in his tone. And I hate to ask for his help in any way. Looking around, though, I realize that I hate being lost even more. "I'm lost," I finally say.

After a brief pause, he asks, "all right, well, where are you?"

"Well, if I knew that—"

"—you wouldn't be lost. Yes, I know," he cuts me off impatiently. "I mean, what are you near? Where did you go today? I assume that at some point you were not lost."

"I was at the Eiffel Tower about thirty minutes ago. But I walked away from it."

"In which direction?"

"The away direction," I say brazenly. I am very self-conscious about my directionally-challenged nature that's followed me through life. It's not my fault that Boston, while lovely, was built like a one-way curving nightmare.

He is silent for a long moment. "You really wear on my patience, do you know that?"

I smile, pleased that I wear on his patience. Because he definitely wears on mine. "Do you see any signs?" he prompts after a moment. He almost sounds eager to help me. Or find and annoy me.

I look around and spot a sign, a pretty large one just in front of an office building. "Yes," I say excitedly. "Yes, okay. Here's one."

"Yes?" he urges me, bursting with impatience.

I open my mouth to read the sign, but stop, suddenly self-conscious. "Don't make fun of my accent. I never learned French. Though I was great at Spanish. All A's."

"Miss Gray."

I sigh and look at the sign. I guess, to his point, this really isn't the ideal time to boast about my good grades fifteen years ago. "It says 'A Vendre,'" I say. "Is that a restaurant you know or something?"

He's quiet for a moment. Then he bursts out laughing.

"What?" I ask, growing concerned. "Where am I?" But he only continues laughing. I've never really heard him laugh. It's actually kind of a nice sound. I wasn't sure he had it in him, honestly. "Oliver, pull yourself together," I beg, staring at the building and this oh-so-humorous sign. "I warned you about my accent."

"It's not your accent I'm worried about," he says, still rippling with laughter over the phone line.

"Where am I?" I order through gritted teeth, hoping my frustration is making its way through the phone line and into his ears.

"For starters, you're in front of a building that is for sale," he says. And then he bursts into laughter all over again as I begin slowly turning all shades of red. I walk to the sidewalk behind me and take a seat, shaking my head at that darn sign. Of course I had to choose *that* sign to read to *this* man.

"Stop laughing," I plead, though I start to feel the beginning waves of laughter bubbling within myself. "I don't speak French. It was an honest mistake that anyone could have made."

"I feel like it could only happen to you, Miss Gray."

And then we're both laughing. Really laughing. Somehow, after feeling on the verge of crying fifteen minutes ago, I'm having *fun*. Sitting on a Paris curb. Completely lost. On the phone with Oliver, of all people. Wiping my eyes, I reach into my bag and remove my camera to take a picture of the sign. This sign – this stupid, uninformative sign – made Oliver Burke laugh hysterically – no small feat with someone like him. This sign definitely needs to be documented. It needs to be remembered.

chapter eleven

I embarked on this adventure completely on my own, yet I never seem to be *alone*. This fact was the very reason I was so excited to have the full afternoon to experience Paris in my own way. Seeing the Eiffel Tower, walking along the Seine, taking thousands of photos all around the city. Every incredible moment was mine and mine alone.

Having someone show you around, however, has its benefits too. Even when that someone *is* Oliver Burke. It eliminates the option of getting lost, for one thing. On top of the directional benefit, Oliver actually knows stuff. A lot of stuff. From history and culture to local hangouts, he has this city down. He's like the tour guide from the Tower of London tour – just an endless stream of trivia.

"I assume you'll want to get your camera ready for our next stop," he says, breaking into my thoughts.

At his words, I reach for my camera as we round a corner. "What's next?"

"The Arc de Triomphe," he says with a bit of pomp and circumstance, gesturing toward a proud, stately and gorgeous structure just as it falls into view. After snapping a couple of pictures, I decide immediately that the Arc de Triomphe is, like the Eiffel Tower, a great candidate for another cleverly angled photo. In silence we walk until we are directly before the building. Perfect spot. I sit down, placing my photo bag and purse beside me. I peer through the lens at the building and start to lean back.

"What are you doing?" Oliver asks, standing over me with an expression that seems to be questioning my sanity. "You're going to lie down on the ground for a photo? You do know that it's about ten degrees outside."

"For this shot, I'd lie on the ground naked," I say, immediately regretting my word choice. I mean, you don't just say things to guys that could cause them to think of you, you know, naked. Especially one day after said guy very nearly caught you naked. I pull the camera away from my face and peek at Oliver. He's just staring at me, shaking his head in clear disbelief, his cheeks much redder than before. That could have something to do with the cold though.

Oliver clears his throat and cocks his head to the side, the teasing glint in his eyes that I am becoming familiar with, returning. "I honestly can't believe you're on the ground, taking a picture," he says, stuffing his hands in his pockets.

"Oh, you should see the shot I got of the Eiffel Tower. I probably got bubble gum in my hair, but I don't care. The picture was that good."

I peer through the lens again and begin snapping away. For all my talk about a great shot being worth any sacrifice, my butt is starting to freeze on the cold pavement.

Oliver squats down and leans over me. "This entire album better be bloody publishable for all the effort going into it," he says.

I look at him again, smiling. He smiles back, that crooked smile of his that I am getting to see more and more lately.

I stand upright and tuck my camera back into its bag as we begin walking. "Now that you've located me and brought me back to civilization, you can head back to Jessie's. You don't have to babysit. I mean, it's Christmas—"

"A time for family and loved ones, you might say?" he asks, a knowing smile playing across his lips.

I ignore his blatant jibe at the absence of Cary in my afternoon and nod. "Yes."

He runs a hand through his mess of dark curls and sighs, looking at the ground as we walk. "It's okay," he says finally. "I don't mind...this."

I nod, staring solemnly, awkwardly ahead of us as well. "I don't mind either."

Twenty minutes later, I scoot into a booth at a hole-in-the-wall café that Oliver assured me would be open today.

I rub my hands together, breathing warm air into them. "It's freezing out there."

"Says the girl who was just laying on the cold concrete for a photograph," Oliver quips, removing his jacket and scarf and placing it on the booth beside him.

"I think this calls for a warm white mocha, don't you?"

He raises his eyebrows. "You seem to switch up your coffee order daily."

"Not usually," I say, fiddling with the menu. "Just on this trip."

The waiter walks over and hands us a drink menu. I only know it's a drink menu due to a black and white drawing on the cover of martini glasses with an olive garnish.

"Parle vous englais?" I ask the waiter, who nervously shakes his head and backs away, as if I've just asked him for his life savings.

Furrowing my eyebrows, I try to figure out how to order my hot drink. Perhaps if I talk slow and use hand gestures—

Before I can formulate a plan, Oliver says something to the young man in rapid French and with a nod the waiter hurries off.

"That was good." I say to Oliver, leaning forward. Though I shouldn't be shocked he speaks French. His sister lives here. He seems to know the city remarkably well. "Do you speak French or just know how to order in French?"

"I speak it, though not well."

After a moment, the waiter returns with three drinks – a cappuccino for Oliver and two white mochas for me. I look at Oliver incredulously. "You ordered me two?" I ask.

"Don't you always order two?" he asks, looking unsure – almost boyish.

"Yes," I assure him, kind of touched he's paid attention. "I always get two." I grab the first of the white mochas and take a slow, cautious sip. It is hot, so I blow on it before attempting a second sip. It succeeds in warming me, making me feel comforted and safe, here inside this little restaurant.

"I do have to ask, though," Oliver says, sitting back with his cappuccino and fixing me with a curious look. "How do you sleep?"

"I'm immune to the effects of caffeine," I share. I have to explain this to a lot of people. Apparently most people only drink a cup or two a day of coffee.

His smile widens as I shrug innocuously.

"So, where is your husband today?" he asks.

I sigh, all positive feelings toward this man nearly vanished. "Oliver, if we played a drinking game for every time you asked that question, I'd be wasted this entire trip."

"I'm sorry," he says. And he actually looks like he means that. "But I have to ask."

"*Why* do you have to ask?" The words seem to explode from inside of me. But he infuriates me. One moment he is completely helpful and friendly, and the next he's just nosy and annoying. "You make it sound like you're being ordered to ask this. So please, Oliver, tell me. Why do you have to ask?"

He sighs and places his cappuccino back on the table before staring down at his lap, a look of regret etched on his face. "I just want to understand," he finally says quietly. "Understand what is going on with you two."

I laugh haughtily. "Is that part of your job?"

He breathes in deeply but still avoids eye contact. "You have no idea," he mumbles.

"You are the concierge at my hotel," I explain slowly, like I'm explaining to one of my third graders that it's not okay to pull on another third grader's braids no matter how long and 'pullable' they look. "I know this is basically the first vacation I've ever taken and all," I continue, "but from what I understand, concierges sit at a desk and recommend good restaurants to guests or give maps to people like me who get lost in a parking lot and explain how to get from point A to point B."

"I helped you today when you were lost," he adds, like that's a point in his favor. "And we're at a good restaurant now."

"In Paris," I point out. "The hotel is in London. Again, I'm not that well-traveled, but - "

"I'm very hands-on," he says lamely.

"With everyone?"

He looks at me and I just stare right back, my arms folded across my chest. Waiting. He doesn't say a word, though. He looks like a million things are on the tip of his tongue but he seems to think better about saying each one of them out loud. "How would you like it if I played twenty questions with you every time I saw you?" I ask.

"You did ask me my last name that one time."

"That was one question, Oliver," I say, exasperated. "Let's try one more."

"Okay," he says reticently. "What do you want to know?"

I lean back and smile. This might be fun. "Last night, Jessie said working at The Chaizer must be hell for you. What did she mean?"

He shakes his head and laughs sort of humorously. "You don't miss anything, do you?" he asks.

"I'll answer your questions if you answer mine."

We stare at each other, locked in our stupid stalemate, for what feels like an eternity, when the waiter returns to take our orders. Oliver orders quickly in French, while I stare blankly down at my menu. I really don't feel like asking Oliver for advice right now, and he's not exactly offering to translate the menu either. Probably because I've just asked him a question that most likely annoys him, that he has no desire at all to answer. I choose the first dish I see and then hand the menu to the waiter who, seeming to sense the tension at our table, rushes off quickly. I look back at Oliver expectantly.

"Fine," he says after a long moment. "I talk now. You talk later."

"That sounds reasonable."

"Jessie," he starts, in a tone that lends an unspoken *'who I am going to kill later'* tag to it, "can be dramatic. What she called 'hell', I would simply call 'annoying.'" He looks up at me, meeting my gaze and sighs. "She was referring to something that happened three years ago," he explains. "When I got married."

"You're married?" I ask, my eyes wide as saucers. I am having trouble processing this information, though I'm not sure why. It's not like Oliver's an old friend or even an acquaintance. He is allowed to be married with kids, and I shouldn't be shocked. Though if he were, I'd like to think he'd spend the holidays, you know, with *them*.

"Was," he corrects me. "For a very short time," he hastens to add. "Apparently she didn't want to get married at all, but she never let on. She thought it'd be bad form to cancel the wedding." He clears his throat and looks at me. "She was afraid of what people would think. So she went through with it."

I watch him intently as he speaks. His face is a perfect mask, like he's just relayed a story he heard that had absolutely nothing to do with him, rather than a bad memory from his own past.

"Anyway," he continues. "She was supposed to meet

me at the airport but she never showed." He shrugs and looks down at his lap. He's clearly done talking about this topic. But I'm not.

"She stood you up on the way to your honeymoon?" I ask. I feel like something is twisting my heart, as he nods in confirmation. He leans back in his chair and fixes his gaze on some unseen space between us. And I can see it. He's not so good at pretending. He is not as detached as he wants to appear. This experience hurt. It probably still hurts.

Still reeling from shock, I ask, "how could anyone do that?" He looks up at me, his mouth falling open in shock at my burst of emotion. "And to someone they loved enough to marry?" I add. "Not that marrying someone equals caring for them. Clearly it doesn't. I mean, look at every celebrity couple ever."

At his quizzical look, I hasten to add, "Not that I'm suggesting this woman didn't love you. I'm sure she did! She just seems...."

I trail off. I'm sure I've already insulted him with my ramblings about how his ex clearly *didn't* care about him and how she could be likened pretty easily to Britney Spears, like he needed to hear that when he probably agonized over it himself on a daily basis. "I'm sorry," I stammer quietly after a long moment of silence. "That story is just— "

" – in the past," he says calmly.

"I don't get it," I press, fidgeting with my napkin. "Jessie's right. Working at The Chaizer must be hell for you. Happy honeymooners everywhere, making out in the lobby, in the hallways, even at the front desk. Why do you do it? She seemed surprised you worked there, so I assume it's not your normal job."

Leaning back in his seat, Oliver fixes me with a small smile. "That's two questions," he says.

"Come on," I urge.

"It's just a temporary job," he says quickly. "Now you."

I sigh, recognizing a closed case when I see one. Well, he answered my question, which, innocent as it seemed when I asked it, turned out to be a pretty hefty one. Now I owe him.

"He's out again with his friend," I say, slowly, methodically picking out each and every word. Lying is not easy. Or pleasant. At all. "He used to come to Europe all the time, but they haven't seen each other in quite a while. They're just, you know...making up for lost time."

"And he can't take you with him?" Oliver asks, resting his chin in his hand, his eyes never leaving mine. "It's your honeymoon, after all. Aren't you supposed to be attached at the hip on these things?"

"I don't know," I admit with a shrug. "But I'm having a really nice time." I peer at him closely before adding, "I think that's what counts."

He regards me strangely, after the words are out of my mouth. Before he can say anything at all, the waiter hurries over, putting two dishes down, interrupting the moment. I break our gaze and look down at my food. Immediately I do a double take. My food has eyes.

"What is this?" I ask when the waiter is gone.

"Prawns," Oliver answers, smiling coyly. "It's what you ordered."

"Oh. Right." I cock my head and look once again at my food, as if this angle will magically make it look more appetizing. It doesn't work. My food is staring at me. "I guess I didn't realize that it had eyes."

He laughs. "Why don't we switch," he suggests.

"You don't have to – "

"I like prawns," he cuts in. "So long as you like garlic chicken."

"I do."

"It's settled then."

I look at him incredulously as he switches the dishes and picks up his fork.

"Do you actually eat the eyes?" I ask, like we're talking about a mega international scandal rather than shrimp.

"It's the best part," he says, his smile growing. "Most flavor." He takes a bite as my mouth falls open.

∽

An hour later, we walk side-by-side down the cobblestone streets that lead to Jessie's little house in a comfortable silence. With my scarf wrapped around my mouth and nose in a pointless attempt to keep warm, narrowing my eyes to keep the wind out of them, I think about the lovely area we had just come from.

"What was the name of that place again?"

"I've told you a thousand times," Oliver says, peeking down at me quickly.

"Come on, I want to add it to my scrapbook."

"To go with the fifty photos you took while there," he says, dryly. "I can write it down for you when we get back to Jessie's."

"And that's great and all, but I really want to master the pronunciation, too, in case people ask."

He looks skyward and releases a long, low breath. "Last time." He glances at me. "The Quartier du Marais," he says in a perfect French accent.

I giggle, which is just ridiculous. I don't giggle. I never giggle. The word *giggle* is so completely flighty and wispy and opposite of all things me. But I can't help it. I love the sound of his French accent. It's kind of cute.

And that area – that quartier – was so quiet and beautiful. We headed there after leaving the café, and I fell in love. Oliver explained that during the holidays, Paris is pretty quiet, because the Parisians leave town to head to family homes in the nearby provinces. And that's exactly how it was in the quartier. Quiet. Still. I heard the echo of church bells ringing somewhere in the city far from where we walked. It felt like the only people alive in the world were Oliver and me. I've never felt like that before in my whole life.

I wrap my arms tightly around myself as the wind whips around us, sweeping through my hair and soul. This really has turned into an amazing day.

"I want to show you one more thing before we go to Jessie's," Oliver says, looking down at me.

"Oliver, I think I saw the whole city today. I think I even possibly saw the whole city backwards today."

He smiles but persists. "You'll love this. I promise."

I sigh and follow him, with complete trust, down a little dirt pathway just a block away from Jessie's. I look up to see where we are heading, but only spot a tiny cottage a ways ahead. A paint-chipped white picket fence lies slightly ajar in the front yard, almost welcoming us inside. Why would Oliver think I should see this?

Then, all at once, it becomes clear as I hear him beginning to laugh. A sign stands proudly on the front yard and though it's barely visible in the twilight, it clearly says "A Vendre." There is a bright red slash through the sign.

"This place," Oliver explains, collecting himself, "is *not* for sale."

I push him lightly, trying not to laugh at myself again. He playfully, gently tugs on my scarf, which causes it to unravel a little, exposing my red nose.

"Did you buy this place?" I ask coyly. "Because it's lovely."

"I did not," he says, still smiling. "I know that you like to keep on top of the buildings in Paris that are for sale and not for sale."

I reach up and grab the hat off his head. He makes a move to grab it back, but I back away too quickly. He just stands there, smiling, his eyes bright from the cold and laughter.

I grab my camera.

"You are going to get a picture of this sign," he assumes aloud, as if doubting my sanity.

"I am going to get a picture of this sign," I assure him. And while my face feels nearly numb from the cold, I can still feel my smile getting wider.

I peer through the lens at the sweet cottage that is not for sale and hear Oliver bustling towards me until he's right beside me. Very close to me, in fact. Close enough that I am aware of his smell – a mixture of spicy soap and fresh air – and his height (my eyes level with his shoulder). I hand him his hat and he takes it, but doesn't put it on. I swallow hard, put the camera to my face again and take the picture quickly.

When I look up at him, his smile has vanished. He seems to be done making fun of me, done laughing for the moment – though there is still a spark in his eyes. He looks quietly content as he stares at the sign and then slowly back at me.

"Let's get back," he says.

I follow after him, wondering what happened, what had been happening all day. This nearly perfect day has honestly been completely strange. Trailing behind Oliver, I'm struck with an awful realization.

I don't hate this man anymore. Not even a little.

I'm Hip Now.

Posted by @Delores at 1:57 PM on december 25 on TheGrayBlog

That's right, kids. You all think that I am so set in my ways that you can only tell me big news when you're either drunk (Julie) or about to fly away from me literally (Lucy). And I thought you should know that I am a reformed woman. Maybe it was my makeover the other day (by the way Julie, all my friends thought I looked like Sharon Osborne, THANK YOU...) or the news that I'm going to be a Nana again, but I have a new lease on life. No need to hide from me. I'm quite chill. Case in point:

Julie – who needs a paying career? They are overrated. Make me pretty.

Lucy – next time you want to go on a vacation, I will help you pack. As it is, you probably forgot half the things you needed for exactly this reason.

I love you all, kids. Your hip, cool, newly lightened-up:

-Mom

PS: Julie, if you could put down your air brushes for a bit honey - I am going to need some help with Christmas dinner. Lucy was in charge of the turnips, stuffing, cranberry sauce and seating list. I'll die on the spot if I end up sitting next to Uncle Melvin because Lucy is off in who knows where doing God knows what.

Rock on, mom.

Posted by @Jules at 2:18 PM on december 25 on TheGrayBlog

Help is on the way, Mom.

And Lucy- I can't wait to see you. And if you do ever decide to do another international vacation, don't believe mom. She won't help you pack. ;-)

Love,

Jules

chapter twelve

As the Chunnel pulls away from the station, I gaze out the window. Paris rolls on by, bidding me farewell and Merry Christmas. I still can't believe I just had a two-day getaway in Paris! This whole thing –this whole trip – is just so surreal. Jessie told me to come back someday, that I was welcome to stay with them again (even though I burned a hole in their countertop). I actually have an acquaintance *in Paris*.

"Would you stop smiling?" Cary eyes me from over his newspaper.

I look up at him and tilt my head. "Smiling is not allowed?"

"Not the way you're doing it." He rests his head back and gazes past me, out the window, a sad yet hopeful expression dancing across his face.

I realize it's up to me to keep the spirit high since we have to sit on this train together for hours. "I can't help it," I explain. "If you asked me two weeks ago where

I'd been in this world, the words 'pit stop' would have come up. But now England *and* France. I'm going to be tough to deal with when I get home. That's for sure."

He laughs, refocusing his gaze on me. He shakes his head. "I think it's hysterical, personally," he says.

I pull my knees up against my chest and circle my arms around them before looking up at Cary, feigning offense. "Not everyone does yearly workshops overseas."

"Actually, I mean you. This permanent grin. Ever since you walked through the door last night."

"I had a great day," I answer defensively. Like I should have to defend smiling. "No thanks to you," I add, which makes him narrow his brown eyes at me.

"I had things to do, people to see," he murmurs quietly, unsuccessfully attempting lightness.

"You know, it was your idea to be my 'husband', but I think Oliver is more suspicious of me now than when I just looked like a liar who parades around honeymoon joints alone."

"I don't think Oliver is suspicious of you at all, actually," he says knowingly, crossing his arms and looking at me expectantly. Except I have no idea what he's talking about. Has he been paying attention? Because Oliver is definitely suspicious of something.

I've heard the British are polite and reserved. Not shady and chatty. He's definitely up to something.

"Cary, every time I turn around, he's there. I'm amazed – honestly *amazed* – that he decided to take a later train today."

"And why do you think that is?" he presses, smirking a little.

"Because he wanted to spend more time with his sister—"

" – I *mean*," he cuts in impatiently. "Why do you think it is that he's everywhere you are?"

"Maybe he thinks I'm committing identity theft in his family's exclusive –"

"—and that, *Miss Gray*, is what's hysterical about you."

Before I can ask him to explain, he shoots a smug look my way and hands me a section of the newspaper that he is apparently done reading. "Let it simmer a bit," is all I get in the way of an explanation.

Cary turns his attention back to the newspaper in his hands, quieting the subject for now. I look at the section in my hands and scan for a good headline. I spot an article called "The Honeymooners." We have a winner. It takes me about ten seconds to realize that this is no fluff piece. The article's subhead states, "The famous criminals can now add murder to list of crimes". The article begins with the ominous words "Who will be next?" This question is followed by statements like "their fifth crime, committed on their latest 'honeymoon' in Italy left an innocent man dead" and "police believe the couple is heading to southern Italy then Spain."

The Honeymooners are not a lovey-dovey couple at all. These 'honeymooners' are thieves on a global 'shopping spree' now wanted for murder in addition to their numerous crimes. They've stolen goods from hotels throughout Europe totaling up to seven million pounds. Why hadn't I heard of them before? Apparently they've been on the run for six months. No one knows what they look like or anything about them. Taking out security cameras and moving from place to place quite fluidly have made them something of a nightmare for European authorities. The only way they've been linked to all the crimes is from the note they always leave at the scene of the crime that simply says "Still Honeymooning."

"This is just like Mickey and Mallory." I fold the paper and look at Cary.

"Excuse me?"

"From *Natural Born Killers*." I jab at the headline. "It's them all over. A couple in love but severely misguided and, frankly, nuts."

Cary chuckles and folds the paper in his own hands. "I read that one, too," he says, nodding to the article. He looks back at me and smiles. "Don't worry. I won't let the Honeymooners come after you."

"I don't think *I'd* exactly be a target for these guys. My 'Lucy' necklace from Tiffany's is about the most expensive thing I have with me and it's only worth a couple hundred dollars. Somehow I don't think they accumulated their seven million pounds pulling petty crimes."

"I think you might be right."

"I would've pegged you more for *Legally Blonde* than *Natural Born Killers*."

I swat him playfully and close the newspaper. "I like a lot of things, for your information. I'm not that predictable."

He looks down at me, the smile leaving his face as he meets my eyes. "I think you're right about that."

"So you never did tell me what happened with Anne," I say, looking up at him.

He stares out the window as his expression quickly grows grim. "Nothing happened," he mutters miserably. He rakes a hand through his hair, agitatedly, and sighs. "I come all the way out to Paris to visit her, she invites me out, and parades around with a date in front of me the whole time I'm there."

I frown, thinking about that. When I met her, Anne seemed so mature. But I am getting the distinct impression that she's toying with poor Cary.

"You know, it's funny," he says after a long moment. "I really don't think Anne would play mind games with me. We're friends. At the very least, we are really very good friends." He suddenly laughs. "I'd be very turned off if that is what she was doing."

I peer closely at him, knowing he's leaving something out. "But?"

"But," he adds, grudgingly, "I can't help but wish that were true."

❧

Four hours later, we're back on British soil. Cary helps me and my bags out of the taxi and we walk into the familiar charm of The Chaizer. I'd spent the last half of the Chunnel trip reading all I could find about The Honeymooners. Authorities received an anonymous tip that they were headed to Florence, Italy next. But still, I look around at all the honeymooners heading to their morning Pilates session or couples' massage treatments and wonder what if the crazy couple in the paper looks anything like the actual honeymooners here? Do they call themselves that because they walk around all in love or are they a cranky old couple being a little ironic? The fact that authorities cannot even put a sketch together creates a buzz in my mind at all the possibilities.

I take a seat on the love seat in our flat and turn the

fireplace on as Cary disappears into the bathroom to grab a shower. Looking around the flat, my mind wanders away from thoughts of thieves turned murderers and travels about a thousand miles away to Haley, Massachusetts. To my loft where Mary and Jake are possibly up to no good. I can picture the dark hardwood floors beneath my feet, covering the small expanse of space that was mine. I can practically hear the wood creaking the way it does with every step. I imagine Ricky asleep on the rocking chair in the corner that connects my kitchen to my living room, by the tiny 1950s diner table for two. If I were there, I would scoop him up into my arms and walk to the window where I'd be greeted with a view of...well of the brick-faced apartment building next to mine and the window of Mrs. Suzayaki. But if I peek just beyond the window and the brick, I can see some lights – the city of Boston.

The distant sound of running water signals the start of Cary's shower. Is it possible to miss something so much you can ache inside, while loving the place you are in? I rest back on the soft, velvety cushion on the love seat and prop my feet up, glancing at the large picture window by the bed. The thrill of London outside mixes with a sad little voice that softly says, "But it's not home."

I dig into the pocket of my jeans and grab my calling card. I reach for the phone on the coffee table and proceed to dial a number I know as well as my own name.

"Mom?"

"Well, if it isn't my daughter, deciding to tell me she's alive, after a week." She can't fool me. Her high-pitched voice is scolding, but relieved.

"Mom, you know I'm alive." I fall into the love seat

and put my feet up on the coffee table. "You've talked to the others. And I'm sure Mary has told Jake and he's told you that as of yesterday, I was still, you know, among the living. In London."

I can almost see her eyes darting back and forth as she clutches the phone nervously and searches for something to say. She doesn't like spontaneity. Growing up, we were all made well aware of the evils of spontaneity, having been told elaborate tales about children who lived on the wind and ended up dead or friendless. This is probably the reason I made it to twenty-six years old without ever having done anything truly adventurous.

"Hi sweetie," I hear my dad's voice say into the phone. "Are you having fun?"

"Don, it's not about her having fun. It's about her being careful."

"Tomato, potato."

"That is not the saying! I've told you a thousand times—"

I smile. My parents are so completely opposite from each other. Charles clearly takes after my mother, over-worrying about every little thing. I like to think I'm a bit more free-spirited like my dad. He and I always have loved taking road trips, blasting Springsteen, and generally laughing at all the crazy around us – though we wouldn't change one thing about anyone in our family.

"So," my mom says with measured, controlled calmness. "What is London like?"

"It's fantastic."

"Fantastic like Boston?" she asks.

"Different," I answer honestly. "I guess you might say I'm an entirely different person in London."

She pauses. "You're not slutty there are you?"

Oh, my God. I stare at the phone. Only my mother would say that. "Yes, Mom. I stepped on British soil and became easy," I say, sarcastically.

"Lucy." She sounds downright horrified.

"Mom, you're being dramatic." I roll my eyes, knowing she can't see me and lecture me about how it's rude to. "Anyway, I was calling to see how you are."

"I suppose you've heard all the news," she says in her cheery gossispy voice, sounding much more like my normal mother now. "I'm going to be a grandmother again, have to support poor Julie until she's married as she's chosen a penniless career, and judging by the look of Mary and Jake, be planning yet another wedding probably in a year. I tell you that boy has been hit over the head with the love stick. They've known each other for years. Why now they've chosen to fall in love is beyond me," she gushes all at once.

"Everyone must be really excited." Even as I say the words, I feel a little twinge of jealousy knowing so many exciting things are happening at home and I'm not part of any of it. "And I'm sure Julie has a plan that won't leave her completely reliant on you for life."

"Everyone really misses you, Lucy," she says after a moment. And I can tell that she really means that, which I appreciate.

"I miss everyone, too."

"Now," she says, returning to her business-as-usual voice. "I hope you're being extra careful because they do everything backwards there."

"Actually, Mom, since they were here first, I'm pretty sure that we're the ones doing everything backwards."

"Hm," she mumbles, the way she always does when

one of us ever makes a point she can't argue. "Just don't get run over because of it."

"Hasn't been a problem yet."

I jump when the bathroom door opens. I look up to see Cary walk out, wearing only a towel. My breath catches. Water drips down his toned, tan body. I look back into his eyes when he clears his throat.

"You're kind of staring," he says, smirking.

"Sorry." I turn away, my cheeks flushing from embarrassment.

"Lucy, who is that?" my mother demands from one thousand miles away.

"No one, Mom." I clear my throat. "But I have to go now."

"That was a man's voice," she says. "Lucy—"

"Give my love to everyone there, okay?" I hang up to the sound of protest.

"Okay, you can look now," Cary says finally.

I turn toward him and smile sheepishly.

"Class is only for an hour today. Then, I am coming back here. And you and I can have our own little Christmas celebration."

I sit up straighter. "Really? You'll come back this time?"

"I promise," he assures me, putting his watch on and his wallet in his pocket. "I dragged you to Paris, barely spent a moment with you, and I know that I owe you."

"You definitely owe me."

"What are you going to do while I'm gone?"

"Head to Hugging Mugs, explore more of Kensington, maybe a quick walk over to Hyde Park," I say excitedly, eager to go out on my own and visit those places.

"You're starting to sound like a local," he says, his eyes twinkling at me.

"Right." I can't hide my smile. "A local who only visits tourist attractions."

Something wonderful stirs deeply within me. I am returning to favorite spots in this foreign city. A sense of freedom and independence dances through my veins, energizing me as I get ready to go back out, forget about my own little world in Haley, Massachusetts for awhile. And seize *this* moment.

chapter thirteen

The next day, as I step outside The Chaizer into the morning sunshine, I am sad to report that it still hasn't rained. Not once. In London. London, a place known for its rain. And Prince William. It's almost as if my mother called Mother Nature and told her, mother-to-mother, to hold off until I left, just to spite me for embarking on this adventure. Well, I don my turquoise raincoat anyway and walk to Hugging Mugs for my daily fix.

Once I'm seated with my two iced caramel lattes, I pull the postcards from my pocketbook that I purchased in Paris. *Eiffel Tower. Moulin Rouge. The Louvre. Notre Dame. Arc de Triomphe. Champs de Elysees. Paris at Night.*

Paris at Night. I stare at that one – the orange glow of a city alive reflects peacefully in the inky waters of the Seine River. I walked along that river with Oliver, when he first found me after I'd gotten lost, after the "For Sale" moment. We'd seen Paris at night together, exploring that beautiful, quiet quartier before walking back to Jessie's house. I smile.

It's strange that I didn't see Oliver last night – or yet today. Maybe he's spending extra time with his little sister. And this is a good thing.

I pull the cap off my black pen and start crafting my words about the trip to my niece and nephew, Mary, my mom and my third grade class, regaling them all (as much as one can regale with the tiny allotment of space on a postcard) with stories about my adventures through Paris and London so far.

Re-entering the lobby, I still see no sign of Oliver. Maybe he's been fired for stalking guests. I walk up to the desk, where Polly sits, reading *Romeo & Juliet*. She looks up when I approach, huffs rather haughtily and closes her book.

"If you're going to ruin this one too, I'll just go get Geoff and take my break until you're gone."

I raise an eyebrow and regard her curiously. "You don't already know how *Romeo & Juliet* ends?" I ask.

She narrows her eyes at me. "What can I do for you, Miss Gray?"

"Oh, you remember me."

"It's hard to forget someone who's not only married to that hot guy, but also has Oliver asking about you and everything that you do *nonstop*," she mutters under her breath, placing her book on the counter. She leans forward and looks at me, folding her hands together. "To what do I owe this pleasure?"

"Oliver asks about me?" I ask, ignoring her question. "What does he say?"

"What does it matter?" Polly says, exasperated. "You have the most gorgeous man I ever laid eyes on married to *you* for some reason that eludes me. Can't you just leave Oliver to the rest of us mere mortal women?"

I laugh, which really seems to upset her. But I can't help it. She can't be more than sixteen years old. "I'm sorry. You're right," I eventually say, controlling my laughter. Polly just blinks at me, clearly waiting to see what it is that I want.

I smile kindly at her and wave my five postcards at her. "I have some mail to send. To America," I add for clarification.

"Really? America? Is that where you're from?" she asks, sarcasm dripping heavily from her voice.

"Can I send them here?" I ask, ignoring her remark.

She rolls her eyes and puts her hand out impatiently. I lean the postcards warily toward her, but she grabs them as soon as they are near her hands.

"Will you make sure to send them – "

"No worries, Miss Gray. Your postcards are as good as on their way now."

"Okay," I say. "Have a great day, Polly." I genuinely hope that kindness can outweigh teenage angst.

She waves before turning her back to me, my mail clutched tightly in her hand.

I turn around to head back outside and nearly collide with Kiki.

"Lucy!"

"Kiki," I say, smiling uncertainly. Every time she says my name, I feel like she is about to ask me if we could be Best Friends Forever. "How did you like Paris?"

"Oh, Paris is one of my favorite cities," she says, nearly bubbling over with enthusiasm. "We've never been on Christmas, of course, so it was a plus. I hate the city in summertime. Too many people. This was just right." I smile, thinking of the calm and quiet emanating the streets of Paris on Christmas, trying to imagine it hot, sticky and filled with people. "I was just about to head out and do some shopping on my own because my new hubby is a complete *workaholic* and even though he said he wouldn't do any work on this trip he…" she trails off, as if remembering she's venting to someone she barely knows. She rolls her eyes and smiles. "I bet your husband is the same way. Is that why he's never with you?"

"Kind of."

"Well – if you want to come, it'd be a lot more fun with company."

I glance at the front picture window of The Chaizer that overlooks Kensington High Street. "I was going to jump on the tube, go downtown, walk around, maybe take in a show later."

"That's perfect," she says excitedly. "I'm going to the West End. The theater district is over there. I think." She gazes skyward. "Anyway," she says, shrugging, returning to our conversation. "You can shop with me and go see your show later."

An hour later, I find myself in Piccadilly Circus. Shopping. Well, window-shopping, in my case. No need to go broke because of my vacation and inability to calculate the exchange rate. I gaze around this plaza reveling in its character, its charm that reminds me a little bit of home. A thousand miles from home, I feel for a moment like I am in New York City. I used to go to the city once a year at Christmastime when I was growing up, one destination in mind: FAO Schwarz. I had to see what new developments there were in Toyland. Even then, I understood what a hip metropolis the Big Apple was.

Twenty years later in London's Piccadilly Circus, I am struck with that same kind of awe. Everyone is so stylish. All the trends that will no doubt make their way westward in about six months are sported in high style. It seems like giant buckles and patterned fedoras are making a comeback. Everyone looks classy, smart and just so worldly. And they all seem very important, like they are on their way to merge mega-corporations or solve global warming. And the stores are huge here.

Aside from the energy of this city and the look of the people it is instantly obvious that this is a different place entirely. Everything seems brighter and bolder. Signs in bright orange and blue decorate my line of vision. Those famous bright red phone booths are scattered all around. The streets look cleaner than those of New York. On the labyrinthine side streets, where people live, charming balconies rest right outside the windows on every storey of apartment complexes boasting adorable flower baskets. Yes, this city is a vibrant place. I'm even happy that it's sunny. Much as I crave getting soaked in a London rain, these bold, bright colors would not beckon this American in the same way on a gray, dreary day.

"You do that a lot," a voice says, breaking me out of my reverie.

"What?" I look up, seeing Kiki waving a hand in front of my face, a strange grin on her face.

"Zone out. You look like you've never left your house before."

I smile feeling my cheeks redden. "I've never been to London."

"I've been everywhere and believe me, *this* isn't that special," she says, laughing like that was the best joke ever. "If you'd ever been to Venice or Buenos Aires or *oh*, Vienna, you'd know what I mean."

I smile and shrug, because really, what do you say to that?

"Oh God," she says, horrified. She places a strand of her pretty brown locks behind her ear. "I'm so sorry. I'm not trying to say you're not...or that you are...that you're not...um...."

I laugh. "Well-traveled?" I offer. "I'm not." I laugh and she visibly relaxes. "This is the beginning, I think, of me changing that about myself."

She smiles shyly at me. I glance down at a bag in her hands, a purchase from the store we just left.

"So, what was the final verdict?"

"I bought the best pair of jeans," she squeals. "These babies cost two-hundred buckaroos."

My mouth falls open. First of all, who in the world still says the word *buckaroos*? Secondly, is she referring to dollars or pounds? Because the latter would be laughable for a pair of jeans.

"That's in American dollars," she says, reading my expression.

"Well, don't ever put them in the dryer," I say.

"Or gain weight," Kiki adds.

I laugh at that, which seems to make Kiki really happy. She links her elbow with mine and sighs. "I'm so glad you came out with me, Lucy," she says. "This is fun."

"I agree," I say honestly.

"Anyway," Kiki says, rolling her eyes playfully. "I'm going to need a pair of pumps to wear with these babies." She grabs my hand and pulls me toward a hole-in-the-wall shoe boutique near the shop we just came from. "And I'm going to need your opinion."

Kiki tries on nearly every high heel shoe the store has on display. From too high to too brown to too pretty, I learn quickly that she is very indecisive.

I sit, my gaze transfixed on a pair of boots hiding against the back wall of the shop. Knee-length, black leather. Think Julia Roberts circa 1990. When I first saw *Pretty Woman*, once upon a time, I always wanted high boots. Black boots. Woman of the World boots. My mom told me I couldn't have them because as the movie illustrated, they were hooker's wear. And I'd never gotten around to buying them myself. I couldn't buy them now. What would I even wear them with? In my teen years, I could've pulled off the short skirt and high boots look. But now, I'd be laughed out of Boston if I tried to walk around looking like that. My chocolate brown Uggs are the only boots I can really trust.

"You should buy them," Kiki says, sauntering up to me, following the line of my eyes.

"What would I wear them with?" I ask, still looking longingly at the boots, reminding myself of the budget that I really should be on at this point.

"Jeans, a long skirt, a short skirt, a dress..."

"What wouldn't I wear them with?" I joke.

"Pajamas," she answers coyly. "They're hot," she concludes, pretend-slapping my arm. "Seriously, do it."

"They're not really me."

She places both hands on my shoulders and turns me toward her, holding my gaze for a few moments. "Sometimes it's really great to just not be yourself." Something passes over her expression just as she closes her eyes for a moment. "Besides," she adds. "When in London, right?"

That night, I walk into The Chaizer wearing my new boots with my most comfortable dark jeans and a silvery-colored sweater, smiling. I swear, since I arrived, I think a grin may have actually become a permanent fixture on my face. Humming ABBA, still feeling enlivened by the magic of *Mamma Mia* I am blissfully unaware of anything as I head toward my flat.

"A penny for your thoughts?" a deep, familiar voice asks.

I stop in my tracks and look over toward the concierge desk, as Oliver walks around and leans casually against its back. As I get closer, he smiles and pulls a hand from his pocket, revealing a penny.

"That's just a saying, you know," I say, feeling, for the first time since I met him, actually happy to see him. It's been nearly two days. And the last day we spent together was probably the best day, well, ever.

He pockets the penny. "I know," he says. "I was just engaging in a childish ritual stemming from pure boredom."

"If you're referring to flipping pennies to see if they land on heads, that is not childish."

"Ah. My mistake." He thrusts his hands back into his pockets and stands up straighter, clearing his throat. He eyes me closely and for once, I don't feel uncomfortable under his scrutiny.

"Did you just get back?" I ask, unraveling my scarf. "From Paris," I clarify.

"A little while ago," he says, nodding. "Where did you just come from that put such a massive smile on your face?" he asks. "You didn't even notice me when you walked in, and when you did see me, you didn't even grimace."

"I don't always grimace when I see you."

He considers this, but seems doubtful.

"Well, you usually have it coming to you," I amend.

"I went to see *Mamma Mia*."

"That musical about the disco band?"

"Disco band?" I ask, appalled. "KC and the Sunshine Band was a disco band. ABBA is legendary – and the musical was amazing," I gush. Oliver seems a little taken aback by my enthusiasm, but I barrel on because, well, I need to tell *someone* how great this show was. "It more than made up for the Meryl Streep version. They wove all the songs into the story so effortlessly. They even worked in 'Super Trouper'. That's not easy, believe me. If only they could have worked 'Fernando' into the playlist. I mean, 'there was something in the air that night, the stars were bright, Fernando.' That's good stuff. But," I sigh. "Alas. Well, at least 'Fernando' is in the second movie."

He shakes his head, pressing on. "Who'd you go with?"

"I went alone," I mutter, staring up at him. "How tall are you?"

"What?" He looks at me like I'm crazy. It could be the wine I enjoyed at the show. Or the new sense of comfort I feel around Oliver. Maybe it's the boots. All I know is that suddenly I am hyper-aware that he is actually kind of tall.

"I don't think I've ever noticed how tall you are," I explain. "You look tall. Taller than Charles, and he's six feet tall."

He shakes his head. "Who's Charles?"

"My brother."

"Ah," he says, just as his cell phone rings. "About

six-two," he answers me, flipping open his phone. "Burke," he says into the mouthpiece. "I am, yes...very good, very good," he says, a dark shadow passing over his expression. Whatever he is hearing on the other end doesn't seem to be good news. "See you then," he says, tapping the phone to end the call. He squeezes it tightly in his palm as he stares at the ground intently.

He's going all weird again, I can tell. He has that look like he's about to ask me a bunch of pointless questions.

"I'm actually going to turn in for the night." I turn and begin heading to my room, knowing he'll follow me even before he actually starts to.

"Look," he says quickly. "I'm not trying to...I'm just trying to...."

"Make up your mind, Oliver," I say, forcing a smile. "Are you trying to or not?" I throw a glance over my shoulder at him.

"Can we just talk about a few things?" he asks quietly, seeming suddenly both serious and nervous. And he has that look – like he wants to bombard me with a thousand questions again. After our day in Paris, I kind of thought we were past that.

"When Jessie visits, take her to see *Mamma Mia*," I offer. "You won't waste your money."

"Lucy."

Can he stop saying my name? As it is, I feel like a fourteen-year-old girl with a schoolyard crush when he says it. Or when he speaks French. Or smiles. How can a man that does nothing but get under my skin manage to make me feel this way?

"Sleep well, Oliver," I say, reaching the door to my flat.

Just as I pull my key out to unlock the door, it opens.

"Hey, Babycakes," Cary says seductively. I bite the

inside of my cheek to keep from laughing at him in front of Oliver. "I've got the champagne and strawberries and…" He straightens, pretending to just notice Oliver. "I should have known." Oh, he's laying it on thick.

Cary looks at me accusingly. I look back at Oliver who is looking at Cary like…well, if looks could kill, Cary would be sprawled out on the floor right now.

Cary tugs at my sleeve to get my attention back. He smiles and nods his head in silent invitation. I walk into the flat. The two men exchange one more scathing look, before Cary closes the door.

"Babycakes?" I look at him incredulously. "You know, when you finally make it as an actor, you're going to be one of the ones that spends most of his time in rehab."

Cary smiles innocently.

"What was that about?" I demand, taking off my earrings. After a night at the theater, walking around in my new boots, I can't wait to pull on sweats and relax. "Oliver looked at you like you were vermin."

"I'm assuming he didn't follow you around today," he says, walking toward the tiny kitchenette, grabbing a banana.

"I didn't see him at all, for once." I sit at the table in the nook, removing the new boots and massaging my sore feet. "How did you know?"

"He didn't follow you today, because he was busy following me."

My hands freeze mid-massage and I drop my foot, looking intently at Cary.

"Are you sure?"

"Positive," he says smoothly, biting into the banana and taking a seat beside me at the table. He hands me a bottle of water. "He doesn't know that I saw him. I was wearing sunglasses and was very nonchalant about it."

I sit back and consider this. "He followed *you* to-day?" Something tightens in my stomach as a bad feeling washes over me. Oliver definitely suspects us of something. "He was outside Anne's studio when we walked out at the end of class," he explains. "I filled her in and she acted cool and collected." Suddenly, Cary breaks out into a wide grin. "She was more than willing to play along."

"Play along?"

"You see," he continues, "I've given him a little distraction from this whole lying about our identities thing."

"And what would that be?" I can tell that he's excited to tell me something. I can't imagine what. It seems like this whole situation just amuses him. It doesn't seem to aggravate him like it does me.

"He thinks I'm having an affair with Anne."

"Why would he think that?"

He smiles shyly and excitedly as his cheeks immediately flush. "Because he saw me kiss her," he says quietly, his gaze meeting mine.

I nearly choke on my water at that. "You kissed Anne?" I squeal, delighted. Because as much as Anne's been tormenting Cary emotionally for the past few days – or years – he is obviously just so in love with her. This kiss was a dream come true for him. Finally.

"Part of the act," he assures me, coolly, waving a hand like this was merely an acting exercise and not a monumental moment in his life.

"How was it? What did she says afterward? Was this the beginning of something? Of a relationship? Are you going out on a date finally?" I ask, not caring that I'm bombarding the man.

He laughs, half-shrugging and tilts his head at me. "I have no idea," he admits. "And honestly, tonight, I don't care."

I smile, happy that he looks so happy.

"So," Cary says, shifting his tone as he leans forward with his elbows on his knees and fixes me with a serious look. "Did you see how he looked at me just now?"

At my confused look, he gestures toward the door to our flat. "Oliver?" I ask. "He looked mad." His expression was pure poison. "That doesn't make much sense," I wonder aloud. I sit back in my chair and fold my hands in my lap. "Why should he care? He doesn't even know Anne."

Cary opens his mouth, but seems to think better of it. He just searches my expression, places his hands on his hips, and finally utters, "let's just sleep on that one."

Fuzzy little bastard

Posted by @Jake at 10:17 PM on december 27 on TheGrayBlog

Well, Lucy, the cat is out of the bag. And I'm not talking about Ricky. No, I'm referring to the reason you went to London. And I'm telling you...Prince William is taken. Prince Harry is taken. Kate and Meghan pretty much won that one. The whole world watched their weddings, they've created new life. It's not happening. So come back, okay?

Okay, okay...the real cat that's out of the bag: me & Mary. And...I can explain. It's not what you think.

Hope you're having fun. I know you're taking lots of pictures. I expect to see them all.

-Jake

PS: I don't think Charles has released the breath he's been holding since you left. I've explained, you know, that you're 37 or something. Ouch. Mary just slapped my arm. Apparently you're 26. Well Charles doesn't seem to care how old you are. Yes, that was my point......

chapter fourteen

There are actually many great things about going on a honeymoon alone. So there are no crazy lovemaking sessions. Or romantic kisses by sunset in an exotic, foreign locale. Okay, in many ways, a honeymoon alone is actually just a regular vacation that anyone could take.

But this "on your own" thing has its merits. Last night, standing outside the theater *Mamma Mia* played at, I felt nervous. Why wouldn't I? I've never even gone to a movie by myself before. But there I stood, frozen at the entranceway to the Prince of Wales Theatre on Coventry Street. Families rushed in from the cold, couples, their hands intertwined, excitedly embarked on a date night that no doubt began with dinner and wine, friends laughed together heartily as they bustled right past me. Finally, I walked in, my head held high. After my ticket was scanned, a feeling of relief and confidence washed over me. And at the precise moment the first familiar notes of ABBA strummed, a total sense of rightness filled me. Everyone in the theater faded into the darkness. Being alone didn't matter. Being there did. As the character of Sophie sang "I Have a Dream," it was suddenly clear why I was on this journey at all.

"Earth to Lucy," Cary says, waving a hand in front of my face. I blink quickly and snap fully back to the present.

"Sorry. Still reeling about ABBA," I say with a smile as we walk together down Prince Consort Road en route to Royal Albert Hall. While yesterday was mine alone, today is ours – mine and Cary's. We're taking on London in a big, very touristy way.

"Do you have your camera?" he asks. "I've always wanted a picture in one of these things." Cary runs quickly over to one of those old-fashioned red London phone booths.

Laughing, I pull out my camera to capture the magic of Cary pretending to be Clark Kent changing into Superman.

"Excuse me," I say to a passerby. "Can you take a picture of my friend and me?"

The older man sighs but nods resignedly.

"You don't have to," I say.

"Well, I've already stopped, haven't I?" he asks in a grumpy, impatient tone.

"Fantastic point."

I laugh, handing my camera over to him, explaining how it works. I rush over to Cary, who's smiling in amusement at the whole exchange.

"I have a feeling we're going to be beheaded in this picture," he mutters in my ear. I elbow him gently and tell him to smile at Grumpy.

"Watch the birdie," the man says before snapping

the picture. "Okay," he says the moment he's done, "please come and retrieve your camera now." He's grumpy but efficient.

Once I have my camera back, Cary and I continue taking pictures of each other in the phone booth – pretending to have the most intense transcontinental conversations, hanging out of the doorway, staring at the phone itself in shock. The whole thing makes me feel like I'm thirteen. It's so silly, and somehow that's why it's so fun.

"You know, I almost didn't come this year," Cary says quietly a little while later, sitting on the stony steps at Hyde Park, across the street from Royal Albert Hall.

"What do you mean?" I ask, staring at the Hall, wondering what kinds of music have filled this air before. Maybe someday I'll return and see a show there.

"To London," he explains. "To the workshop."

"Why?" I ask, still gazing at the round, dominating structure before me that is as much a staple of London as the queen. "Everything here is so incredible. The history, the theater, the music, the squares, the posh neighborhoods, the parks," I finish, glancing behind me. Even in winter, not cast in glorious colors, this place looks so peaceful and nice. "Don't you love it?" I wonder.

"Of course," he says with a shrug. "But I've seen all of this a thousand times. These places you're seeing for the first time, I've seen them before. For me the pull here was not about the scenery or about touring around. It was about love. And you know – as time goes by, it just hurts more. Why would I put myself through that again?"

"So why'd you come?" I finally ask.

He looks at me. Studies my eyes, my expression. "I

had a feeling that maybe this year would be different."

My eyebrows shoot up. "A feeling?" I ask skeptically.

"Yes." He looks at me very seriously then, all humor from before gone from his expression. "And I'm glad I went with it."

"Well, aren't we a pair?" I ask, chuckling. "You had a *feeling* and I came all the way here because a psychic basically told me that I needed a life."

Cary pulls closer to me as he laughs. Really laughs. I honestly feel like I've known him forever. Well, I guess I nearly have. Though I never really knew him back in our school days. I thought he was a conceited jerk. But my God, he's a complete sweetheart. A romantic and a naturally good person.

"Who knows, Cary? Maybe this time things will turn out differently."

He shrugs, absentmindedly playing with a tear on the knee of his jeans. "Sure. And maybe this time the classes will pay off and when I get back to New York I'll land more than just supporting roles in off-off-Broadway shows."

"A lot of actors would kill to get work off-off-Broadway," I say encouragingly. "Anyway, you're doing it right. You're taking classes, improving, and you're following your heart. It's what you want to do, and you're going after it. Plus, you aren't starving, or on the streets, so that's a good sign," I joke, knocking my knees lightly against his.

He drops his head and laughs quietly. "Told you that you were an optimist," he says.

"Look, you've successfully convinced a lot of people that we're married and you're not even attracted to me. If that's not the sign of a good actor—"

"I find you very attractive," he says, almost sounding offended.

"You have known me since the second grade and you barely knew that I was alive before this trip," I point out.

"Maybe so," he says. "But just trust me on this one. Once I finally got to know you, you honestly drew me in. I think you're beautiful and funny. Though as far as *we* go," he says, gesturing between himself and me, "I feel this is exactly right, like we were always meant to be friends."

I nod because I feel the exact same way. Handsome, sweet, and charming as he is, I have nothing but friendly feelings for him.

"And just so you know," he continues, "there is someone you've met here that is attracted to you, who might act on it if he didn't think you were married."

That gets my attention. I look at him again. "Who?"

He offers me an impatient look in lieu of an answer.

I balk out loud as comprehension dawns. He's talking about Oliver. "Cary, Oliver Burke thinks that I'm a complete liar – and okay, he's kind of right about that, although usually I'm very truthful – an identity thief, *and* he seems to want to find me out and, I don't know, put me in jail. Plus, I nearly burnt his sister's bathroom down. Let's not forget that."

"Oh, I don't think I'll ever forget that," he says. "I just think that despite all of those very tiny details, there might be something there." He's enjoying this too much. "I see it in his eyes."

"Well, you're wrong." I stand up, suddenly feeling cagey.

"Try not to be so upset about it," Cary says, following suit and standing too. "There are worse things than me being right about this. He seems like an okay guy."

"He is," I say. Too quickly. But Oliver is a good guy, despite some of his frustrating tendencies. The way he is with his sister...the way he's helped me out more than once since I arrived, going clearly beyond the expectations of his job. And he *is* a good looking guy. With his unruly dark curls, constant five o'clock shadow, scruffy style and soft brown eyes....

Cary chuckles softly beside me as we head into Hyde Park. A little girl in a pale blue petticoat walks hand-in-hand with her father. Runners and bicyclists battle the cold for their sport. Three young teenage girls are sitting on a bench a little ways away, bundled up in sweaters, hats and scarves of the brightest colors – the golden memorial behind them glistening in the sunlight – gabbing a mile a minute about life and love.

"You know, nearly every time I look at you, you have this look on your face, like you're blown away by every sight. Except half the views aren't that fascinating. Like those girls on the bench, for instance," he points out, following my stare.

"They just remind me of my sisters and me."

"How many sisters do you have?"

"Two. Julie and Marian."

"Ahh, the infamous Marian, who just married Tom," he says, coyly.

I sigh and look at the girls again. The older of the three is telling her sisters to shut up because they're giving her a headache. "We used to walk down to Faneuil Hall and sit there for hours on the steps, drinking iced coffees. We had to drink them away from home because my mom told us coffee would stunt our growth. She said she didn't want people thinking she was in the business of raising hyper midgets."

He laughs and then bites his lower lip, studying me. "You miss them, don't you?"

"My sisters?"

"Your whole family."

"We yell at each other. Everyone is always in everyone else's business. Sometimes there are so many of us, it's work just to feel visible. I am constantly told what I should do to better my career and my dating prospects. And my wardrobe. They're all overachievers which can be so annoying—"

Cary just stares at me intently, solemnly, and waits.

"I miss them a lot," I finally admit. Because I do. Warts and all, my family is one large and in charge brood. Life is too quiet without them.

We stare ahead at miles of park. Shifting the conversation to Cary's own wacky family, we walk past the park's famous Peter Pan statue, Diana Memorial, the flower gardens, the Serpentine Pond, and then back to the Royal Albert Hall. Things I never thought I'd see in a million years are at my fingertips, before my eyes, and all around me. It won't be long before *this* is what I miss.

෨

"You know what happens at the Serpentine Pond on New Years, right?" Polly asks, after I've told her all about my day at Hyde Park with Cary. She is prepping decorations to put up in The Chaizer's ballroom for the New Year's party tomorrow. She grabs a bag full of black and silver stars and breaks it open like it's some kind of personal enemy of hers.

"What?" I ask, leaning my elbows on the counter of

the reception desk.

"At midnight on the new year exactly, all these people jump into the Serpentine – many of them *naked* – and go swimming," she explains.

"That sounds really fun actually," I say. "The swimming part, not the naked part. Although in this weather, you couldn't pay me to partake."

"It's disgusting," Polly says, staring at me until I make a face that she clearly takes for concession to her side of the argument. "And it's mostly these old, wrinkled men that do it."

I laugh as a mental image comes to me. "I may have to venture over there after midnight to check it out for myself."

"Why? Are you some kind of pervert? Are wrinkly old men your...your preference?"

"What?"

"Hi, ladies," a familiar voice interrupts before I can even grace her asinine question with an answer.

I turn to see Oliver walking, hands in his pockets, towards us. I take a deep breath, realizing that for the first time since I met him, I'm actually nervous to see him. And not at the thought that he might question me nonstop about my husband and my marriage, or ask where Cary is again. No. I'm nervous because...well, he looks nice. As always, his dark, wavy locks are falling carelessly in all directions, grazing his forehead just above his left brow. He's wearing a dark grey sweater over a tee shirt with dark jeans, and something in his walk just says "I don't care" in a way that's kind of....

I close my eyes, cursing Cary and his big mouth for planting this seed in my mind.

"Aren't you two chummy now?" Oliver asks, looking pointedly at Polly.

"She came up to the desk and just started yammering on about her day with that hot hubby of hers," Polly explains, beginning to string the black and silver stars on a long clear wire.

"Listen," Oliver says to me, aside. "Can I talk to you?"

He walks away from Polly towards the concierge desk that he never seems to sit at. I follow, waiting expectantly for him to say something once we've stopped. Anything. Instead, he looks around, almost like he's looking for something – or someone. He seems uncomfortable and extremely unhappy. Finally, he stares down at me, his dark eyes blazing.

"Okay," he begins in a tight voice. "I know I'm not your favorite person. And, well, you're not exactly mine either, Miss Gray. So I don't know why I'm even here right now. I shouldn't be," he says quietly. Conspiratorially. All of it in a rush.

In all, it isn't shaping up to sound like an admission that he just can't stop thinking about me or has a maddening crush on me. Yet, I still have knots in my stomach because, well – he's speaking with such urgency. He seems so tense and conflicted.

Kind of how I'm starting to feel.

"Okay," I say encouragingly. Because I honestly have no idea what else to say to him at this point.

"I'm not sure if you're...who you say you are," he mutters carefully. Slowly. He stares at me, waiting for something. A look, perhaps. I try to keep my gaze steady, to keep him from finding whatever he is searching my face for. "Do you see what I'm getting at?"

"I think so," I say, deliberately. Even though I am

positive I have no clue what he's talking about right now.

"This whole thing is just...it's a problem," he says. "I have a job to do, and I'm not supposed to care one way or the other how it turns out." His gaze falls to the ground and he shakes his head almost sadly. "I really can't believe I'm here right now. This could screw up everything. And I'll definitely be sacked."

"You know, the last thing you said that made any sense was 'can I talk to you,'" I point out.

"Have you been honest with me?" he asks, suddenly.

I stare at him. I didn't expect that. Such a bold, blunt question. And of course I haven't been honest with him for one millisecond that I've known him. I open my mouth to say something, but don't know what to say. All I can manage to do is chew on my lower lip.

He sighs, running a hand through his hair. "I didn't think so," he says softly.

My heart is hammering so loudly in my chest, I wonder if he can hear it. This conversation is spiraling out of my control. The instinct to run is becoming strong.

Plus, this man completely unnerves me every time I am near him. Suddenly all of it just seems so stupid. Every lie – pretending to be a honeymooner to stay in this hotel, pretending Cary is my husband – it all just seems so dumb. I want to get it over with, tell him that I've been lying since we met. And then add casually that I'm single and ready to mingle.

No matter how many times I open my mouth to tell him, it won't come out. I guess when you tell a lie long enough, it seems impossible to ever just admit the truth. Even when it's a harmless little white lie. And especially when you sort of care about the person you've lied to, and what they think of you.

"Here's what I think," Oliver continues, looking at me again. His cheeks are flushed. "You are in way over your head and...." He trails off, looking at some space between us, shaking his head. I can almost see his mind racing.

I just stare at him numbly, trying to figure out *what* he is possibly talking about. The conversation has actually gotten stranger than when it started. I didn't think that was even possible.

"I can't help you," he finally spits out, seeming almost bowled over with some kind of inner torment.

He puts his hands on my shoulders and I freeze. I am almost positive my heart has stopped beating altogether. How pathetic is that? He is touching me on my *shoulders*, for God's sake. For the way I feel at this very moment, he may as well be making out with me.

He searches my face intensely. "Just be careful," he says, almost in a whisper.

And then he is gone.

I stare after him as he leaves The Chaizer, wondering what on earth just happened. "What was that all about?" Polly asks, rushing out from behind the desk and making her way to the concierge desk to the get the scoop. "I tried to listen in, of course, but I didn't get a thing."

I just stare at her, shocked she's admitting to eavesdropping. Or attempting to eavesdrop.

Instead of answering her, though, I just continue staring at the door, squinting my eyes, Polly's voice becoming no more than an echo inside a loud ambient vacuum.

Suddenly I think of everything – my promise to Mary

to own this adventure and be Marian, my worry about being kicked out for checking in with a fake ID, the Chaizer's policy about exclusivity for honeymooners, and Oliver's strange, ominous words. And I wonder, for the first time, what would happen if I decided to tell the truth.

chapter fifteen

The next day, Oliver's words are still ringing in my
ears. They have all but put me in a tizzy. Warnings
to be careful, assertions that I'm in over my head and
allusions to my lie – it's a wonder I got any sleep last
night. For safe measure, I call my brother, Charles, for
some legal perspective from Cary's cell phone. It's *immediately* obvious, however, that he can't remove the Big
Brother cap long enough to think like a lawyer.

"I told you that you shouldn't have stayed there
alone." Somehow even now, at twenty six years old,
I do not merit an adult tone from my older siblings.
Or my parents. "You should have come straight home
when I said to."

I pull the phone away from my ear, Charles's deep
vibrato hurting my eardrums. "Charles," I say, putting
the phone cautiously back up to my ear. "Calm down.
Nothing's happened." *Yet*, I add silently so Charles
doesn't have an aneurism.

"Really?" he asks disbelievingly. "Nothing? That's why you're calling me for legal counsel?"

I count to five to myself just as I do in class before dealing with the kids in particularly stressful situations – like when Liam put gum in Hannah's hair or when Liam pulled the fire alarm causing the whole school to evacuate and the fire department to visit. Once I'm calm, I ask my brother, "Did it ever occur to you that maybe I've made a few friends and I'm just seeking advice to pass on to them, since it would be free of charge coming from my brother, instead of, you know, a strange lawyer?"

"Friends." I can practically hear the air quotes over the line. "I've heard that a million times, Lucy. Cora has 'friends', too, that wanted to know at dinner – last night, in fact – why parents 'wrestle with their door closed' on Saturday mornings. So don't pull that with me. You don't have friends."

"Well, now you're just being mean," I say, grabbing the red nail polish I tucked away in my makeup bag's side pocket and pulling the cap off. I prop my feet up on the bed and begin prettifying my toes to distract myself from Charles's needless worrying.

"You know what I mean," Charles says, his voice a mix of apology and impatience.

"I'm just curious, Charles, about what happens when a person gets caught for, um, identity theft."

"Identity theft." Now he sounds horrified. I don't think I've helped my case at all.

I roll my eyes as he laments that I was such a good kid, and never gave him so much as a worry in high school, unlike Julie and Marian. *There. Left foot done.* "But I knew you were too easy," he says insistently. "I knew your drama would just come later."

"You know what?" I ask, cutting him off after I've painted the toes on my right foot, too. Cradling the phone between my ear and shoulder, I screw the cap back on the nail polish. "Forget I called."

Honestly, I'm beginning to worry that Charles might hurt himself obsessing like this. I once overheard two teachers talking in the teacher's lounge about how it was possible to actually induce a stroke on yourself. I don't know much about it – or if it is even true for that matter – but Charles is the perfect candidate for such a thing. And I am not exactly helping. "I'll be home in a couple of days and then you can rest easy."

He sighs. I imagine him massaging the bridge of his nose with his thumb and forefinger, eyes closed – possibly counting to five like I was a few minutes ago. "Lucy, what do you need to know?" he asks after a moment, sounding defeated but much calmer. I smile. No matter how often he flies off the handle, he always comes through for me. And for everyone. He really is the best big brother. I just hope I don't give him an ulcer because of it.

An hour later, Cary and I head to the lobby – which, like the ballroom, is fully decked out in black and silver shimmery decorations for the New Year's Eve bash tomorrow – for another day of touring. At least that was the plan. As we near the exit, I notice someone walking toward us from the couch area and turn to face her. Anne Benedict.

I nudge Cary gently and tilt my head in her direction as she strides up to us, a nervous smile plastered on her face, her eyes never leaving Cary's bewildered face.

"Anne," he says. He looks very thrown seeing her here. "Did I miss a class or something?" he asks. "I thought we were off until the last class on the third."

"Oh," she says, shrugging.

I could swear she's blushing. Maybe I should walk away.

"That's not it," she explains. "I mean, I'm not here about anything to do with class."

Now Cary's perplexed expression turns to one of concern. "Are you all right?" he asks.

She nods and rolls her eyes in self-deprecation. "I have these tickets to a show tonight," she explains quickly.

Cary still looks confused, though I'm starting to see what's happening here. And I'm delighted.

"Two tickets to be exact," she says.

Cary looks down at the tickets in her hands in interest. "Billy Elliot," he enthuses. "Great show." He still doesn't quite get it.

"I thought maybe we could go together," she finally says. She throws a desperate look my way, like she's asking for help, and I can't blame her. Cary is being completely thick right now.

He blinks a couple of times and looks at me in confusion. "To study spatial blocking or style?" he asks, turning back to her. I try very hard not to just kick him into understanding.

She shakes her head. "No. Just...to go," she says quietly. Her face is completely flushed.

"That sounds nice," I say encouragingly to Cary.

He finally gets it. I know because he looks like he's been sucker punched. And sometimes that is exactly how love should feel. He looks from her to me. "But we were going to—"

"We," I interrupt him, "were going to do some things that I can definitely do on my own."

I smile at Anne and she smiles back appreciatively.

"What kind of wife would I be if I kept you from a possibly wonderful date?"

Cary bends to kiss my cheek and whispers a very sincere "thank you" in my ear before finally putting Anne out of her misery and leaving The Chaizer with her.

At Hugging Mugs, sipping my caramel latte, I ponder what Charles said. Basically I haven't done anything wrong. I am not charging a credit card that is not mine. I am not trying to get any kind of monetary gain by pretending to be married at this resort. I haven't committed a crime and attached Marian's name to it. In short, I'm just a liar. And that's reassuring. You know, in a humiliating sort of way.

I turn the copy of the *London Times* that was left at my table – the same table that I've now sat at a few times – and peer at it casually as I drink. Another article about the Honeymooners grabs my attention. It's just a small article stating all the countries they've hit so far – France, Germany, and Spain. They are now rumored to be in Italy.

"So," I hear Oliver's voice say.

I turn in my seat and look up at him, feeling a touch of anxiety at the sight of him. The last time I saw him, I basically admitted that I am lying about something. What if he's coming in for his closing? "So," I say back. I gesture towards the empty seat across from me in silent invitation.

"How many more days are you here for?" he asks, taking a sip of his coffee.

At my quizzical look, he smiles and I just stare at him. How can this be the same guy from yesterday? Yesterday he acted beyond intense and incredibly cryptic. He was almost...protective toward me. Worried. Torn.

Now I look at the man sitting before me. He is smiling in that particular, knowing way of his. His eyes twinkle. Just a bit. Kind of like they had in Paris when he found me after the "A Vendre" debacle.

"I leave on the third," I finally say.

"Let's see," he says, placing his coffee down and folding his arms atop the table. "You've seen Westminster Abbey, Hyde Park, the Tower of London—"

"And here I thought that it was just in my head that you were following me all this time," I say, though I can't help smiling.

"You do tend to get chatty about all things London, Miss Gray. You've mentioned your whereabouts to me in that excitable way of yours. You know, in passing."

"Fair enough. Though you have *tended* to follow me. In passing," I shoot back, casually.

"And you've been to Piccadilly Circus," he barrels on, ignoring my last remark. "And on a red double-decker bus, and—"

"—and let's not forget Paris," I add, resting my elbows on the table, my gaze meeting his.

"Of course," he agrees. "Paris is unforgettable."

I'm not sure if he means that the city is unforgettable or our time there was. Or both. "What are you getting at, Oliver?" I press.

"You don't have much time left here," he says as an imperceptible look passes over his features. "And I'm just wondering if you've really seen the city."

I shrug. "I've walked it. Ridden it. Shopped it." I lean

forward and pierce him with a suspicious look because I know he's getting at something. "You tell me."

"If you have some free time today, I'd like to show you a few more spots is all," he says. He rests back in his chair and shoots a smug look my way. "Unless you and your husband—"

I hold a hand up, for once cutting him off at the pass. "If I agree, will you shut up?"

⌘

Two hours later, we're still strolling the corridors of the National Portrait Gallery – our first stop on the Oliver Burke Tour of London – and my mind is racing. It's an absolute dream in here. Some of the art looks like something my students could have created. Apparently the content of the painting was the draw when the gallery assembled their collections, not the actual quality of the work. But in general, I'm flabbergasted. Some of the portraits are stunning. And the photography collection mesmerized me. As expected, there are many royal likenesses including, of course, Princess Diana and Queen Elizabeth I.

What I especially adore are the portraits depicting literary legends like T.S. Eliot, Virginia Woolf, Shakespeare, and so much more.

A Brontë sisters' portrait stops me. It was painted by their brother, and I just stare at it, absorbing that fact, and marveling that so much artistic ingenuity existed in this one family. The girls that brought the world the love and angst of legendary characters – characters continuously revered thanks to the BBC – happened to also have a brother with sizable talent, too.

"What, your family doesn't compare?" Oliver teases, leaning against the wall and staring down at me.

"I just find all of this fascinating. Though what literary buff doesn't?"

"Literary buff?" he asks, looking shocked as he pushes himself forward and stands tall again.

"I majored in literature," I explain defensively, crossing my arms. "I wanted to teach because—" I look around me at the many people milling about, looking in awe, like me, at various works. "I want kids to *want* to learn and to understand who these women are," I exclaim, gesturing toward the Brontë sisters painting. "Who Heathcliff and Catherine are, for that matter. And Jane and Mr. Rochester."

"Easy there," Oliver says, laughing gently. "I just wasn't expecting someone who spouts about literature to currently be taking up *The Cat Who Went to Paris*."

"Oh." My cheeks flush as I smile. I look away from his amused stare and look into the earnest faces of the three Brontë sisters once more. "Well, I'm not some literary snob who can't sit down occasionally with a breezy read," I say with a casual shrug.

"I see," he says in an interested tone as we make our way out of the gallery.

As we exit, I gaze up at the sky and smile and shiver all at once. It's flurrying. It's not exactly a London rain, but right now it'll do. It's quite a bit colder than it was when we headed into the gallery. I put the hood of my raincoat on my head, happy for an excuse to finally use it.

"I'm glad you aren't a literary snob," Oliver says, though I can see he's stifling a laugh, looking at me hooded in my turquoise parka.

"My old college boyfriend," I say, ignoring his look,

"wouldn't be caught dead with *The Cat Who Went to Paris*." I laugh as Colin Randall's image flickers to life in my memory like an old VHS tape – not sharp, a little snowy, but very loud and almost too clear on the details that matter. I can picture his low ponytail, wire-framed glasses, button-down-collar-shirt-over-tee-shirt-and-cargo-pants look. I can hear his deep voice and often-snide laughter. And I can easily recall his eventually annoying inability to talk about *anything* other than our major. Wow...I honestly haven't thought of him in years.

"Real catch?" Oliver says easily as we make our way toward the Underground, the *tube*, at Charing Cross Station.

I laugh, still lost in hazy movies of my college days. "He would play these games – like which siblings would you rather spend an afternoon with, the Brontë sisters or the Brothers Grimm?" I say, in a faux-snobbish voice.

Oliver throws his head back and laughs heartily. "Ouch," he says, putting his gloves on and buttoning up his coat. It's gotten a great deal colder since we went into the gallery. "He must have been fun at college parties."

I smile and look up at Oliver. "Actually he was," I admit. "When he'd drink, it was like a happy little vacation from reality. His major was suddenly flip cup and I can't say I minded all too much."

He nods, considering this. "So you did not enjoy his literary games?"

"God, no," I say, too quickly. "Don't get me wrong. I loved reading classics and poetry, getting lost in worlds of propriety and hierarchies that defined everything – even love – for men and women. Analyzing the customs that used to navigate society. I mean, I got to read Jane Austen as homework!"

Oliver nods, but seems more amused than understanding exactly what a privilege that actually was.

As we descend the stairs to the tube station, I rub my gloved hands together hoping they get warmer faster if I do this. "After writing a twenty page paper on a twelve word haiku, I just wanted nothing more than to drink a cold beer and watch *I Dream of Jeannie* or *Gidget* like a normal girl."

As we board the train, Oliver is laughing. After a little prodding, he says, "I just wouldn't imagine the 'normal' viewing habits for American college girls to include sitcoms from the 1960s."

"I threw in an episode of *Sex and the City* every now and then, too," I add, to which he twists his mouth and looks down in consideration, but says nothing more.

The train is so crowded, we have to stand. I hold onto a pole for balance as Oliver steps aside to make way for a woman with a young child in tow before resuming his stance as the train begins rolling along.

"Thank you, Oliver," I say.

He looks over at me in surprise. "For what?" he asks.

"For taking me there. I am not sure how it is possible that I missed it since I arrived."

Oliver grins widely and leans toward me, his grip on the pole still tightly securing his steady footing. "I thought you might feel that way given your behavior at the Eiffel Tower and Arc du Triomphe."

"My behavior?" I ask. "I took a few photos of iconic landmarks."

"You dropped to the freezing ground and took about a *thousand* photos. And I'm sure you'll only frame one," he adds, shaking his head.

"Probably," I admit, smiling. "I'm sure one will be perfect."

"Anyway," he says eventually, leaning away again. "You're welcome."

⁓

It's not the perfect day for an outdoor stroll. To be honest, it's so frigid that my chest burns every time I inhale. Every word out of our mouths, every breath we take leaves a little trail marking the frostiness in the air.

Cold as it is, I don't mind our ramble down the Queen's Walk, a quaint pedestrian-only path thrilling with energy today. It's lined with traditional dolphin lamp posts. The Waterloo Bridge is now behind us. Oliver knew, considering the die-hard ABBA fan that I am, that I might enjoy that bit of scenery. This path, flanked by the Thames River, leads us now into Green Park, the reason for our visit.

"Being that its name is Green Park, you'll have to imagine it in the warmer weather," Oliver says, smiling as we take in the scene before it. The dusting of snow covering the ground has footsteps traipsing through in every direction. The trees and bushes are barren, and it all feels very subdued and quiet. Very *un*-green.

"It actually used to be called Upper St. James here," Oliver continues. "This is my favorite of the London parks." He stops just past the park's entrance and looks around almost nostalgically before shivering and fastening his collar a little higher on his neck. He doesn't seem at all ready to head indoors, though he's obviously freezing. I know I am.

"It's rumored this park got its name," Oliver is saying, as we continue walking through the winter wonderland, "because the clever wife of King Charles the second thought her dear husband had picked flowers here and given them to a woman who was *not* her. To cast her revenge, the Queen had every flower in the park pulled and no more flower beds were planted. Ever."

I grin widely because Oliver makes it all sound like a fairy-tale. The flowers were all banished from the land by the wicked queen! "She sounds like a very strong, independent, absolutely frightening woman," I say and he laughs, though I'm not sure it's at my joke. "You know, you should have been a tour guide, Oliver," I say, peering up at him. He rolls his eyes playfully and looks down at me.

"What?" I exclaim at his look. "You seem to love the city's history. Plus, you're really not a very good concierge."

He shoots me a reproving look at that, but ignores my jibe as he barrels on. "My mother was a city guide, actually." We walk in silence as I wait for him to continue. "She loved London's history and took her turn doing different types of tours all while we were growing up. She did walking tours, tours of the Tower of London, of St. Paul's – even the big red bus you seem so fond of," he finishes.

"That explains it," I say.

"What?"

"When you are talking about this stuff, you're very animated. Like you're perfectly happy."

He shrugs and gazes far off into the distance, his expression clouding briefly. It clears almost instantly, though.

"Maybe it's time to head indoors."

This whole day has just flown by. Oliver's still picking at his fish and chips as I push my plate away, stuffed to the brim, and lean back. I had the best shepherd's pie, though it was called cottage pie. Why don't we call it that at home? It's so much quainter and more appealing! Oliver holds a finger up to the bartender who nods. We're getting another round of pints.

Who knew a pub in a tiny alley off Kensington High Street called Filthy McGee's could be so adorable? Because it is. Old photographs from the 1800's line the walls. The barmaids from back then look fierce and serious, staring out at me while the men look round and jolly. Dark, ancient-looking wallpaper with faded gray roses lines the walls, darkening the room which seems to be lit mostly by candlelight and lanterns. There's an empty gin bottle on every table with a single flower in it beside an empty wine bottle that's being used as a candelabra. It's possibly the coolest establishment I've ever stepped foot in!

In the corner, a man plays piano, singing a surprising number of American classics. Right now, he's rocking "Piano Man" as the rest of the band is setting up. Oliver glances at the band and then at his watch, a small smile twisting at the corners of his mouth as he looks back toward me.

"Do you know that guy?" I ask, nodding toward the piano player.

Oliver shakes his head and puts more malted vinegar on his French fries. "I come here sometimes," he says. "He's very good."

The waiter brings our new round and I tap glasses

with Oliver before taking a sip. The froth sticks to my upper lip and I try to wipe it away casually though Oliver eyes me with that amused look of his and I know my attempts at sophistication are all for naught.

"How often do you get to see your sister?" I ask.

He looks surprised by the question as he sips his beer. "I don't know," he says, his brow creasing slightly. "Three, four times a year, I suppose."

"That's *it*?" I ask incredulously. I can't imagine seeing anyone in my immediate family only a couple of times a year.

He smiles and tilts his head at me. "Not everyone lives as close to their family as you do," he points out.

"Fair enough." I take another sip of my beer. "When did Jessie move to Paris?"

Oliver stops smiling, clenching his jaw, and I can feel it. The big brother overprotective vibe, I mean. It's easy to spot, having two big brothers who used to look exactly like that whenever a guy showed any kind of interest in me. Which wasn't all that often, but it did happen on occasion.

"She moved there for Giancarlo, didn't she?" I prod, smirking a little.

He nods, looking none too pleased about that. "About two years ago," he says.

"Two years ago?" I asked, surprised. Even Charles only took a couple of months to adjust to any of my past boyfriends. "Maybe it's time you started liking the guy," I suggest. "He seemed really sweet."

"Sure," he says sarcastically. "I'll just start liking him. He's about seven years older than Jess. She left school to be with him, promising that she'd go back as soon as summer ended. Well – three summers have come and gone," he exclaims, shaking his head in disappointment and some fury. I recognize that pretty well, too.

"They seem happy," I point out gently. "But you're right to want what's best for her," I add, to which he looks at me, an imperceptible look on his face. "She should finish school. From what I can tell, your opinion obviously matters a lot to her."

"It used to," he says quietly. "My dad died when I was about nineteen," he says plainly, his face devoid of emotion. He seems practiced at keeping his emotions safely masked. "Jessie was..." he cocks his head back to think. "Twelve?"

"And your mom?"

He looks down, his mask faltering – just a bit. "She passed away a few years ago."

"It's just the two of you?" I ask quietly. My heart goes out to him. And I understand instantly why he worries about his sister as much as he does.

He nods and shrugs, like he's trying to shrug it all off and pull that mask back on. But it's not back on. Not really. He looks at me and I can see it all clearly.

"I suppose I was meant to be like a father figure at that point. Turn her out right," he says sardonically. "But I don't think I did too good a job. This guy she lives with...he's a painter." At my nonplussed look, he leans forward. "A painter," he repeats raising his voice a tad, as if I just hadn't heard him the first time. Still, I say nothing. "An Italian living in Paris. He's a bloody artistic *nomad* and he's dragged Jessie along. He took advantage of her ideals about romance, her longing for stability."

"Maybe," I interrupt, "his focus on his own dream will be good for her. Maybe she'll decide what she wants to do and go for it. And maybe he'll support her as she's supported him because maybe, just maybe, those two are actually in love."

He narrows his eyes at me. "So, I should just applaud them for being so...so bold and daring as to shuck every practical path out of their way? I should pat him on the shoulders, shake his hand, say 'good job, man. School really wasn't her bag, anyway?'" His emotions are beginning to seep through in an explosive way and I find myself laughing. At his look, I clap a hand to my mouth, but my eyes betray me.

"Sorry," I say, my face returning to normal. "But no – I obviously do *not* think you should applaud them and turn your back." A small laugh escapes my lips. "Just the opposite. Don't turn your back. Do what you do best. Annoy the crap out of her."

That at least earns a smile – well, the hint of one anyway – as he leans back, waiting for more.

"She might roll her eyes at you for telling her what to do but I promise you, as a younger sister myself – she'll appreciate you for always wanting what's best for her."

He still says absolutely nothing for a long moment. "You know," he says. But I never get to hear what he's about to say because the band interrupts the moment with an announcement that it's time for a little bit of holiday fun.

Oliver smiles, cheering up instantly from the conversation before. He looks at the band and then back at me. "This is why I brought you here."

I take a sip of my beer and look at him, "The band?"

They begin to play a few notes of "The First Noel" and I lean into Oliver. "Do they know Christmas was a few days ago?"

"They do this kind of Irish holiday jam every year. I figured you might like it."

I turn in my seat and face the band. They have the attention of the whole restaurant now, as the piano starts playing.

"It's pretty," I whisper, my eyes still glued to the band. The pianist samples little pieces of different Christmas songs as a female vocalist hums quietly into the microphone. A bit of the melody from "Silent Night" gives way to "It Came upon a Midnight Clear" and the songs remind me of home for a moment.

My mind goes blank as the band suddenly comes alive. I mean really – drums, harmonica, flutes, piano – the song has taken on a sort of Ye Olde Irish Jig vibe and the whole pub seems celebratory. Oliver takes a sip of his beer and smiles at me as a female vocalist sings to the piano player.

I laugh and look at Oliver. "I love this!" I sway a bit like the rest of the room, elated at the atmosphere. The flowing beer, the laughter, the camaraderie—

I suddenly jump as the whole pub – and I mean *everyone* around me, except Oliver – joins in the jubilant chorus that I don't recognize. Oliver puts a reassuring hand on my shoulder and laughs.

It's like I've suddenly gone to an Irish house party. Oliver joins in the next chorus, though not with the enthusiasm around him. That wouldn't be fitting for him at all. But he leans into me and says the words clearly so I understand them. By the last chorus, I'm able to join in, while waving my beer around like everyone else.

"That was the coolest thing. Ever. Period. Bar none," I exclaim once we step outside the pub and begin walking. My ears are still ringing. The outside seems like a quiet wintry vacuum compared to Filthy McGee's. It's so dead out here. So subdued. Inside, even the candles were dancing at each table. In there, the air was charged and alive. A natural high seemed to take over the whole place. I can't seem to wipe the smile off my face.

"They do that act every night between December twenty-third and January third each year," Oliver explains as he zips up his coat. He still seems to be on a natural high, too, if his smile is any indication. I've never seen him so truly relaxed since we met. "Minus Christmas day itself, naturally. It's their claim to fame."

Cars slosh on by and I gaze up at a street lantern, seeing the flurries hitting the glass bulb. It's snowing again. "I feel like I'm wearing out the words 'thank you,'" I say, turning towards him as we begin walking carefully along, toward the hotel. "I mean, every time I turn around, you've surprised me with something really amazing."

He waves a hand dismissively as if to say it's all no big deal, that he does this for everyone. But something in his expression reveals far more than he'd ever dare tell. He does seem a bit pleased at my confession.

We walk along, quietly, but my heels are having a lot of trouble on the crooked cobblestones. Maybe I shouldn't have worn the new boots out today. It really is slippery and I knew I'd be touring around, though I didn't plan on the Oliver tour, which definitely in-volved more walking than I'd planned to do. We're both walking at a snail's pace. It must look kind of funny to the people who keep bursting out of nearby pubs and whooshing past us. "Oof," I squeal as I nearly lose my balance completely this time. Oliver firmly grasps my elbow and I lean into him, thankful for the support.

"Maybe a taxi would be good," he says casually. He's probably done the math and realized that at this pace it'll take approximately six hours to walk the five blocks to The Chaizer.

"I can walk quickly," I protest, rolling my eyes. I yank my arm free from his grasp and take one very confident step ahead, and instantly slip on the icy ground. Oliver grabs me, his grip on my arms tight and reassuring. He laughs and looks down at my boots.

"These aren't exactly snow boots." He steadies me and glances quickly up at the flurries. "Not really made for ice," he adds. He stares down at me, suddenly looking almost nervous.

"They're new," I explain feeling a cold rush course through me. "I thought they looked good with these jeans."

"They do," he agrees. His eyes widen like he didn't mean to say that. His eyes have this look in them now, a look I've never seen before.

Now in addition to being all off-balance, I can barely breathe. It's the cold, obviously. Except, coincidentally, the moment Oliver's grip on me tightened, my heart rate skyrocketed and my breathing became more shallow. And, of course, that does nothing to help me gain steady footing on the icy ground, which is made clear when I trip yet again while trying to continue our walk. Oliver uses his other hand – the one not already supporting me – to steady me. I look up at him. His eyes look intensely, darkly brown. And serious. As he gazes down at me, those dark eyes capture mine. My throat has gone completely dry as my heart hammers against my ribs as if it's trying to break free. It's *freezing* out here and yet my cheeks are burning.

Oliver touches my cheek with his hand, tilting my face upward just slightly as he quickly bows his head. Before any coherent thoughts, objections, suggestions, or excuses can even begin to form, he's kissing me. I close my eyes and kiss him back, putting one of my hands on his face, noticing how rough his stubble is and how soft his lips are. I can hear cars passing by, people down the street hollering and my own breathing. I wrap my arms around his neck and pull him closer. He quietly groans as the kiss deepens.

This is what we should've been doing all along. Not fighting or lying or avoiding. Just kissing. Right from that first moment.

Oliver suddenly pulls back like he's been burned. He extracts my arms from around his neck and just holds them, staring at me wide-eyed, remorse etched on his face. He shakes his head sort of numbly.

"I'm sorry," he eventually says, barely audibly. His hair is sticking out every which way thanks to me. "I shouldn't have done that."

I shake my head. "Oliver, it's okay—"

But he just shakes his head again and steadies me, a business-like look on his face. He looks so torn and he won't meet my eye, no matter how hard I try to get his attention. When he's sure I can stand without his support, he walks a few feet away towards the sidewalk and holds his arm up, hailing a nearby taxi.

He mumbles something to the driver, hands him something and opens the backseat door. I cautiously walk toward the cab.

Realizing himself, he takes a step toward me. "Do you need—"

I hold a hand up, stopping him. I am embarrassed enough. I don't need his help walking to the taxi that is ten feet away! It's not the quickest of walks or the most elegant, but I manage. I get in the cab and look up at him expectantly.

"I'm heading in another direction," Oliver explains. He barely looks at me as he says it.

"Oh," I say with a slight wobble in my voice. I clear my throat and look at him, eyebrows raised in a 'whatever' kind of way. He's finally managed to really look at me and I can see the questions, the uncertainty, the apology and the doubt in his eyes. "See you later then," I say, closing the door. The moment we pull away, I close my eyes and rest my head against the seat.

What was that? The moment the question forms, the answer does too. It was quite simply the best kiss I've ever had in my life.

I crease my eyebrows and concentrate on removing all thoughts of Oliver from my mind. The scenery outside is very pretty. Let me just breathe in and out rhythmically and focus on that. Yes, good idea. Snowy London streets, closed shop-fronts, young people dancing around gaily—

Except...my lips still tingle. It's hard not to think about a man when your lips still tingle from the kiss he laid on you four minutes ago.

The moment I picture it – because I can't help it – I smile to myself against my better judgment. That was a good kiss.

"That sodding bastard."

The taxi driver laughs suddenly and I close my hand

over my mouth. "Sorry." I squeak out. "I didn't mean to say that out loud. I swear I'm not crazy."

"Quite all right, miss."

"Incidentally," I say, looking at his reflection in the rearview mirror. "How was my use of the local vernacular?"

He stares at me through the rearview mirror and his eyes are still shining with laughter he seems to be holding in. "Very good, miss."

I nod proudly. Serves Oliver right.

The honeymoon is almost over

Posted by: @Marian at 9:18 PM on december 31 on TheGrayBlog

I only have a couple of minutes until we head out for drinks. I can see everyone's been writing on here, but I'll have to read it when I get back. Just wanted to drop a word to say we are excited to see everyone soon... but sad to see our honeymoon end. We are having a blast. Everyone should go to Greece, especially Mykonos and Santorini. We are so tanned (sunburned) and about ten pounds heavier to boot thanks to our new-found love for Baklava.

Lucky for you, we've been keeping a journal. So far, we've written 32 pages.. When we get back, we'd like to have a family dinner and read it to everyone.

Ugh, Tom got the weirdest email alert from his credit card company that his Visa was charged in London. That was our second honeymoon option. I don't know. Seems a funny coincidence. But he cancelled it and reported it stolen so we should be all set.

Don't mess with the Boltons.

Love to all.
XOXOXOX

Marian

chapter sixteen

C ary finally returns to the flat. The next morning. And oh, does he have a smirk on his face as he closes the door behind him. Sitting in front of the crackling fire, applying curl cream to my wet hair, I look at him knowingly. I've only been awake for an hour and already it looks like this is going to be a good day complete with a juicy, romantic story.

"How was your date?" I ask innocently, as he takes his coat off. I jump to my feet excitedly and stare at him.

He laughs and walks into the kitchen, opening and closing cabinets. I'm not sure if he's actually hungry or just avoiding the question.

"You know that we don't actually live here," I point out.

That earns me a look. His confused gaze meets my playful one.

"I just mean, you won't find food in those cabinets."

He grabs an apple from the fruit bowl and sits at one

of the chairs at the kitchenette table and looks at the apple like it's the most fascinating thing in the world before finally biting into it.

"I know that look," I prod. "I've even worn that look myself a time or two. Things went well. Really well."

He leans back in his chair as he finally looks at me, chewing, but not saying a word.

"Of course it went well," I add. "It turned into an all-nighter."

He cocks his head to the side and looks thoughtful, like he's considering my words very carefully, measuring the truth in them.

This is insane. If he were Mary, he'd be halfway through the story already. "Cary." I can't handle it anymore. "Talk to me."

He smiles at me and allows the truth to make its way to his eyes. "Things went well," he concedes. He runs a hand tiredly over his cheek. "But I'm not a girl, so I might not gab about every little detail like you undoubtedly—"

"Just a rough idea of what you did, who said what, and how the night played out would be fine," I say defensively. I grab my makeup and sit next to the coffee table cross-legged, setting up my mirror. "Want to grab breakfast?"

"Shower, shave, then food," he says like an automaton.

I wave him off. "Go." As soon as I hear the water running, I turn my attention back to my makeup. As I pull the cap off my mascara, there's a knock at the door.

In the ten steps it takes to get to the door, the knock gets more insistent. Maybe it's Oliver. I mean – after last night, running off like he basically did, he *should* try to knock down my door and...and apologize what was basically a Kiss and Run! And then he should admit that he can't get kissing me out of his mind! I open the door, my stomach in knots of excitement—

But it's not Oliver.

It's Kiki. And she looks a bit frazzled. She normally looks so elegant, so classic. Gracefully beautiful like a ballet dancer or a movie star from the golden days of cinema.

Today she looks like she's on day five of using the nicotine patch.

"You okay?" I ask her, furrowing my eyebrows in concern. I stand aside so she can enter.

Once the door is closed, she looks around the room. "Is your husband here?" she asks tentatively.

"Yes," I say slowly, glancing towards the bathroom, where the muffled sound of Cary's singing and water can easily be heard through the closed door. "He's showering."

"I won't be long," she explains. She smiles and for a moment, she looks a little bit more like herself. Like the woman that I met in our hall that first day, who I had lunch with after our run-in at the Tower of London, who I shopped with. I guess she's become a bit like a friend. And I don't really like seeing her looking so...*off*.

"Kiki, take as long as you need. We're just going to grab breakfast when he's done. Feel free to come."

"Thank you, Lucy," she says genuinely, softly. In her eyes, I can almost detect a mixed range of emotions. Sadness, gratitude, fear....

Maybe she had a fight with Dan or something. "Can I just use your phone actually?" she eventually asks.

"Sure," I say, gesturing toward the phone in the kitchen.

She smiles appreciatively and sits at the table very primly, her hand on the receiver but not moving to make the call she came here to make. She looks up at me after a moment. "It's just kind of private," she says shyly.

"Oh," I say, blushing instantly. "Of course." I walk back toward the fire and sit by the coffee table. I unscrew my mascara once again, and look at myself in the mirror as I apply it. All I can hear is the crackles in the fireplace, the shower running and muffled, hushed tones coming from the kitchen where Kiki is still hunched over, her back to me.

The poor girl. From the moment I met her, she's just seemed so *lonely*. I'll have to make sure to get her information before I go home so we can keep in touch.

"All set," she finally says. She looks much more relaxed now that she made whatever phone call she came here to make. "Thank you so much."

"Great," I say, standing. I walk toward her. I smile at her and wait until she looks at me. "Any time."

"I'm so glad I met you," she says. And there it is. That look. Like she's sad even though she's saying something really nice.

"Me too," I say, touching her shoulder encouragingly. "Are you going to the New Year's Eve Party tonight?"

She nods nervously, like I just asked her if she's going to attempt to go into orbit without oxygen.

"We can hang out together," I suggest, hoping she'll get excited or something.

I'm not even sure she heard me though. She opens the door in a daze and looks across the hallway at her door. "I should get back," she says quietly.

And then she's gone. Just like that. I turn away from the door, but stand in the kitchen, unmoving, thinking about Kiki. Honestly, what is her deal? One moment she's begging me like she's sixteen years old to have lunch with her, to go shopping with her, to spend time with her. And at other times, she just seems a million miles away in some strangled emotional battle with herself.

"Who was that?" Cary asks, walking out of the bathroom, showered, shaved and dressed.

"No one," I say, brightening. Cary's ready for breakfast. Which means he's going to tell me what happened last night. "Let's go."

⁓

Polly's hanging decorations as we pass through the lobby and past the ballroom. Oliver is nowhere to be seen.

"I don't get it," I say to Cary as we step outside into the frigid air. It's not nearly as cold yesterday and a good deal sunnier. "The Chaizer is relatively small compared to some hotels. Why does it host a big New Year's party?"

"Didn't you read the pamphlet?" Cary asks, putting his arm around me as we wind our way down Kensington High Street toward the restaurants in search of a breakfast spot.

"What, you did?"

"It's been on the desk the whole time. I like to know where I'm staying."

"What did it say?" I challenge him.

"Just that The Chaizer is kind of a big deal," Cary says shrugging. We stop to browse a menu but keep moving since it looks a little pricey. "I'm surprised you didn't see the story, actually," he adds. "It's pretty romantic."

"Do tell," I encourage him playfully, gazing up at him as we walk.

"It opened in 1930 or '31," he says slowly, uncertainly. He shrugs, giving up. "Well, it was around the time of the Great Slump anyway – or as we call it, the Great Depression. The owners – a middle-aged husband and wife who were *very* wealthy...had apparently seen a young couple forgo a honeymoon since they couldn't afford it. They opened The Chaizer in London, Venice, Madrid and Paris – their favorite places. The concept was very cheap but nice honeymoon accommodations in the name of love and love alone. Since the grand opening was on New Year's, they threw a big party on the first anniversary and it's been going on ever since. It's by invitation and obviously open to guests as well."

I look at him suspiciously. "And you did not just make that up?"

"Scout's honor," he says smoothly, as we find a restaurant finally. "The only one still open is the one in London. It's much more expensive now, too. I guess the 'in the name of love and love alone' concept died when the owners did," he says wryly, wrinkling his nose like he regretted the joke the moment it escaped his lips.

"So all the other locations closed but they still have a big to do about New Year's?"

He nods. "It's their claim to fame."

Once we give the waiter our order, I lean forward, my hands crossed, resting on the table, and fix Cary with my most interested – yet casual – look. "What happened with Anne?"

He chuckles and shakes his head at me. "You're relentless."

"Listen, you owe me a little something." I say desperately. "If it weren't for me, she might have taken back her offer to go out altogether. You were *that* slow."

He nods. "I'll give you that," he agrees. "I did not think she was there to ask me out. I had honestly given up on her. I thought she was dating that guy in Paris and – I don't know. I decided she was a friend. Nothing more. And I let her know it."

"You what?" This isn't shaping up to be the next great love story for the ages like I'd hoped.

"Calm down," he says. "I mean, I told her yesterday morning. We had a workshop for two hours and I went, did my part. No flirting. No extra moments. No idle conversation." He smiles, remembering. "It was hard, actually. But I did it. And after class she did ask me if anything was wrong. And I just told her that everything was fine. That she was a great teacher and friend – and when I head back to New York in a couple of days, all her advice will come in handy."

"How did she react?" I ask, sipping my coffee and staring wide-eyed at Cary. Because, while he's six foot two and handsome in a rugged sort of way, I know he's not that tough. Especially when it comes to Anne. He's been like a schoolboy this whole time over her. For him to put her off like that could not have been an easy task.

"She didn't seem happy," he admits. "But, it honestly didn't matter anymore. Coming here, knowing it was not going to lead to anything was hurting me."

"So she came to her senses," I gush, "and asked you out. She let you know she *was* interested. Yours for the taking if you still wanted her."

He roars with laughter at that, throwing his head back. "Your head is honestly up in the clouds, I swear," he says, once he's controlled himself.

"Well, it's true," I argue, defensively crossing my arms. "I was there. She came to make a move."

He smiles coyly. "Oh she made a move, all right," he concedes devilishly.

"Were the tickets for real? Or were they just a ploy to get you alone?"

"They were for real," he says slowly, looking amused at that question for some odd reason. I thought that it was a perfectly logical thing to ask.

"Okay," our waiter says, sidling up to us with our dishes. "Fruit salad and wheat toast for you," he says, placing my dish down in front of me. "And eggs over easy, toast and bacon for you," he says to Cary, placing his dish down. "Enjoy."

"Well, then what?" I ask, as I lather strawberry jam on my toast.

Cary smiles. "We went to the show and she was very nervous," he remembers, his eyes crinkling. "I honestly felt bad so about twenty minutes into the show, I took her hand. After that," he says, his voice dropping to an almost husky whisper, "it was electric."

I swallow my toast. "Electric?" I ask, confused.

"We've been friends for six years. Good friends," he explains. "We've never held hands. We've barely touched, except for flirtatious little swats and taps. Hugs and kisses in greeting. It's always been friendly, and it's always been more or less how we are with everyone else. This – this was a new level. Jeez, I could barely breathe. It was electric."

My heart feels like it's swelling inside my chest with

total joy for him. I can see a look in his eyes. A new look. And I love it.

"We were supposed to go and have dinner. When we left the show, though, she was cold. It was freezing outside last night."

"I know," I agree softly, my cheeks flaming at the memory of my own late night walk outside in the cold.

"I put an arm around her to keep her warm and she looked up at me. I guess she didn't know that I'd...be so forward so soon. But when she looked up," he says, looking at some invisible spot between us, clearly back in the moment. "Our faces were so close. So I bent down and kissed her."

"Oh, Cary," I squeal excitedly. "Good for you."

"I kissed her with six years of pent up emotion," he adds, smiling, finally letting his absolute elation at the turn of events yesterday shine through his eyes. "I kissed her like my life depended on it." He taps the table and I jump at the sudden thump that causes our silverware to clank against the dishes. "I kissed her in a way that warmed her *right* up."

"Sounds like a good kiss," I say after a moment. My heart's racing at the thought of this kiss and it didn't even happen to me. I just pictured the whole scenario in slow motion and black-and-white! "What did she say afterward?" I finally ask.

He laughs and grabs his fork. "She cancelled dinner," he says and then he begins eating his eggs. "That, my dear, is all you're getting on the subject." He winks at me playfully. "I want to hear about your night."

I open my mouth, but close it again. I don't know where to begin. To be honest, I don't really want to re-live it. After hearing about Cary's AMC movie channel smacker, I am a little embarrassed about what happened last night outside Filthy McGee's. I mean...it doesn't sound so promising when a guy kisses you and then can't stand to be around you for a second longer.

"What?" Cary says, the lightness leaving his expression. Concern creases his features as he puts his fork down and tries to get me to look at him. "Lucy."

I finally do. I look up at him and roll my eyes. "It was nothing," I say quickly, moving my hair behind my ears.

"What was nothing? Did something happen last night?" Now he honestly seems a little worried.

"Oliver and I...kissed," I explain hastily.

The moment the words are out of my mouth, Cary's brow clears and he begins to smile. "I told you—"

"It wasn't anything like *your* kiss last night," I add. "He broke off the kiss, put me in a taxi and basically ran off with his tail between his legs." I shrug. "Not exactly going to make us runner ups for kiss of the year."

"Was it a good kiss?" Cary asks, deadpan.

I nod, feeling a little embarrassed. I've barely divulged anything to him and my stomach's in knots, my throat feels tight and I can't seem to find the words to describe how I feel about any of it.

"You do realize why he ran off, don't you?" Cary asks, leaning back in his chair, serious as ever.

I shake my head. "He seemed dazed when he pulled back. A little nervous, confused, and something else," I say, furrowing my brows, my eyes darting back and forth, searching. "I can't put my finger on—"

"It's because of all this nonsense," Cary says, almost angrily. "He likes you, Lucy. It's obvious."

I gaze dreamily at Cary. "I don't remember Prince Charming putting her in a cab," I joke.

"He thinks you're married," he says impatiently. Suddenly he's acting like our dumb charade is, well, dumb. Cary, who's been the biggest cheerleader of the plan since he arrived at The Chaizer and made the whole thing up to boot! Not that anyone really bought it.

"Come on, Cary," I retort, putting my toast down and resting my elbows on the table. "He can't honestly think that we're married. I am sure you're a great actor, but neither of us has really pulled off an Oscar-worthy performance."

"I think we've done okay," he says, wounded defense written on his face.

"I think we phoned it in," I say gently. "The fact that last night we were both out kissing other people is kind of a testament to that fact."

"Maybe he isn't sure if we're married," he admits. "But he knows that you're lying about something. You are right about that. And I can tell you," he says, squinting his eyes and leaning forward toward me. "He's lying about something, too. *That* is why he ran away."

"You lost me."

He sighs and puts a hand through his hair. "He likes you. He kissed you. But this thing that you've both left unsaid, this *something* that is hanging in the air, what you're not telling him and what he's not telling you... *that* is what came between you last night."

I nod, considering this. It makes sense. Oliver's been trying to pull the truth out of me since the second I arrived. And it's such a lame truth.

"If he's at the party tonight," Cary says, cutting through my thoughts like a knife, "just tell him everything. Tell him how you feel. Tell him that *we* aren't married. Tell him that you like *him*. And end this trip knowing that you came out here and really went after what you wanted."

I look at him wide-eyed. Tell Oliver everything?

"I'm telling you," he says after a long moment. "It's the best feeling."

chapter seventeen

I swear, these boots are going to get me killed. Every fifth step I take seems to result in a slight stumble. But they look so good with my emerald green and silver vintage dress – the one I bought when Cary and I went shopping. That feels like ages ago. I have to wear these boots. These are my London boots. They are the boots I was wearing when Oliver kissed me last night. And they are the ones I will wear tonight for good luck.

As I put the finishing touches on my makeup, I see Cary's reflection in the mirror as he walks up behind me. Through the reflection, he takes me in and lets out a low, appreciative whistle.

"You look beautiful," he says. He squeezes my shoulders gently and I turn to really look at him. My breath catches because he looks absolutely unbelievable. In gray pants and a black button down, he looks like he just stepped from the pages of my favorite fairytale story to attend the ball with me. Or, more accurately, the pages of *GQ*.

"So do you," I finally say. "Is Anne coming tonight?"

He nods, trying to stifle a smile. His fingers graze the tips of my hair and he looks at me curiously. "Straight?" He suddenly looks around the room nervously and breathes in dramatically.

I swat his arm. "There's no fire," I say defensively. "I happened to get it straightened by a professional down the street."

He laughs. "A very safe choice."

His phone chirps and he grabs it from his pocket, walking away as he answers. I walk to the fireplace and plop myself down on the couch, resting my feet on the coffee table. I grab *The Cat Who Went to Paris* from the end table and open it, but I close it immediately. I can't concentrate. We'll be heading down to the ballroom at any minute now. Entering the party.

Oliver could be there.

Oliver, who I kissed last night.

Oliver, who I plan to tell everything – the moment I can get him alone.

My stomach coils itself into endless knots as I stare dazedly at the dancing flames in the fireplace.

In a flash, I remember it all. *That night* – the night of Marian's wedding – I felt something inside at that crazy psychic's ramblings. She talked about signs. She talked about fate. She seemed to stare right into my soul.

I know. It sounds nuts. I *know*.

But that night as I'd lain in my bed, I'd felt an emptiness and a longing so strong that it ached. I so *wanted* to believe her.

Maybe that was enough. Maybe it was enough to just believe in something like that. Something intangible and just so promising. So I did. I believed in those signs from fate. I believed in taking chances. Just like she said.

That night was perfect because of that. Because I believed. And I paid attention. I changed.

But now...I can't leave everything to fate, can I? If I want something, then I have to step up. Be honest. I have to grab it for myself.

And anyway, it's all so silly. I'm sure Oliver will understand. Right? If he really likes me at all, he'll be relieved that I am a single woman who just told a little white lie.

I look over at Cary as he approaches me, clutching my book to my chest.

"Shall we?"

❧

We walk into the dimly lit ballroom and my nerves take a backseat for a moment as I look around, taking in the scene of The Chaizer's New Year's party. I'm impressed. It looks immaculate. The silver and black cut-out stars I'd seen Polly stringing at her desk are draping the windows and hanging in various spots, their shimmer matte catching the warm lighting causing them to twinkle a little. Everything seems to be cloaked in black and silver. A crystal chandelier hangs low, setting a romantic tone to the room, which just today looked like a normal room. At the center of every table, which is covered with black tablecloths, are black candelabras filled with silver pillar candles. The hors d'oeuvres tables are topped with clear vases filled with silver balls. The only color in the room seems to be coming from the Christmas tree in the corner, which is adorned with turquoise and silver balls.

As I step further into the room, I notice a champagne fountain in the far corner. The gold bubbly liquid spills into a mountain of toasting flutes. Loads of people are already here. There must be nearly one hundred guests at this party. The women all look so trendy and sleek in their cocktail dresses, while the guys look cool and sophisticated. So many of the partygoers are sporting Happy New Year's hats. I can't believe it's already New Year's Eve. Another year is almost behind me, and at the last moment, this one became a pretty interesting one.

I make my way over to the hors d'oeuvres table. As I grab a cracker with cheese, I jump, noticing the ice sculpture in the corner – two swans forming a heart with their necks and faces. This place really does go all out for this annual shindig.

"Seriously?" Cary asks, sidling up to me, his gaze fixed on the ice sculpture. "Love birds to decorate the ballroom of this love nest?" he asks incredulously, shaking his head.

"You said it was a big deal," I say, looking at him, nibbling my cracker.

"I had no idea," he says, grabbing a cracker and cheese himself. He leans against the table and looks out at the dance floor.

As I scan the room nonchalantly, I don't see one familiar face.

"Looking for Oliver?" Cary asks smugly. I glance up at him and grimace at the smirk he's wearing. "Come on." He holds out his hand. "Let's dance."

As Frank Sinatra croons "The Way You Look Tonight," I take Cary's hand and smile, allowing him to lead me to the dance floor.

He pulls me into his arms and begins turning to the music. I look around, taking it all in...the cascading silver and black décor shimmering around me under the warm glow from the chandelier, the safety of Cary's arms, our new friendship, this beautiful resort, the magic of London...

"My trip is coming to an end," I whisper to Cary, gazing up at him as the reality of those words starts to hit me like a sucker punch. "I'm going to miss you. I'm going to miss all of it," I admit.

He squeezes my hand reassuringly and in his gaze I detect understanding – and reciprocity. "Have you had fun?" he asks, his expression remaining serious, even as his eyes gleam knowingly.

"You know it," I say, smiling. "This trip is the best thing I've ever done."

"Well, it's not over yet." He pulls me closer to him.

We twirl and swing and have a grand time as Frank Sinatra becomes Louis Armstrong and then, for a modern twist, Maroon 5. The sadness and nostalgia quickly give way to unprecedented joy. After all, I only have two days left. There's no time to waste.

"Hi."

I turn quickly and find myself face to face with Anne, who's looking at Cary like a love struck teenager. "Anne," I say, giving her an appreciative once-over. "You look fantastic." Her hair is swept up in a 'do straight out of the 1940s. Her pewter floor-length dress hugs her curves perfectly. A long pearl necklace droops low to her bellybutton.

She finally looks away from Cary and looks at me. "Thank you, Lucy," she says with a small laugh. She somehow looks lighter than every other time I've seen her. Like a weight has been lifted. Like she's free. "I know you two are sort of undercover," she says, winking. "But would it be possible for me to cut in for a song?"

I smile at them both. "Of course."

Cary touches my arm as I turn to walk away. "Thank you."

I smile sincerely, reveling in his perfect moment. "Give me your phone," I say. "This deserves a picture."

He pulls his phone from his pocket and hands it to me. The two of them smile at me and I take a photo that definitely will not require a filter. It's perfect. Cary pulls Anne close, and begins dancing with her as I walk away.

A waiter hands me a glass of wine as I approach the outskirt of the dance floor. I can't help but stare at Cary and Anne. They are so cute. She says something that makes him laugh and kiss her on the cheek, and she cannot hide her happiness at the kiss. I shake my head, mesmerized. What took them so long to make that move to be together? They are just so clearly *right* for each other. I pull the phone up and take another picture of them.

"So, here you are," a familiar voice says and I jump. My God, this man has an uncanny ability to just appear out of *nowhere* constantly.

I look up at Oliver and instantly feel my heartbeat quicken. He looks so handsome – and nervous. Shuffling his feet as he looks around the room at everything but me, I see he is dressed up for the party in a smart, dark suit. He emanates the class and ease of the men here who are dressed to the nines. His dark eyes are now glued on Cary and Anne curiously. When I say nothing, he looks down at me. Our eyes meet for the first time since our kiss. As my eyes lock with his, my mind goes completely blank. Any possible thoughts die on my tongue as I just look at him.

"Did you have a nice day?" he asks casually. As his cheeks flush, I can see he feels uneasy, too. I can see he could not care less about how my day was. He's just looking for something – *anything* – to say to kill the post-kiss awkwardness.

"It was relaxing," I say at last. "I didn't do much of anything." I cock my head sideways and smile at him. "Incidentally, I didn't see you once sneaking around. You know, like you normally do."

He shrugs. "I was called away today," he says quietly. "On business."

I shake my head. Because...*really?* A concierge called away on business? This is just ridiculous. We are both clearly lying! And...we clearly like each other. I think it's about time to just get it all out in the open.

"Oliver," I say, in a rush. "We need to talk."

He looks downward, toward the dance floor, peers once more at Cary and Anne, and nods in agreement.

"I think we need to clear the air," I add softly, honestly, also looking at the dancing lovebirds.

"I think that's a good idea," he agrees solemnly. But he doesn't move. Doesn't look at me. He's just staring at the people on the dance floor almost longingly.

"What?" I ask, following his gaze.

"How about we dance," he suggests. He releases a long breath, like just saying those words relaxes him a bit. He smiles tentatively at me. "And then we talk."

I smile and blush, slipping Cary's phone into my purse. I take the proffered hand and try to ignore the butterflies in my stomach as we make our way to the dance floor.

"It's just that this is one of my favorite songs," he explains. Is it me or does he sound nervous?

I nod and smile. My head is buzzing so loudly, I can't even hear the song he's talking about. "Okay," I say.

When he stops, I turn to face him, and he's staring down at me, a mix of emotions flitting across his expression as he tentatively pulls me close, takes my hand, and begins slowly swaying to the music amidst the throng of couples and families at the party. I feel just the lightest touch on my lower back. Suddenly, I feel a bit like a teenager as we begin to dance.

It feels different being in his arms. With Cary, I felt secure and comfortable. The warm embrace of someone who's become a good friend. With Oliver, I feel anything but comfortable. And yet, there's a feeling of rightness about being this close to Oliver that makes my chest muscles constrict as if my heart is truly swelling.

"I'm sorry about last night," Oliver says halfway through the song.

I shrug, looking at the other dancers on the floor. I gaze up at him finally. "It's okay. If you felt—"

"It's hard to describe how I felt. How I've...been feeling." He looks like he means that, too.

I nod, looking up at him. "I know what you mean," I say. "And I think that things will be clearer after we just talk about it. About all of it."

He nods and very subtly pulls me just a little bit closer. He's holding me like he's afraid if he lets go, we'll lose everything. My heart is thundering against my rib cage. I wonder if he can feel it.

"I hope so," he says. He half-smiles at me as our eyes lock.

"Burke," a deep voice says from behind me. Oliver

jumps, looking over my shoulder at someone. He drops my hands and takes a small step back, away from me like the junior high chaperone just ordered us to leave room for the holy spirit.

I swivel around to see who's gotten Oliver so spooked. I don't recognize the man. He's a thin, tall man with slanted blue eyes and graying hair. And he's looking at Oliver with a grim expression.

"What are you doing here?" Oliver asks, darting a quick, nervous glance at me, before looking once again at this man.

"Who is this?" I ask Oliver.

"Is this her?" the man asks. "Room 708?"

Okay, this is getting weird. "How does he know my room number?"

"You don't understand," Oliver begins saying to the man. But the man grabs my arms and pulls them behind my back.

"Hey." I look at Oliver in shock, and pull my arms free, seeing handcuffs in this guy's hands. Was this man honestly just trying to handcuff me? Right here in public? And why does Oliver know him?

"Oliver, what is going on here?" I ask.

"Karl, please," Oliver says, taking a step toward me, toward this man.

"I have been trying to call you," the guy says to Oliver. "We got another lead a couple of hours ago from the hotel. It was the female half again. Said she'd be at the party at this time, with her husband. The phone call was made from Room 708. The credit card holding this hotel room was just reported stolen earlier today. You've suspected this woman the whole time—"

"Oliver...." I look at him closely and feel like I'm

seeing him for the first time. He doesn't look like himself. He's standing taller, looking (if it's possible) more serious, more fierce than I've ever seen him look. I have no idea what these two are talking about, but it's obvious that it's that *thing* that Oliver has been lying to me about. "What is he talking about?" I finally ask him.

Oliver doesn't even look at me. He's just looking at this guy with a dark expression on his face now – his face which had worn such a nervous, almost tender expression just minutes ago, while we were dancing.

"What's going on here?" Cary asks, walking up to us, Anne holding his hand, standing a bit behind him, looking on curiously. "Are you okay?" he asks me.

"I've been telling you," Oliver starts. But the guy takes a step toward him, cutting him off instantly.

"I know what you've been saying. But I also know evidence, Burke. She's been lying all along. You said that. The call was made from her room. Her credit card is a stolen one. I was sent here by Griffin to do what you can't seem to do. To take the Honeymooners in before they can do anything else."

The man grabs my arms again, tighter this time. It feels like a grip of steel, but I feel almost numb. My head is swimming with the implications of the words I'm hearing.

Those articles. That crazy duo, the Honeymooners. *They think I'm one of them?* My mouth falls open in shock, but no words come. In a flash it all becomes clear. Oliver – he's a cop. He must be. I swivel my head around to face him – really face him – and our eyes lock as the truth falls down around us.

He looks down at the grip on my arm and looks back at the guy. "Get your hands off her," he orders quietly.

"You'll take her in then?" the guy asks, his grip on me loosening. "Because I really don't want to take your case. I don't."

At that, I look at Oliver, lost for words. Through the confusion, something is bubbling up in my chest. Hurt, I think. His case? That's what this was? Hot tears of humiliation spring to my eyes as the room feels like it's closing in on me. I can see a few other couples staring at us nosily. Oliver takes a step toward me but I take a step away as the hurt gives way to anger. A lot of anger.

"Was that what you wanted to talk about – your belief that I'm one of the Honeymooners?" My hands ball into fists as I just stare at him and force him to hold my gaze. "The *Honeymooners?*" I repeat incredulously. "Are you serious?"

I yank my arm free from that guy's grasp and hit Oliver in the chest with both hands as hard as I can, knocking him into the other guy. They both move toward me, but Cary – who looks beyond confused, but definitely protective – rushes forward and knocks them both back forcefully.

And then I run.

chapter eighteen

I know, I know...you shouldn't run from cops! But I can't even handle what just happened. Honestly. I cannot process it.

As I fight my way through the crowded room and back into the main lobby, the last few minutes play themselves over and over in my head like some kind of nightmarish tableau. Oliver never liked me. He thought I was a criminal. An actual criminal. The kind that commits crimes.

I head up the stairs, taking them two at a time. These boots were definitely not made for running. They're killing me. New blisters scrape against the leather folds that are jutting into my heel, leaving my skin raw and aching. But I don't care. I need to go home. *Now.* Charles was so right. I never should have left.

I cannot believe that Oliver thought I was a criminal. How's that for an answer next time my mother asks me why I'm still single: "Well, Mom, men seem to think I'm a traveling wacko on a giant thieving spree – who also happens to be a murderer – which, you know, creates trust issues."

I finally arrive on the seventh floor out of breath. I grab my key from my purse and head towards my door in a rush. I don't know what I think I'm going to do. I mean, the cops are downstairs. I may have escaped, but I can't fly. I have to go back down there. Who cares if I pack my bag at this point? I probably should have run outside and hailed a cab. See – this is why I couldn't be a criminal even if I wanted to. I can't even escape properly.

I jump when I hear a door open as I put my key in the door. I turn and see Kiki and Dan laughing, all dressed up. They are clearly heading down to the party now.

"Lucy," Kiki says when she notices me. "Are you coming to the party?" she asks sweetly, holding her husband's hand.

Knots twist in my stomach as something dawns. What that cop said. The phone call.

"You," I say, taking a step toward them. "It was you."

Recognition dawns on Kiki's face as I take another step toward them. Now she looks afraid. And she has every right to be.

"You made the phone call from my room. You're the reason the cops were just trying to take me to jail," I say passionately. "You're the reason they think I'm one of those Honeymooners."

Dan takes a step toward me and the moment I catch his eyes, I realize what I've just said. Because if I'm not one of the Honeymooners but the Honeymooners are here and the woman just planted a lead from my phone to out them to the cops, then that must mean that –

"Oh, my God," I whisper, taking a step back. But Dan is too quick. He grabs me and before I know it, he's shoved me into his flat. He slams the door behind Kiki and turns around to face her.

"What did you do?" he screams. I can't even speak for shock. These two haven't been able to be in a room together without making out without a care as to prying eyes. They're The Honeymooners?

And now it all makes sense. Kiki's loneliness and sadness, her strange quirks, her constantly being on her own....

And the places she mentioned traveling match the ones mentioned in those articles. It's why those articles felt familiar. How did I not figure it out?

I look at Kiki, who's sobbing and looking both ashamed and just so defeated. And I realize why I didn't figure it out. She doesn't look like she could rob a Girl Scout, let alone a bunch of multimillionaires.

"I want out of this," she says dramatically, flailing her arms wildly, trying to appeal to her husband. "You said we'd stop. But we never did!"

"You told on me?" Dan asks, shaking his head in shock. He seems like he's used to always getting his way. And marrying a woman who would betray him like this is beyond shocking – it's a crime to him. "After everything we've been through, you *reported* me to the cops?"

"That guy in Florence died," she argues. "What was I supposed to do?"

"You didn't complain when you got his wife's three million dollar necklace."

I edge my way towards the front door. Because I need to get back downstairs. Tell Oliver that he was spying on the wrong side of the hallway all this time. And then go home. I just need to go home.

"Where do you think you're going?" Dan asks, running toward the door before I can whip it open and run for my life away from these two. I trust Kiki not to hurt me. But Dan seems seriously unhinged.

"It seems like you two are having a private conversation," I explain. I hope I sound convincing and not like I'm terrified to be anywhere near him. Which of course is exactly how I feel right now. "I really don't think I should be here for it."

He laughs at me like I just told the best joke. I almost feel like laughing myself actually. Because this is a joke. It really is. Me being suspected of their numerous crimes, which include murder, by the way, and the guy I like being the main cop on the case, the one most suspicious of me. The fact that any of this is even happening because a psychic at an 80's themed wedding basically said a couple of vague, silly words that she probably said to every other guest at the wedding – it's comical.

But I don't laugh. Because while I was only mistakenly suspected for these crimes, Dan here is actually responsible for them. And he's very scary up close. His white-blonde hair is so perfectly gelled that it looks like a helmet. His eyes are so dark, they are almost black. His skin is so pale, it's nearly translucent. He looks kind of like a weasel – except totally built and muscular. And really intimidating.

"You've just told me the cops are downstairs," he says, lightly, like this is no big deal. "Do you honestly think I am going to let you go anywhere?"

"Well, we can't stay in here forever," I point out.

"You have to go down there eventually. They'll still be there, no matter when you leave."

"And if I have you, they can't hurt me," he explains.

Did I just go from suspected thief to unsuspecting hostage? My stomach coils. I feel a little sick. These kinds of things just don't happen to normal people. And that's me. I am normal. More than that. I'm boring. I'm just plain, old Lucy Gray. Miss Reliable. Last year on New Year's Eve, I went out for drinks with Mary and at exactly one in the morning, I went home and curled up with Ricky.

Dan physically blocks the front door to his flat with his body as he grabs his cell phone and begins dialing furiously.

I turn around and take a couple of steps toward Kiki. She is crying less hysterically now. But she still seems upset. I sit down next to her on the bed and look around their place. Everything is so immaculately placed. There are no clothes overflowing the suitcases like in my flat. There are no coats dangled over chairs. It barely looks lived in and they've been here at least as long as I have.

"I don't understand," I say to Kiki quietly after a moment. "You told the cops where to find him, but you didn't tell them your names?"

She looks me in the eye and bites back another sob. She is nervously ripping the tissue in her hands.

"It's hard to explain," she finally whispers. "I couldn't say his name. It was bad enough to send the leads in. I mean – I led the cops to my own husband."

"But that's just it," I burst out. "You led them here. Why not just give them all the information so they could have focused on the right people?"

"It was like – as long as I didn't say his name, I wasn't

being disloyal. I wasn't a bad wife, I was just an informant," she explains, her chin quivering. She rolls her eyes at herself self-deprecatingly and laughs. "I know it's stupid," she admits. "I know that now. And I am so sorry that you got mixed up in it."

"That's not entirely your fault," I admit. "I wasn't being completely truthful since checking in. My lie was harmless and stupid, though," I quickly add. Because she looks momentarily excited at the idea of her new friend being a criminal in hiding like her. "I'm just a horrible liar and it seemed to tip off the cop here, I guess."

Oliver. I still can't believe it. All the times he was there mysteriously. The times we'd spent getting to know each other. He'd just been chasing a lead. And *that*...is just so humiliating.

I look over at Dan. He's pacing around the room, mumbling to himself. "Is he really dangerous?" I ask Kiki, as the ball of fear in my stomach springs to life again at the sight of him. At the idea that I am, right now, trapped in here with him.

"He isn't really," she says emphatically, her love for him shining in her eyes. "But if he's desperate...." Her eyes look distant. "That's how that other guy got killed. Dan got desperate. And he honestly didn't mean to even *hurt* that guy. It just – oh, it all got out of control."

I bend forward, putting my face in my hands, eyes closed, and try to breathe. "It all got out of control," I repeat calmly, even though I feel anything but calm. This situation is already so far out of control, it's not even funny. And he really looks desperate right now.

I have to do something. I am *not* going down to the lobby as a hostage. I just need to think.

I have nothing. I am dressed in a flimsy vintage dress with high heel boots that are making my feet truly ache. Well, that's something anyway, I guess. The boots. If need be, I can stab Dan with a heel. They *are* pointy.

Okay, this is another reason I'd be a terrible criminal. My weapons suck.

I breathe out and look down at my lap. My purse is lying there. No weapons in there. Just lipstick, some cash, my passport –

And Cary's phone.

Oh, my God. I still have Cary's phone!

I unzip my purse quietly and peer inside. There it is. Dan is mumbling quietly in the corner to whoever he's talking to. And I have no idea who to call. I don't exactly have Oliver's cell phone number. Or the number to the front desk downstairs. Is the number 911 here for emergencies?

I wrack my brain until it hurts. There must be a number I can call. What numbers have I called since I've been here?

Eyeing Dan closely, I subtly move the phone so it's in my hand, secured so he can't see it. I start scanning through the recent calls and see one number appear numerous times. Anne.

I place the phone on the bed, and angle my body to block it from Dan's view. I make it look like I am just chatting with Kiki. "What is your room number?"

She looks nervously at her husband and then back at me. "711."

I push the little green phone button, which dials the selected number. Oh, please let her hear her phone ring and answer. As I wait, I lean into Kiki and force her to meet my gaze.

"Pull yourself together, Kiki," I whisper. "I need you."

Again she peers at her husband before looking at me again.

"You were trying to do the right thing," I say gently. "When you called the cops and left those leads."

She nods. "I was," she says adamantly.

"You still can do the right thing," I tell her. "Just, *please*, play along with what I do."

She seems confused, but nods all the same.

I lie down on the bed and pretend to cry. I'm instantly reminded of the first time I ever met Cary. It was a theater audition in the ninth grade. I was trying something new and he was the star. No one was ever as good as Cary. I was supposed to cry. Cary had to try so hard not to laugh at me and my bad acting. I can't fake cry. I know I can't. But my God, I'll try right now.

I cradle the phone next to my lips. I can hear a voice muffled against the comforter of the bed. Anne. Hopefully.

Kiki pats my shoulder. "There, there," she says. She looks up at her husband. "Well, what do you want me to do?" she asks him loudly. She risks a look down at me and then looks back at him, a look of determination on her face. "She's upset," she explains. "Wouldn't you be? She got mixed up in *our* stupid mess."

"I can't deal with you right now. You report me to the police, and you're comforting the only woman who can save me," he spits out in disgust. "I feel like I married a crazy person!"

"*You* feel like you married a crazy person?" she shouts.

While the two of them go back and forth arguing about Kiki's loyalties, I turn my attention to the phone, hugging it to me. "Tell Oliver," I whisper into the receiver. "Room 711. Room 7-1-1," I repeat slowly. "Room 711. Tell Oliver."

Then I pretend to cry again, so that Dan won't suspect me of anything.

"I should never have let you in on it. I was doing just fine before I shared my life with you," Dan is saying. I can hear his voice getting closer. I pull the phone closer to me and hide it under my chest but I don't dare end the call. Just in case.

"You insisted that you loved me and would accept me for who I am. For better or for worse," he says in mock imitation of his wife. "You kept saying 'for better or for worse.'"

"I didn't think you were a criminal," she argues, crossing her arms, sounding a bit mad now herself. Good for her. Better late than never. "I thought 'worse' would be like bad moods and the flu."

"And you didn't mind it all too much when you got money and jewelry from the whole deal, did you?" he challenges her. Still, his voice gets closer to us.

"You know what?" she says, still rubbing my back. "I should have. I should have said something sooner. I should have turned you in the moment you told me. You're a liar and a...a bad man," she says. Her voice has a slight wobble, but the intensity behind her words never falters. "I thought I knew you," she continues, wiping a tear angrily from her cheek. "You barely flinched when that man died," she says. "You barely cared. I can't believe how stupid I was," she says. She seems so angry. At herself, really. "I shouldn't have phoned in vague leads."

"Damn right you shouldn't have."

"I should've been specific," she throws back, like he's stupid. "I should've given them our names and our room number. Then they could've just come to our room and taken you away, and Lucy wouldn't be here right now, crying her eyes out."

She knows that I'm not really crying, right?

"Tell Oliver," I whisper again, toward the phone. I have no idea if my message is going through, but I have to keep trying. "Room 711—"

"What do you think you're doing?"

I jump at the sound of Dan's voice. He's right over me. Shit. I stare up at him, my eyes wide as saucers. Because if he was scary before, it's *nothing* compared to this moment. He truly looks murderous. And, well, he is a murderer. So...this is no good. I feel like I could throw up. Who knew crippling fear could make you nauseous?

"Leave her alone," Kiki says, getting to her feet.

"Kiki, I swear to God!"

"She didn't do anything. Just leave her alone!" Her eyes are wider than I've ever seen them, filled with tears and fear, but still, she takes a step toward him to place herself between her husband and me.

Her friend.

Well, okay, plan one is in the bag. Who knows if it was successful? I begin to unzip my boot because it honestly is the only other thing I can think of.

I look at the boot that is now in my hands and shake my head in disbelief.

In one swift move, Dan grabs Kiki by the shoulders and *flings* her – honestly flings her – out of his way. She falls hard to the ground and pulls herself into a ball, crying desperately, helplessly.

He sets his eyes on me and before he can reach out to grab me, I grab my boot like a baseball bat and swing it as hard as I can at his face. I feel the impact of the boot connecting with his face. He falls back, toward the front door to the flat, holding his eye. That's all the head start I need. I turn on my heel and wobble unevenly in one boot toward their balcony. I need to get out of this room, but I cannot run past him. The man is seriously pissed at me right now if his language is any indication. And in case I didn't mention it already, he's killed before.

As the frigid winter air instantly freezes my skin – especially my right foot – I close the balcony doors behind me and run to the balcony and look down. There's no fire escape. No easy access to another flat. There's just a ledge. A ledge to my right. It's pretty wide but *it's a ledge*. A real live ledge. Seven stories high. I am just going to stand on the balcony and hope for the best. I unzip my other boot and step out of it. Because if I do need to resort to the worst, I'll definitely need even footing. As my left foot tingles from the fresh wave of coldness hitting it, I shiver. It is freezing out here. I know that help must be on the way. Someone is going to bust into Flat 711 and take him away—

I jump when I see the balcony door begin to move and instinctively run toward the ledge. Oh God. I lift one leg over and freeze, closing my eyes.

This trip has been surreal in so many ways, right from the beginning. But...this is insane. Absolutely insane. I cannot climb onto the ledge. I can't.

But when I see Dan's face as he stumbles outside, I do it. I lift the other leg over. Somehow in the middle of my ice-cold panic, I manage to steady myself on the ledge. I secure my hold on the building's stucco fixtures and slowly let go of the balcony.

And then I begin to move away from Dan.

And away from safety.

chapter nineteen

I cannot believe it. As I stand on this ledge – yes, ledge – seven stories high, I think about that crazy psychic once again. If she had said that following fate's signs could lead me down a path of mortal danger, I probably would've just stayed home. Because this is so not what I came out here to do. I bet her name is not even a good one like Zelda or Esmeralda or Endora. Or Raven. Her name is probably Colleen and she probably does kids' birthday parties in addition to weddings.

With the tiniest, most careful steps, I scoot away from the balcony. Finally, I stop. I can't walk anymore. I'm far enough away from Dan. And my legs feel like Jell-O. They are so cold and are shaking so much. I slowly turn until I am no longer facing the building, but facing out. I close my eyes and breathe in. I can hear Dan yelling, but I won't focus on him. I can't. I just need to breathe. And stay calm.

I plant my feet steadily into the concrete, lean firmly

back against the building and slowly lower myself until I am sitting. As my legs reach out in front of me, my calves dangle over the ledge. I open my eyes and look out. They have different scenery than we do on this side of the building. Well, of course they do. It's a different side of the building.

From our balcony, you can see Kensington High Street. A city skyline greets me every morning when I wake up. This view seems to be more woodsy and dark, completely devoid of the energy oozing throughout the rest of the city.

I hear a loud bang from the direction of the balcony and I startle. When I look over, my heart nearly rolls over in relief at the sight before me. It's Oliver and the other cop. Oliver grabs Dan, and thrusts him angrily at the other guy, saying something to Dan that I cannot hear. In his voice, I hear anger and something else. It almost sounds like fear. The other cop takes Dan back into the flat, leaving Oliver out here. He looks around frantically for a moment and then looks back inside the flat. I suddenly realize what he's looking for. Me.

"I'm over here," I croak, my voice weak from the cold.

He stops and when he sees me, he rushes to the side of the balcony, his eyes wide.

"Lucy," he breathes. "Are you okay?" Even as he asks the simple question, he is already pulling one foot over the balcony. Then the other.

"You don't have to come out here," I say. "I can get back on my own."

Except I can't. Try as I may, my body doesn't seem to be cooperating. I'm rooted to the spot. Or frozen to it at least.

"Don't move," he warns, edging toward me carefully. When he's close, he turns and lowers himself down slowly until he's sitting beside me. "Are you okay?" he repeats. Out of the corner of my eye, I can see him studying me. But I don't look over at him. I can't.

I swallow and nod. "I'm okay," I say at last. "I guess my call to Anne went through?"

He puts a hand through his hair and releases a long, exasperated breath. "Yes," he says. "I came up as fast as I...." He breathes out again. I can practically see the nerves coursing through him. "I am so sorry," he finally says.

"I can't move," I tell him, cutting off his apology.

"What do you mean?" He peers at me and I can see a nervousness in his eyes that I've never seen before.

"I think I am literally frozen. My boots are over there," I explain, eyeing the balcony. "I can't move. I mean it. I may actually turn into a statue," I say all in a rush.

"We don't want that to happen," Oliver says, some of the nervousness gone from his voice now. He shifts his body and begins removing his suit jacket. When it's off, he holds it out towards me, gently placing it behind me, helping me get my arms in. The warmth from the jacket immediately takes effect. It doesn't take away the cold. I breathe in Oliver's scent and feel a slight amount of comfort. After a long moment, I look at him.

"You're a cop."

He nods, but doesn't break eye contact. "I've been undercover here since about two weeks before you arrived. I received leads in my case and it seemed the notorious Honeymooners were heading here for the holidays."

"The leads were right." I'm quiet for a moment, thinking about the article from the paper. "Except the leads said they were going to southern Italy and Spain."

He takes a deep breath, his nerves seeming to relax a little. "I fed a false lead to the media, so the Honeymooners wouldn't know we were close."

I shudder as a breeze seems to penetrate my skin and freeze my bones.

"And... does your family own this hotel?"

Oliver shakes his head. "No. I think Geoff wanted to justify my behavior."

"It wasn't a good strategy. Most owners don't drill their guests."

I shoot him a hesitant smile – our familiar, old banter making me feel both happy and sad at the same time.

His gaze bores into mine with a different kind of intensity. Now, he's surveying me. "You aren't on your honeymoon," he says. "And you two were never—"

I sigh and shiver at once. "I'm here on vacation," I admit, feeling suddenly foolish for ever having lied about something so *normal*. My God, I took a vacation. Why couldn't I have told him that right from the beginning? "Cary's a friend."

"I don't understand," he says quietly. "Why—"

"It was my sister's reservation. It was spontaneous. And I never do anything spontaneous. I guess now we can see why that is," I say, attempting to joke at this ridiculous situation. "It all happened so fast. And I was going to tell the truth, but the receptionist said they had a policy, that you had to be here on your honeymoon, that the reservations were non-transferable – and my friend Mary made me promise."

"Made you promise what?"

"To go with it," I say, feeling exasperated as the last few weeks finally flood out into the open. "To be Marian. To check in and stick to that story. To have a little adventure for myself for once." I close my eyes, feeling foolish. Mary was trying to be a good friend. But there was clearly a point where I should have come clean. And I didn't.

He nods slowly, resting his head against the building. As the truth hangs in the air, I want to cry. Everything had seemed so nice. Our time together. Our kiss. Our dance. It all seemed so promising. But none of it was real. We were both lying this entire time.

"Lucy," he starts.

"I think I can get back inside now." I pull my knees to my chest and plant my frozen feet into the concrete and begin standing. I cannot be here anymore. I can't listen to anything he has to say because he's just going to do that thing that I hate. He'll let me down gently. Apologize for leading me on. Tell me it was part of some undercover magic he was trying so he could close this case and get on with his life. He gets to his feet quickly and immediately grasps my arm to help steady me.

Once I'm standing, I nod to him and we begin making our way toward the balcony. Once he's there, Oliver climbs back over to safety swiftly, turning his attention to me. He grips my arms and hugs me toward him, pulling me toward the balcony. In spite of the fact that I am still on a ledge seven stories high, I feel safe now. I manage to make my way back onto the enclosed balcony and let out a breath I didn't even know I was holding. And then I bolt inside, desperate for warmth.

Inside, that guy from downstairs is handcuffing Dan, who is looking at Kiki with a wounded and angry expression. She's sitting on the bed, crying.

"I am sorry for how this all went down," the other cop says when he notices me. "And to ruin your New Year's Eve," he adds. "We do need you to come with us and answer some questions."

I nod and excuse myself. I need to change out of this dress and put on multiple layers. I need to grab my things, too. Because I am not heading back here.

When I leave the police station, I'm heading home.

❧

Three hours later, I am still at the police station and I still have not had a chance to answer the detective's questions. I am sitting in a waiting room going stir-crazy. I have to say, some very unsavory characters hang out in police stations at three-thirty in the morning on New Year's Day. Drug addicts mostly. A few hookers. Some underage rebellious types.

But at least I'm warm. And not on a ledge seven stories high.

I haven't seen Oliver since I left Kiki's hotel room. In that room, he looked at me like he wanted to talk. He'd stepped toward me like he wanted to come to my room and wait for me while I changed. But I hadn't encouraged that. I mean, what was there to say? Just that he had been confused. That he'd simply gotten too close to his case. He'd admit he suspected me of something I didn't do and tell me that now he felt bad that I ended up on the ledge of a hotel as a result. And I'd tell him that I was embarrassed because I had stupidly thought that something nice – something *real* – had been happening between us.

"There you are," Cary exclaims, rushing into the waiting room and throwing himself into the seat beside me. "Lucy – what the hell happened?"

I look over at him. "They're making you answer questions too?"

He shakes his head. "No," he says. His face looks pale and his eyes look concerned. There's an almost wild look in them. I guess this isn't how he thought his night would go. "I had no idea where you were. I've been trying to find you."

I sigh as tears spring to my eyes. I just want this night to be over. I cannot believe I ruined his night with Anne. His perfect date with her. "I'm sorry, Cary. I took everything and left," I explain lamely, not daring to meet his eyes. "I didn't even think about leaving a note. And – oh no, I had your phone," I realize out loud, putting a hand to my forehead. I grab my purse and begin rummaging through it. It's not here. "Where is it?" I ask. Of course. It's probably still in the flat.

"Do you think I care about a cell phone right now?" Cary asks. "Lucy – Lucy, stop," he says, grabbing my hands. "Look at me."

I do. And I don't hide anything from him. I let the tears fall and the apology show. "I *am* sorry, Cary," I say sincerely. "This turned into a big mess and you ended up in the middle of it."

"Pretending to be married was my idea, remember?"

I laugh, remembering how he'd stormed into the lobby and kissed me – a move that started our whole charade.

I shake my head. "So you're okay, then?" I ask, turning my attention to him. "They didn't try to handcuff you or anything?"

"Oh, they did," he assures me with an amused smile. He sits back and relaxes visibly as he talks. "Or at least that other cop did. Oliver just kept asking me where you'd gone. He looked in our flat and couldn't find you, came back down and drilled me. When Anne's phone rang with my cell number, I said it had to be you and Oliver grabbed it and answered." He shivers. "The guy went pale. I'm not sure what you said, but he took off, demanding the other cop come with him."

"Cary, that was the most insane thing," I say. "If I didn't have your phone—"

He grabs me and pulls me into a hug. "I know."

"So how were you not able to find me?" I ask. "It's been three hours. And I was at the Chaizer for a little while."

He places his arm around me and smiles. "Because," he explains. "Someone said a woman was on the ledge and I ran with the rest of the crowd outside."

Oh, God. There was a crowd down there? I never noticed. I stare at him wide-eyed.

"Lucy, the whole ballroom and just about every guest cleared out. The crowd on the sidewalk was insane. Seeing you up there was pretty incredible."

I manage a small smile. "You know I'm resourceful," I say. "I'm sure you knew I had it all under control."

He laughs. "Oh yeah. I wasn't nervous at all." He squeezes my arm and leans forward until our foreheads are touching. "I'm glad you're okay," he admits quietly.

"Me too."

He pulls back and takes my hand again, holding it securely in his own. "It was hard to get back in to see you. The police had sectioned off the hotel, the crowd was just so big because by the time the Honeymooners were taken out, everyone in nearby pubs, restaurants, hotels, you name it – were on the sidewalk at our hotel."

I close my eyes and lean back in my seat. I still can't believe it all. It's been hours. Midnight has come and gone, a new year has started. And I'm sitting at a police station in central London because of this whole mess.

"Incidentally," Cary adds after a moment. "Geoff from reception said that the police are paying for your room since you were instrumental in catching the actual Honeymooners."

He's got to be kidding me. I was instrumental? I was their number one suspect until a few hours ago.

"I imagine they felt a little bad that an innocent person ended up climbing out onto a ledge to get away from the actual bad guys because they let you get into harm's way."

I shake my head in disbelief. The more I hear, the bigger the knot in my stomach becomes. I don't owe a penny for my hotel stay now? Oliver convinced them to pay for it?

"Miss Gray," the receptionist says, walking through the door that Cary just came bursting through ten minutes ago. The middle-aged woman looks tired and like she'd rather be anywhere but here. I sympathize only too well on that front. "Detective Cameron is ready for you."

"Finally," I mutter, standing. I look down at Cary. "You should go," I say. "Salvage what's left of your New Year's."

He smiles softly at me but doesn't budge. "I'm not going anywhere."

I smile at him appreciatively. "Thank you."

The receptionist walks toward me. "Also," she says, "your barrister is here."

I look at her like she's grown a second head. "My *barrister*?" I ask. Do they give anyone going in for questioning a lawyer in London – even innocent people who didn't ask for one? "But I don't have a law—a barrister."

She shrugs. "He was just using the restroom. He'll be in here in a moment." She turns toward the door and smiles. "Oh, here he is now."

"Hi, Lucy."

As if my night couldn't get worse, my barrister does in fact walk through the door. And it's my big brother.

chapter twenty

*C*harles, to his credit, doesn't lecture me in front of the other cops. Or Cary. He just sits there quietly as we tell Detective Cameron our story. I can tell that he wants to. Lecture me, that is.

"So to synopsize," the detective says in a dry voice, "you did not phone in the leads to the cops, you had no idea your neighbors were the Honeymooners, and you were both pretending to be honeymooners to stay in the resort to avoid–" he looks at his notes and makes a weary, almost annoyed face – "'staying in a hostel where people pee on suitcases.'"

"And to avoid paying an asinine amount of money to stay somewhere last minute at Christmas," I add. "But remember – Kiki *did* phone in the leads. Even though she was severely misguided in love, she tried, in the end, to do the right thing."

"Kiki," the detective says, thinking. "Oh, right – her alias." He nods. "Her name is actually Susan Sinclair – a name you'll undoubtedly hear when the story makes papers."

I exhale deeply and place my chin in my hands. The end of my vacation ended up being a story that will make papers. Of course. And Charles is here to see it all unfold.

"Can I go now?" I finally ask in a voice fraught with emotion. I've never been so embarrassed or tired in my life. Or so sad. "I've been here all night."

I sneak a look at Charles. He must be exhausted too. He just flew in and the dark shadows under his eyes speak volumes for how much sleep he's gotten. But he doesn't even look annoyed. Just concerned. And supportive.

The detective looks his notes over once more and stands. "Yes," he finally says. "Sorry to take so long, Miss Gray."

I walk out of the interrogation room with Cary and Charles, pulling my suitcase behind me.

"Maybe I can get the airline to change my ticket," I say to Charles. "I wasn't supposed to leave until the third."

"Don't worry about that," Charles assures me, putting a hand on my back. "I have it all taken care of."

"So you're not coming back to The Chaizer?" Cary asks, eyeing my suitcase.

I shake my head. "I'm sorry, Cary. I hope it doesn't screw things up for you."

He sighs. "I could probably get Anne to agree to let me stay with her," he says with a wink. He looks quickly at Charles and pulls me aside, out of his earshot.

"Listen," Cary says quietly. "I've been to London so many times before, but this was the best visit." He stares at me intensely. I can see he means that. "Because of you."

"It was good for at least a little while, wasn't it?" I admit.

"Thanks to you, I am finally not waiting around for life to happen. I learned that from you. So when you go home, remember that. Forget this mess. It's not worth thinking about."

"You better keep in touch with me," I say coyly, pulling him into a fierce hug.

"You're the one who has yet to accept my friend request on Facebook."

I laugh. "It'll be the second thing I do when I get home."

Cary nods and smiles. "After you kiss and cuddle Ricky."

I laugh. "You know me so well."

As Charles and I finally get outside, we begin heading toward a taxi that is pulled over, lights flashing.

"Charles," I say, horrified. "Has this guy been waiting this whole time?"

Charles holds his hands up defensively. "I had no idea what was going on, Lucy," he explains. "I got to the hotel and they said you were at the police station. I grabbed a cab, and when I got here, I told him to wait. Once I found you, I wasn't exactly thinking about the taxi anymore."

"Charles. The fare's going to be—"

"Lucy."

I stop and look behind me. Oliver runs out of the police station – no coat, no gloves – just the same outfit he was in before, minus his jacket.

I take a step toward him. "I gave your jacket to the receptionist," I tell him.

Oliver eyes Charles, and I see the confusion in his gaze. But it clears in an instant when he looks back at me.

"I don't care about my jacket. I just wanted to…"

I swallow. This is just what I wanted to avoid.

"What?" I ask quietly.

"I've been tied up with the Sinclairs," he explains. "I wanted to see you. See if you were alright."

"I'm fine," I say adamantly. The last three times I've seen the guy, he's acted like I am some doll marked "Fragile". Someone he has to make things right with. Coming from Oliver, of all people, it really stings. I kind of miss the guy who pushed my buttons without giving a thought to my feelings. "You don't have to check up on me anymore. I'm not your case. I'm not your anything. It's okay if you go back in there and just deal with the Sinclairs."

His eyes flash and he steps toward me. "Is that what you think?" he asks, his voice almost hoarse. "That you were just a suspect in all of this?"

"Wasn't I?"

He looks down at the ground momentarily. "At one point, yes." He looks back at me, a small smile playing at the corners of his lips. "Of course. You were incredibly suspicious." He looks so handsome. So sweet. He's just making everything harder. He's making it all worse.

"I really have to go, Oliver."

"I owe you—"

"You don't owe me anything," I say softly. I turn and begin heading toward the cab.

"So that's it?" he asks. I turn around to face him again. He looks almost hurt. But what is there to be hurt about? Everything about our relationship from the moment we met was a lie. There really is nothing to say.

"That's it," I echo. "You go back to your normal life. And I go back to mine."

He walks toward me until he's close enough to touch. "What about that kiss?" he finally asks.

"What about it?" I ask, my eyes flashing in indignation, humiliation and about a thousand other things. "We were two people who lied to each other about everything, Oliver. We drank too much beer after a great night with great music. It was snowing and it was London. And you ran away as fast as you could when it was over, in case you forgot."

"I didn't handle it very well," he admits, his expression darkening. "But that was because—"

"Based on what you thought you knew about me, I completely understand why you felt the urge to run far away from me. But listen. There was nothing there. Not really. Nothing real."

He nods and looks away just as I feel something on my face. Rain. My London rain. I look up and marvel once again at the beauty of timing. When I look at Oliver, he is staring at my face, smiling sort of sadly. He knows.

"Have a safe trip back," he eventually says. He holds my gaze for an interminable moment and then turns and runs back into the police station.

I release a long breath once I'm safe inside the taxi with Charles. Rain patters against the car, leaving sad trails along the windows as we speed away. "Auld Lang Syne" softly buzzes in the background and it's chock full of nostalgia and hope tonight.

"That's the second man to mention kissing you on this trip," Charles mentions casually, leaning into me.

I laugh and look out the window again. That's just great. On top of everything, my brother probably thinks

I'm a floozy. I rest my head back and close my eyes.

"Just get it over with," I plead.

He looks down at me in surprise. "Get what over with?"

"The lecture. The 'I told you so'. The big brother run down on why I should never leave home again without your permission."

To my surprise, he doesn't laugh. Doesn't use my opening as his opportunity to say all of that and more. He just stares at me, blinking, tired and something else. Something I can't quite put my finger on.

"What?" I ask, when the silence becomes too much.

"Do you really think that I came all the way here to say 'I told you so'?"

I just look at him as something aches inside. I rest my head on his shoulder and close my eyes, relishing the comfort of his unconditional love, as the taxi rushes down London's streets, heading for the airport.

The rescue mission is complete

Posted by @Delores at 9:18 PM on january 2 on TheGrayBlog

Lucy is home. Not that anyone will tell me ANYTHING. All I know is that Charles left after apparently reading Marian's last blog entry. He wrote a quick email to say that Lucy is fine, completely IGNORING all of my other questions about WHY she left to begin with, where she's been, what she's been doing...

At times like this, maybe we should think about staging an intervention. Maybe Lucy has some kind of fight-or-flight problem, and if something triggers it again, who knows where she could end up?

Mom

chapter twenty-one

New Year's Resolutions

- *switch to one iced coffee a day*

- *wear brighter colors*

- *don't steal anyone's honeymoon*

- *don't get mistaken for a criminal*

- *only eat one croissant a day*

One week. One week is all it seems to take for life to get back into a rhythm resembling "normal." Preparing lesson plans, sorting through photos from the trip, and hiding out with Ricky has been a great way to ease back into everything following the drama from London.

I haven't had to deal with twenty questions from probing family members either because for once, Mother

Nature seems to be smiling on me. A blizzard has more or less trapped me in my loft and trapped everyone else in their homes too. Plus, I still don't have a new cell phone. I guess I got used to being disconnected (mostly) when I was away. I haven't exactly been barging into the cell phone store for a replacement just yet.

In all, it's been kind of a quiet return without any fuss. Sitting by candlelight, Ricky purring on my lap, I stare at the thick mass of snowflakes falling heavily outside my window. In the building just next to mine, I see Mrs. Suzayaki smoking in the window. When she notices me, she smiles and waves. It feels so nice to be home. And yet I do miss it.

London.

I finally stop burning with embarrassment when I think about my trip. As I look at my pictures on my computer, I am floored. It went by in a flash. And it really was amazing. Cary's right – I'd be stupid to let the events of the very last day taint any of it.

I continue scanning through the photos from the trip. I can't believe how many I took. There must be over a thousand pictures to sort through.

"Come on, Ricky," I say, patting the ottoman of my reading chair. I sit by my tiny Christmas tree with my laptop on my tray table and put the photos in slideshow mode. I pet Ricky as my trip plays out before my eyes with music. This is my story. My story to go with the stamps in my passport.

A knock on the door interrupts me and I pause the slideshow and jump up. I slip on my candy-cane slippers and pad over to the door. I look through the peep-hole and see Charles staring back at me. He's checking up on me no doubt.

"Hey, big brother," I say, opening the door.

"Hey, woman of the world" he says, pulling his hat off, and rubbing his hands together to warm them. He's taken to calling me 'woman of the world' since we got back. I like the nickname actually. Even though two destinations don't exactly make me anything of the sort. "Tuesday night dinner isn't happening at Mom's tonight."

I look out the window at the snow and laugh. "I figured as much."

"It's happening here," he adds, scrunching his face up apologetically.

"What?" I swat Charles's arm and glare up at him. "How could you let this happen?"

"You try to stop Mom when she's on a mission," he says, laughing. "Don't worry. I didn't tell anyone anything. I just ran ahead to warn you."

"They're *here?*" I exclaim.

Before he can say another word, my mother's shrill tones echo in the hallway outside my door and I fight the urge to climb out the window to hide at Mrs. Suzayaki's house. Our fire escapes do connect, after all.

I open the door as my whole family bustles in, complaining about the cold and the blizzard. I hunch my shoulders and prepare for what's coming – the incessant questions, the lectures, all of it. But instead I'm just hugged. I mean it. They all begin hugging me at once. My mom, Jake, Mary, Julie, Marian, Samantha, Cora, Tristan, my dad – all of them.

"How was London?"

"Tell me everything."

"Did you see Prince William and Kate?"

"Were the French people rude in Paris?"

"Was the food good?"

They're all speaking at once. Samantha – three months pregnant Samantha, my beautiful sister-in-law – begins unwrapping take-out containers. I'm so confused. We've never had Tuesday Night Dinner here. I've offered my place up since I moved in four years ago, but we've always done it at my parents' or at Charles and Samantha's place.

"Oh, are these your pictures?" Julie squeals, looking at my computer and petting Ricky who hasn't budged at all, in spite of the commotion in his living space.

"Yes," I say, walking toward her. I stop in my tracks when I realize that *everyone* is following me. I look over my shoulder and they all freeze too – looking confused.

"Is something wrong?" my mother asks. She eyes the computer screen, which is frozen on a photo of Cary and me inside of a red London phone booth. "Are there indecent pictures on there?"

I roll my eyes. "Of course not," I say. "You have to stop thinking that any one of us could just become slutty all of a sudden, Mom."

"Yeah," Marian agrees. "I've always found that so disheartening."

"I'm just living in the present," my mom says defensively. "This is not the 1950's."

"Have you looked around Lucy's place lately, Ma?" Jake asks. He looks at my *I Love Lucy* posters and *Honeymooners* (of all things) tin signs. "It's basically the 1950s in here."

That's when I notice it. Jake and Mary, I mean. They're holding hands by the front door. And I realize that Mary was right. There's something here that's just so *right*.

"Who's the hottie?" Julie asks, gesturing toward the

photo of Cary and me.

Mary walks over to the computer and gasps. "Cary Stewart," she answers.

"You know him?" Jake asks her.

"He was sort of a fixture in our class. Every girl's dream."

I smile. Knowing Cary now feels so different than just thinking I knew him. His personality makes all the difference in the whole Cary picture.

"Mary reached out to Cary to ask him to keep an eye on me in London," I explain, linking my arm through Mary's even as I roll my eyes playfully at her.

I regard her closely. She somehow looks different. This in-love version of her is so assured and confident – almost more mature somehow.

"So you and my brother, huh?" I say casually, smirking at her.

She stops in her tracks and just stares at me. "Is it weird to see?" she asks, almost shyly. And Mary is never shy. With me anyway.

I wrap my arm around her shoulders and tug her to me. "It's only weird to me that you guys look so perfect together and we never figured it out at any point in the past twenty years."

She laughs. "I know." She stops and turns to me, her brown eyes wide and incredulous. "I swear Lucy, it was that stupid psychic at the wedding, telling me I had already met the man of my dreams."

That stops me and in a nanosecond the smile fades from my face. "The psychic?"

"It sounds so stupid, I know," she whispers intensely. "A psychic that probably works at the Haley Mall with a crystal ball and everything. Listening to her makes me, like, a crazy person, right?"

In her eyes, I see it all only too well. The hope. The uncertainty. The self-deprecation. And I get it. Oh, do I get it.

"I don't think it's stupid at all," I assure her.

A little while later, we are all eating Chinese takeout, gathered around the laptop in the living room. Mary is sitting in the chair, while Jake sits on the chair's arm with his arm draped lightly over her. My parents, and Charles and Samantha are sitting on the couch. Marian and Tom have pulled two chairs from the kitchen into the living room and are cuddling little Tristan, who's telling them some very animated story. And Cora, Julie and I are relaxing on the floor, leaning against the couches. I've set the laptop up on the entertainment center, right in front of the TV, hit "go" again on the slideshow and now – we're watching my trip play out before us like it's a movie. And that is just so much better than watching it alone.

"That was the coffee place that I went every morning," I explain, looking longingly at a photo of Hugging Mugs.

"I'm glad you're back," Julie whispers to me.

I rest my head on Julie's shoulder and stare at the photos. "I am too."

After a few more London photos tick on by, Julie looks at me. "I guess you heard my news."

At that, I turn to look at her, to meet her gaze. "Yes," I say. I shake my head. "I had no idea that you were so –" I search for the right words. "–Unfulfilled," I finally say.

"I wasn't," she says, shrugging, scrunching her nose up. "I liked being a doctor."

"But you didn't love it."

She catches my eyes with her own hazel ones and fixes me with an intense look. "It was Marian's wedding, actually, that changed me."

"Oh God, you too?" I burst out, and Julie looks shocked at my words. "Did the psychic tell you to drop the scalpel and pick up the lipstick...or was she completely vague and odd, leaving you to have to figure it all out yourself?" I feel my cheeks flush because...this is ridiculous. "I hope Marian paid her really well for all the lives she uprooted."

Julie grabs my arm and waits patiently until I meet her gaze. "Okay, first of all, in case you don't remember, I made fun of Marian endlessly for every aspect of her '80s wedding, and I absolutely ridiculed her choice to have a psychic," she explains slowly. "I wouldn't have been caught dead in that woman's tent having my palms read or seeing my future in some loony lady's crystal ball."

I look down, a little embarrassed. "She didn't read palms, actually."

Julie laughs. "It was before the wedding," she says. "The makeup artist's assistant did the makeup for Marian's two friends and that one junior bridesmaid, remember?"

I nod, remembering how thankful I had been that the makeup artist herself would be doing mine and Julie's makeup in addition to Marian's. Her assistant had seemed pretty hung over.

"I saw them after she was done and they were all near tears. They looked like tangerines."

"We all looked a little odd that day," I say to that, careful to keep my voice low so that Marian doesn't overhear.

"They looked really bad and they seemed really sad about it," she recalls. "So I snuck into the bathroom with them and fixed their makeup. All of them. You know I've always loved doing that anyway," she adds.

I nod, listening.

"I like being a doctor. I do. I've delivered great news to patients, witnessed babies being born, seen lives saved. But honestly – at least half the time I drove home in tears. The other side of it – the sad news side – was too much. Plus, no one looks good in hospital gowns under those fluorescent lights. I want happiness. Magic. I want beauty. My world has been missing a lot of that. I cannot tell you how happy and proud I felt when those girls smiled and thanked me. I know it wasn't really magic, but it felt like it."

"They looked great," I agree.

"Please," she says deadpan. "They looked better than all of us. Including Marian."

I laugh. "Hey, you'll never get an argument from me on how good I looked that day."

She looks at the slideshow, but I can tell she's not really looking at it. "When you went away, something just clicked," she says. "You've *never* done anything out of the ordinary. You always stayed in the lines, followed the rules. This was so unlike you. And when we talked to you on the phone, you said it was just something you had to do. You sounded so free." She grabs my hand and really holds my gaze. "I can't tell you how that made something inside of me just snap. You did what you had to do for *you* in some kind of insane moment of clarity or whatever that was. And you didn't let anyone stop you. You didn't seem to care about what anyone thought. Honestly, that's how people should live their lives. Not caring about what everyone else thinks, just doing what makes them happy. So that's what I'm doing."

"Well, I'm glad." I hug Julie to me.

"I'll be going to school for it, I'm going to do weddings, parties, you name it. I'm going to be amazing."

"You're already amazing."

"Thanks, Luce."

"Who's that?" Samantha asks and I look at the screen.

My breath catches as something in my stomach tightens. It's Oliver. The photo I took of him at the end of our night in Paris – when he took me by that For Sale sign that was crossed out. He looks so handsome, so happy. That really was a perfect day. We had a few of those, I guess. At least they seemed perfect.

"Just someone I met out there," I finally manage, tearing my eyes away from the photo. Everyone is looking at me with questioning, interested glances.

"He's cute," Samantha eventually says.

I laugh. "I'll agree with you on that."

I catch Charles's eye and he just nods slowly, a knowing gleam in his eye. It looks like his mind is fast at work. I really hope he doesn't decide to launch into a brotherly lecture *now*. He's been so good throughout this whole thing.

"These pictures are very good," my mom says seriously, looking at the computer. "They look like pictures you'd see in a book at the bookstore."

A new song begins and my heart gives a lurch. It's that song – the one Oliver and I danced to the night that all hell broke loose. Oh, what are the chances? Instead of feeling embarrassed or even sad, the song just conjures up feelings of contentment. Everything about the trip was perfect until that dance ended. And no amount of drama can ever take the amazing memories and stories – the picture-perfect time I had – away.

I rest my head back and let the movie of my trip play as my heart swells. No matter how it all turned out, I don't regret it. Not one moment of it. I mean, my scenery included Big Ben and the Eiffel Tower. I have a million stories to go along with every snapshot.

That psychic told me to pay attention and that's exactly what I did. Without my phone, without the noise of everyone who's ever loved me, I got to have this adventure that was mine and mine alone. I never realized how much I was missing just by being so busy. But nothing changed here while I was gone. Not really. It's all the same. But I'm different.

The comfort of home warms me completely. But I'm already trying to figure out where I'll go next. And when.

As the evening rolls into nighttime, and slideshow time becomes game time, everyone eventually has to get going – lest the worsening blizzard strand them all here. We may have made a Tuesday Night Dinner work, but a sleepover is out of the question.

"I'll see you in two days," Mary says, hugging me. "Back to the grind."

School. Kids fresh off of weeks without structure.

"And then, I want to hear *all* the gory details," she adds, looking at me in her sly, Mary way.

Jake and Mary leave hand-in-hand, chatting idly and quietly as they walk down the hall, toward my elevator as I'm struck with the sudden realization that they're a couple. A full-fledged couple.

After he's zipped his coat and put his hat on, Charles walks over to give me a hug and kiss goodbye.

"Lucy," he says in a lowered voice. "That slide-show…."

"What about it?" I ask him, instantly on guard. I saw

the expression on his face when any picture of Oliver popped up.

"You were so willing to go away like you did and take a chance on your life."

"What are you getting at?"

"I think that you might need to really figure out what that means now."

I pull back and blink at him, utterly confused. "What?"

He smiles and picks up Tristan. "You figure it out, woman of the world."

When everyone's gone, I curl up on the couch and listen to the quiet. I can't believe they all came over here. And no matter how many times I asked people about what they've been up to, asked Marian about her honeymoon, Samantha about the new baby – everyone just kept steering the subject back to my trip. I've never been the center of discussion at our family dinners. Probably because I don't do anything too exciting. Ever. Until now.

I missed them all, but it's good to know that I can leave, do something for myself and come back. Even though everyone's lives have changed while I've been gone, we all come back together. Always.

I think about Charles's words. What is there to figure out?

I went on my trip, I loved (almost) every moment of it, and now I'm back – better for having experienced it.

As I stare at Major Nelson and Jeannie duking it out over her magical mishaps, I know. Of course I know. I know exactly what he means.

I followed my heart when I took that trip. I listened to fate. I ran toward something that I needed. And now...I'm running away.

chapter twenty-two

I walk up the grey paved walkway and through the oak-wood doors of the Bradley Fitzhugh-Simms Elementary School reenergized. I am forty-five minutes early and escape to the teacher's lounge to finish my iced coffee and have my breakfast in silence. Though as all of the other teachers file in, I can see that enjoying a peaceful and quiet start to the new year at school will be impossible. I don't see Mary, unfortunately.

"Hi, Lucy," Ian says, walking over to me, and sitting beside me. "How was your break?" he asks.

I lean back and take another sip of my iced coffee, thinking how to describe it. "Fantastic," I finally say. "Yours?"

He rolls his eyes. "No offense. I mean, I know she's related to you, but your cousin Courtney is a handful," he says, exasperated.

I laugh inwardly. This always happens.

"I guess wedding bells aren't in your future, then," I say.

"Definitely not," he says. "I'm sorry again for going off with her when I agreed to be your date at your sister's wedding. I know how much it meant to you."

I wave my hand dismissively. "It all worked out perfectly, actually," I say, truly meaning it.

When Ian goes to get himself another mug of coffee, I pull a business card out of my pants pocket. Last night, after finishing my laundry, I saw it sitting in the dryer – faded but still legible – Jessie's number from Paris. When I picked it up, something stirred inside and I felt exactly the way I had when I'd boldly decided to go to London. I felt like the signs were screaming at me to do something. To take a chance again. To make my life happen and not just *wait*.

I roll the card over and over again in my hands. I feel like I need to call him. But I have no idea how to get in touch with him. This piece of paper would be a start.

I need to call him because...I like him. I do. No matter how things turned out, I met a guy and fell for him. Finding out the truth doesn't change my feelings. Those, anyway, had been real the whole time.

I check my watch. I still have twenty minutes until class begins. With knots in my stomach, I grab my new cell phone and dial her number – country code first. I agree to the international charge and just wait.

And wait.

Finally it rings. On the fourth ring, the carefree, sweet voice of Oliver's younger sister picks up. She sounds out of breath.

"Jessie?" I ask, tentatively.

I have no idea what's going on around me in the

teacher's lounge. I am just staring at this piece of paper like it's Jessie herself.

"Yes, who's this?" she asks.

"Lucy. Lucy Gray," I stammer. "I stayed with you over Christmas."

She says nothing at all. Oh God, she doesn't remember me.

"I ruined your countertop with my hair straightener," I say, hoping that will jog her memory. "Which I still fully intend to pay you back for. I need your address."

This seems to trigger her memory, if her giggle is any indication. "Of course I remember you!" she exclaims happily. "The girl who made my brother smile – how could I forget?"

At that, something tightens inside and I find myself smiling – not that she can see me.

"You'll have to excuse me," she says. "I just ran in from a jog along the Seine. Still catching my breath."

Oh, of course, I think. A jog along the Seine. I laugh. She's so easy to talk to.

"I don't have a lot of time," I explain. "But...could I have your brother's number?"

"You want my brother's number?" she repeats, like this is a completely odd request.

"I just forgot to tell him something before I – before I left. And I had your number, so –"

She hesitates and then laughs again. "He's switching numbers all the time," she finally says. "Because of his job. I really don't have his most current one. In fact...I don't know where he is right now. Super top secret assignment, if I'm not mistaken. A *life-or-death* matter."

A life-or-death matter? How is she sitting there jogging along the Seine and giggling like a school girl if her brother's on a life-or-death assignment?

"You know what?" she says after a moment. "Give me your number. And when he checks in, I'll pass it along."

This is so not how I imagined this playing out – but I give her my number all the same. At the very least, I can say that I tried to get in touch with him. I tried to make things right.

Before she hangs up, she calls my name and just says, "Hang in there."

With ten minutes to spare before class starts, I leave the teacher's lounge and head to my classroom. I put the piece of paper back in my pocket and try to stay positive. I can't have ruined our moment by running away. It can't be too late to at least tell him that what I felt was real. I open the door to the classroom and look around. It's empty of course. I walk over to the chalkboard and begin writing today's schedule. I hear the door click and brace myself for the noise. The kids are back and I am sure I'll hear their high pitched voices at full volume in a matter of moments.

I finish writing the schedule, shocked that I haven't heard a peep from one student. Fearing the worst, I turn around. Only one desk is occupied. I open my mouth, ready to talk about the holidays when I stop in my tracks. This is no child. Oh, God. I can't breathe. Or speak. My heart begins hammering against my chest. Because sitting in the occupied desk is none other than Oliver Burke.

He looks completely ridiculous sitting, all six-feet-two of him, in an elementary school sized desk. And the sight somehow completely robs me of breath.

After he registers the look of total shock on my face, he smiles and stands.

"Why, hello," he says, looking a mix of shy and confident, if that is possible.

"What are you doing here?" I finally manage.

He shrugs as he walks closer. He looks so laid back right now. So comfortable. In jeans and a dark gray sweater – one of the ones I saw him wear a few times in London – he finally looks off-guard. This is Oliver Burke. No pretenses.

"I came to give you this," he says, holding out a newspaper.

"You came to give me a newspaper?" I ask. I want to stare at his face, memorize it. But I take the paper from him and look at it, thankful that my fumbling hands at least have something to do. The headlines are all about politics.

"I don't understand." I look back up at him nervously.

He smiles and points to the lower corner of the paper. "Right there. Weather predictions. Looks like it's going to rain in London for three weeks."

I smile and shake my head. "That figures." I laugh. "You, um...you came to bring me the paper?" I ask skeptically. "This information is available online too."

He shakes his head, and in his eyes I think I see exactly why he's here. "I came to see you," he says finally. He walks forward until he's right in front of me. "I came to tell you something."

"What did you have to tell me?"

"You were wrong."

That was not what I was expecting him to say. "I was wrong?" I ask, scrunching my face up in confusion. I put the paper down on one of the student's desks and look up at him.

"Yes. You got it all wrong." He stuffs his hands in his pockets and looks at me expectantly, as if he's given me enough information for me to formulate any kind of response.

"I don't—"

"It wasn't the beer. Or the song. Or the snow. Or the city." He bends forward until his face is level with mine and he meets my eyes and forces me to really look at him. "We kissed because something happened between us. Something real and honest."

"It's complicated," I say after a moment. "Because we were not telling each other the truth."

"You said it was all lies. I've been sitting around thinking that I don't think I've ever been as honest with anyone as I was with you." He sighs, sounding almost frustrated. "You didn't know I was a detective. Fine. But you knew about my family and my history. I knew about yours." He takes another step toward me. "I know that you drink two coffees at a time, that you wear a rain coat when you want to tempt fate." He takes another step toward me until our faces are just inches apart. "I know that you're a terrible liar."

I stare at him and shake my head. Because there's something I still don't get – something I've been dying to know since I returned. "How can you like someone that you suspected of those awful crimes?"

He laughs softly and looks at me like I'm quite possibly the stupidest woman he's ever met. "Do you really think that I thought you and Cary were them?" he asks. "Do you honestly think that I ever would've let you into my sister's house – let you anywhere near her – if I thought either of you was dangerous? The whole reason that I stayed back an extra day in Paris was to follow around the Sinclairs. I had reason to think it might be them. But every time I saw them, they just made out a lot. And nothing ever happened in Paris. Or in London. I had no proof, just suspicions."

"Your partner seemed to imply I was your top suspect the entire time."

He smiles. "He is not my partner. And as for keeping you as a prime suspect...let's just say that I was a little less communicative about this case's developments than my boss would have liked."

"If you honestly didn't think that I was involved, then why –"

"Because I wanted to spend time with you," he admits, his face reddening instantly. "I was sure you weren't the Honeymooners. And I was convinced you and Cary weren't a real couple. Finding out what's going on with people is kind of what I do. And I really wanted to see what was going on with you." He rakes a hand through his hair nervously. "But I couldn't call you out without calling myself out, and I couldn't do that. I saw you going out shopping with Mrs. Sinclair, being friendly with her, and she was your neighbor. I couldn't risk my cover or the case."

I blink up at him, taking all of this in, seeing my whole trip in a completely new light.

"I've never let anyone distract me from a case before. That's why I felt so bad," he says, holding my gaze with his now intense one. "You got caught in the middle of the real case – and ended up in danger – because I had feelings for you." In his eyes, I see how upset he still is over that fact. And yet I don't detect any signs of regret.

I laugh and hold his gaze. "You did?" I ask.

He moves in even closer. "Still do."

He inches even closer to my face. If he moves one more millimeter, we will be resuming that kiss we started in the snowy streets of London right here in my classroom.

I pull back, looking around. Something is so wrong here.

"Where are my students?" I finally ask.

He smiles. "Your friend Mary took care of that."

"Mary?" I exclaim. "How do you know Mar—"

"Cary," he explains.

Cary put Oliver in touch with Mary?

"Okay," I say slowly. "Well, where are they?"

"The other third grade teacher, a Mr. Walker, I believe – is taking on the whole class today. You," he says, dipping his face to kiss my lips for a quick moment. Oh wow. "My dear." He kisses them again, his breathing growing more ragged. "Are busy."

And then he wraps his arms around me and crushes me to him – and kisses me fully and firmly with no reservations.

I throw my arms around his neck and kiss him right back.

A million questions buzz through my mind about how this could possibly work, where it could go, but I don't care. Right now, kissing Oliver, I don't care about anything.

I'm leaving it all up to fate.

what a YEAR

Posted by: @Delores at 12:42 PM on december 17 on TheGrayBlog

One year ago, Marian got married and look at her & Tom now – parents! I'm a smidge obsessed w/ baby Calvin. I know he'll be best friends with big cousin, Lulu. I cannot believe she's already six months old. But I honestly cannot believe that Calvin was born ON their anniversary! I knew something amazing would happen because the psychic at their wedding told me so. That's right, everyone. I visited the psychic station and had my fortune told! And you all say that I always play it safe and think that just because I told Marian how odd having a psychic at the wedding was, that I don't have an adventurous side too and wouldn't be caught dead going to see the woman. Well. SEE HER, I DID! She told me that the year would bring new beginnings to my family! SEVEN new beginnings IN ONE YEAR. And so I count:

1. Jake and Mary's relationship (and engagement!)
2. Julie's career (bringing beauty to everyone – just what our world needs, am I right?)
3. Baby Lulu (the sweetest addition to Sam and Charles's brood)
4. Baby Calvin
5. Lucy and Oliver's cross-continental romance (which, now that he moved to Haley is really more of a frequent cross-continental vacation to visit his family – I do love his sister's husband, what a cook!). I forget; are they stopping in Paris after Cary and Anne's wedding?
6. Dad's retirement

7. AND... what?

It's the end of the year, and I only count six. But that psychic was right about EVERYTHING! So... what is someone not telling me? As your mother, it's my right to know!

Love,
MOM

Acknowledgments

There are so many people that I feel forever grateful to – for being in my life, supporting my dreams and helping me see this one through. I got incredible feedback and support from family and loved ones who read this – Bernice Capita, Kathy Sullivan, Alice Sullivan, Jaclyn Leibl-Cote, Damaris Sullivan, Linda Thomasian, Mary Ann Mazzone, Carol Diebold, Sean Kelly, Shelly Marcoccio, Lori Lemke, Lynne Kelly, Dominique Ferrari, Elisabeth Cote, Carola Leibl-Cote and Diana Ditto. Your support means more than you'll ever know!

To my peers and professors at Emerson College – thank you for supporting my thesis project! Thank you to John Rodzvilla, Nicole Christopher, Scott A. Johnson, Erin Dionne, Evva Koyle, and Nora Chan for giving me advice on my book, writing career and being part of the reason my experience at Emerson was truly amazing. And I must give a huge shout out and "thank you" to Jessica Treadway, a mentor and friend who believed in *Honeymoon Alone* from my first submission and built my confidence in it over and over again.

Thank you, Marilyn Sowinski, for bringing Lucy to

life through your amazing artwork and designs. Your creativity endlessly amazes me.

Thank you, Lisa Webster, for taking the time to edit my book; you helped shape it into something that I feel really proud of. Thank you to Martha Osmundson for final proofing and your enthusiasm and encouragement.

This was hard work all around. With four children, work, and writing (plus publishing), I know that I was only able to do this because of my incredible support system. Courtney Gaffney – I couldn't do any of this without you. From the bottom of my heart, thank you for everything you do to support me and my family. Thank you, Lori Egan, for being here for me and helping my life feel a little less crazy.

I feel really blessed to come from a long line of strong women. I thank my grandmother, Alice Sullivan, for reading this novel during one of her trips to Florida, and calling me to encourage me to keep going and get it published. Your support fills me with pride. One of my very first readers was my grandmother, Bernice Capita. She has been in my corner for my entire life, loving the stories I tell and encouraging me with this book more than I ever dreamed possible. I would be lost without your guidance in my life.

I cannot thank my amazing sister-in-law, Amy Burbach, enough for reading and editing drafts of this book over and over. Your dedication to Lucy Gray shows in every page and your commitment to this project has meant the world to me. Thank you, Joshua Chelmo, my very best friend, for listening to me throughout this entire process (and for the past 20+ years). Thank you to my sister-in-law, Damaris Sullivan, for being the cheerleader of dreams that you are – for always inspiring people to take risks. And thank you, Shelly Marcoccio, for being like a second mom and giving me such valuable feedback throughout this whole process.

Thank you to my sister and brother – Jaclyn Leibl-Cote and Dan Sullivan – for believing in me since the beginning. You've always supported my goal to write stories that matter to me. Jaclyn, your feedback was invaluable and I thank you for always taking my writing seriously.

Thank you to my incredible, wonderful husband, John. You are the best person that I know. You were my first reader, the person who told me to get my Masters even though I was pregnant with our fourth child, and you're the one who has gently nudged me forward every step of the way. You're the best. And our four little muses – Nathan, Wyatt, Charlie and Austin – think you're pretty amazing, too. You are honestly everything to me.

And finally – thank you to my parents, Dan and Kathy Sullivan. I wouldn't be who I am without you (and I could not have done any of this without you. I can't stress that enough). My whole life, you have told me that I can do anything I set my mind to. Thank you for that! You have set the most incredible example for me – about what love is and what family is. You are both everything that is right in my world – the two people I still turn to constantly – and I love you both 'tutu mun'.

What's Next?

Thank you for reading *Honeymoon Alone*. If you enjoyed it, please share it with friends, send a review and spread the word.

Nicole Macaulay is at work on her second novel, *Then Comes Life*, slated for 2023 release.

Follow Nicole

 /nicolemacaulayauthor

 @nicolemacaulayauthor

 @nicmacaulay

www.nicmacaulay.com